Praise for the Haunted Bookshop Mysteries

"Full of _____ _____ and p_____ men

"A magnificent cold case mystery"

—Book Review (Great pick)

"Jack and Pen are a terrific duo who prove that love can transcend anything." —The Mystery Reader

"I highly recommend the complete series."

—*Spinetingler Magazine*

"A charming, funny, and quirky mystery starring a suppressed widow and a stimulating ghost."

—*Midwest Book Review*

"The plot is marvelous; the writing is top-notch."

—Cozy Library

The Ghost

AND THE

Haunted Portrait

CLEO COYLE

BERKLEY PRIME CRIME
New York

BERKLEY PRIME CRIME
Published by Berkley
An imprint of Penguin Random House LLC
penguinrandomhouse.com

Copyright © 2021 by Alice Alfonsi and Marc Cerasini
Penguin Random House supports copyright. Copyright fuels creativity, encourages
diverse voices, promotes free speech, and creates a vibrant culture. Thank you for
buying an authorized edition of this book and for complying with copyright laws by not
reproducing, scanning, or distributing any part of it in any form without permission.
You are supporting writers and allowing Penguin Random House to continue to
publish books for every reader.

BERKLEY is a registered trademark and BERKLEY PRIME CRIME and
the B colophon are trademarks of Penguin Random House LLC.
A HAUNTED BOOKSHOP MYSTERY is a registered trademark of
Penguin Random House LLC.

ISBN: 9780425251867

First Edition: May 2021

Printed in the United States of America
1 3 5 7 9 10 8 6 4 2

To all the talented cover artists,
who inspire us to look inside.

FOREWORD

The Ghost and the Haunted Portrait marks the seventh entry in our Haunted Bookshop series, but the truth is our beloved hard-boiled ghost has been haunting the cozy streets of Quindicott, Rhode Island, since 2004. We would like to thank Berkley Prime Crime for the faith they had in this series from the beginning, and our marvelous editor, Michelle Vega, who recently shepherded (pun intended) Jack's return after nearly a decade's absence.

We wish to thank the many loyal fans of the ghost detective, and we look forward to their enjoyment of Jack's adventures on this mortal plane for years to come. A tip of the old fedora also goes to our agent, John Talbot, for his unflagging support and professionalism.

Our long-standing appreciation of cover art from the pulp magazines of the 1930s to the dust jackets and perfect bound covers of today inspired this entry in our series. Many sources helped us, including *Undercover: An Illustrated History of American Mass Market Paperbacks* by Thomas L. Bonn (Penguin Books, 1982) and *Paperbacks, U.S.A.: A Graphic History, 1939–1959* by Piet Schreuders (Blue Dolphin Books, 1981).

Ghosts don't scare us but the many scams and abuses in our industry do, and we thank the Science Fiction

Writers of America (and the MWA, HWA, and ASJA) for sponsoring Writer Beware, a noteworthy resource for authors and one of the inspirations for a subplot in this novel.

As for our novels, you can learn more about them (and us) by visiting CoffeehouseMystery.com and CleoCoyle.com.

—Alice Alfonsi and Marc Cerasini,
aka Cleo Coyle, New York City

CONTENTS

"It's a very good portrait," said Captain Gregg stiffly. "That," said Lucy, "is a matter of opinion."

—*The Ghost and Mrs. Muir* by R. A. Dick (aka Josephine Aimee Campbell Leslie)

PROLOGUE

Shake your business up and pour it. I don't have all day.

—Raymond Chandler, *The Big Sleep*

New York City
October 1947

I WAS TIRED. Dead tired.

Heading for the office, I squinted against the too-bright sun. The autumn chill seemed friendly enough, until I stepped beneath the Third Avenue El, where shadows turned everything meaner. Fighting the shiver, I flipped up my collar and forged ahead, albeit slower than usual.

For the past two nights, I hadn't seen a bed. The punishing hours couldn't be helped. From the moment those Park Avenue parents hired me to find their missing daughter, I knew time was not on my side.

Mom and dad were desperate for good reason. Cops want nothing to do with missing teenagers, especially wannabe actresses who have posters of movie stars glued over their eyeballs. *Runaways* they called them and closed the book, telling families to check the bus terminals.

The coppers weren't wrong. Girls like Millicent typically

caught a Greyhound to sunny California—one was launched every few hours—and after her LA landing, she could disappear for years behind a "stage" name.

I told Mr. and Mrs. Adair as much. They hired me anyway.

Millie was a good girl, they said. She would never run off on her own. They claimed the wrong boy had seduced her with empty promises, and she was bound to come to her senses. When that happened, she could find herself in bad trouble.

It's your dime, I thought and went to work.

It took me thirty-six hours to track down Millicent and Romeo, not in the land of starlets and glamour, but in a fleabag hotel in Paramus.

Millie had a few new bruises to go along with a new attitude. She was more than ready to go home. But first she gladly helped me escort her drunken *ex*-boyfriend to a New Jersey jail cell, where the punk confessed he'd had the perfect grift planned, a fake kidnapping to shake down Millie's parents, one that went south when she refused to play along.

The Adairs were right, after all.

With their daughter safely home, Mr. Adair was so grateful he forked over enough cabbage to keep me in sirloin and scotch for a month.

"I hired you," he said, "because I heard you always got the job done." And since I did, he asked me to accept this "generous reward" beyond my measly per diem.

With a stack of bills and a bookie to pay, who was I to argue? I shook his hand, and we parted ways.

Now I was striding across Third toward a run-down building of cramped offices. I already knew which one was mine because I'd had JACK SHEPARD, PRIVATE INVESTIGATOR painted in simple black letters on the beveled glass door.

I was ready to hit the sheets for a decade or so, but my secretary was off visiting Sis in Myrtle Beach, so I figured I'd check the mail before shuffling back to my apartment.

As I yawned myself up the sagging office staircase, I noticed the eau de ashtray tickling my Jimmy Durante. I figured the stink of smoke came from my own coat, given last night's stakeout at the polluted taproom where I'd waited for Millie's low-life boyfriend to show.

But I was wrong.

As I crested the steps, I saw the little chimney, wrapped in an oversize raincoat, waiting at the end of the long hallway. The young woman stood leaning against my office doorway, the floor around her peppered with her burned-down Luckies, her face masked by a cascade of shiny black hair and clouds of blue smoke.

When she heard my oxfords tapping the tiles, her head jerked up. She might have reacted like a defensive animal, but she didn't look scared. Those hazel brown eyes in her pale doll face were steady as spotlights when they locked onto mine.

"Are you Jack Shepard?" she asked, voice direct and strong enough to echo off the long row of closed doors.

"Who's asking?"

"The name's Shirley . . . Miss Shirley Powell."

"I'm sorry, miss, but you'll have to come back another day. I'm not—"

"Please—" Reaching out, she took hold of my elbow, expression no longer so steady. "I need your help *today*, Mr. Shepard. Please?"

For a moment I stood stiller than Michelangelo's marble. Then those begging doll eyes melted me. Thinking of poor Millie and her fresh bruises, I blew out air.

"Guess you better come in."

Nodding like a grateful puppy, she thanked me for my time, and I fumbled for my keys. Stifling a yawn, I creaked open the door and led the way into my cluttered HQ.

The air was stale, so I opened a window, wondering if the subway would stay quiet long enough for me to hear the girl's sob story.

After a longing glance at my percolator, I threw my fedora on the desk, hung up my trench, and offered her a chair. She refused it with a shake of the head.

"My fiancé is Nathan Brock. Have you heard of him?"

I shook my own head. "Can't say that I have."

"Nathan is a talented artist. A genius, really. Do you know much about art, Mr. Shepard?"

"The art of the con, maybe."

"But you've never dabbled yourself?"

"Dabbled?" I stifled a laugh. "No, Miss Powell. But if I *were* to paint a picture of my life, it wouldn't have flowers or rainbows. The colors would either be foggy gray or blood-shot red. Nothing would ever be black or white. Lines would be blurry, so you'd never know when you crossed one, and—knowing my clientele—an elaborate frame job would be involved."

"I realize you're joking with me, but what you've described is exactly the kind of picture my fiancé likes to paint."

"Cut to the chase, miss. Why are you here?"

"Nathan is in trouble."

"What did he do? Draw a mustache on the *Mona Lisa*?"

"No, Mr. Shepard. He's been arrested for murder."

CHAPTER 1

Cover Story

A dead man is the best fall guy in the world. He never talks back.

—Raymond Chandler, *The Long Goodbye*

Quindicott, Rhode Island
Today

THEY SAY YOU shouldn't judge a book by its cover, but my customers did it all the time.

Most of them say they're looking for books that are well written and insightful, books filled with characters to connect with, and stories that thrill, amuse, enlighten, and entertain. Unfortunately, these intangible properties aren't things you can see from across a room, let alone place in a shop window. A striking cover, on the other hand, you can't help noticing.

During my short career in New York publishing, my more recent years as a bookseller, and my lifetime as an avid reader, I've watched book covers change with the times and the fashion.

Decades ago, painted pictures were enough to grab a reader's attention. Genre-specific cover art (you know what

I mean: the clinch for romances, rockets for science fiction, cowboys and horses for Westerns, tough guys and femme fatales for detective stories) represented the work of America's finest illustrators.

As time marched on, big publishers devoured little ones, and art direction changed. Graphics and photoshopped stock images became speedy, economical alternatives to traditional painted scenes. Brand-name authors were packaged with covers displaying little more than spot art and a title beneath their prominent author moniker.

Then came the evolution of digital and print-on-demand technologies, which allowed self-published authors and pop-up micropublishers to flood the literary landscape. The big New York publishers tried to keep up, launching digital-only imprints and expanding their lists to compete, until the book business began to feel (honestly?) a little bit frantic.

In any competitive business, whenever a new idea proved successful, it was usually mimicked. Publishing was no different, but the digital age had spawned a gaming-the-system mentality not seen since the bad old days of pulp magazine. And some players were clearly less concerned about achieving a creative ideal than with the factory-like grinding out of product—and profit.

Sure, healthy competition was good. *Unhealthy* competition, not so much. A business could withstand only so many predatory participants, people who treated it less like a legitimate trade and more like, well, what a spirited friend of mine might call—

A racket. Is that the word you're looking for?

"Yes, Jack. If racket means caring more about money than meaning."

Money ain't a curse word, honey.

"I'm not claiming it is. We all have to make a living—"

Not all of us. Not anymore.

With a shiver, I conceded Jack was right, in more ways than one.

There was no living to be made when you weren't living. And Jack would know, since he was a ghost.

I didn't mean that he was stealthy or sneaky, or that he "ghosted" me by refusing to return my texts. I meant Jack Shepard was an actual dead man—a specter, a spirit, the departed soul of a murdered detective, gunned down on these premises in 1949 while pursuing a lead in a case.

Raymond Chandler once wrote that a dead man was the best fall guy in the world because he never talked back.

I begged to differ.

On the other hand, there was a possibility that Jack wasn't real at all. That he was no more than a figment of my fervent reader's imagination.

Any therapist would say as much. "Jack is a syndrome," they'd proclaim. The gruff, masculine voice in my head was an alter ego, my way of coping with the stresses of modern living. This hard-boiled "ghost" was merely a distillation of all the colorful characters I'd grown up reading about in my father's library, the kind of spirited soul who was brave enough to speak the blunt or off-color thoughts that I was too polite to think, let alone permit myself to say.

As far as the "stresses" of modern living, I couldn't deny I had a few. Being a widow, I'd endured my share of grief. Now a single mom, I was raising a headstrong boy, who lately enjoyed giving me some. And as a bookseller, well . . . let's just say I was still alive, though the twenty-first century sometimes seemed determined to ghost me.

"We're not dead yet!" my aunt Sadie Thornton liked to declare, usually in a *Monty Python* accent with a cheeky twinkle in her Yankee eye.

She and I were co-owners of a landmark bookshop in the small town of Quindicott, Rhode Island. And as I rolled out of bed one crisp autumn morning, I had the history of modern book covers on my mind for a specific reason.

Turns out, I wasn't the only one.

Yawning my way across the living room, I heard my eleven-year-old son's voice blasting out of the kitchen. He was chatting loudly on the phone, unusual for seven A.M. on a Monday. And my typically morning-grumpy child was actually *giggling*.

"I'm not kidding!" he squealed. "It's a book cover! Here's another one: The picture shows a gorilla . . . No, a *real* gorilla, like King Kong, throwing a guy into a crowd of people way down on the ground. And he's wearing a tuxedo!"

Spencer paused to hear a reply. "No, it's the monkey wearing the tuxedo. His name is funny, too. He's called the Whispering Gorilla."

I stopped in my tracks in the middle of the living room, wondering why the coffee-table book, which I'd left (where else?) on the coffee table, was no longer there. My mobile phone was present and accounted for, as were my empty teacup and black-framed glasses, but the valuable book that had been specially delivered to our shop last night—the one with my handwritten Post-it note that read *Do Not Touch*—was gone.

"This next cover is titled 'Batman,'" Spencer continued, "but it doesn't look like any Batman I've ever seen. There's a dead guy hanging from a rope, with his tongue sticking out. And there's a girl on the floor underneath him." His voice lowered to a whisper. "She's in her underwear. It says *Spicy Mystery* on top of the picture."

I grabbed my glasses, shoved them on, and headed to the kitchen, where I found Spencer still on the phone, standing at the table with his back to me. Before he knew it, I was pulling the oversize volume out of his hand.

"This is not a book for you, young man. And you know that. Who's on the phone?"

"Amy," he replied.

"Tell Amy I'm looking forward to her visit this weekend and say good-bye."

Tapping my foot, I retied my robe twice while I waited for my son to finish his call.

"Now go to school."

"It doesn't start for an hour!"

"Then have breakfast."

"I had breakfast."

"All right, then you can sit down and watch me eat mine."

CHAPTER 2

Table Talk

When your mother asks, "Do you want a piece of advice?" it's a mere formality. It doesn't matter if you answer yes or no. You're going to get it anyway.

—Erma Bombeck

WHILE I LADLED up steel-cut oatmeal from my aunt's slow cooker, my son collapsed into a chair with a frustrated sigh. Once the air went out of him, so did the fight.

"I'm sorry, Mom. I didn't mean to make you angry."

The sincere apology melted me. Spencer was a good kid. Disciplining him never gave me joy. But every child needed boundaries, and since I was his only parent now, I had to hold the line.

"I'm not angry. But I *will* be if you ignore another note of mine."

"I won't."

"You promise?"

He promised. "I was curious, that's all."

I didn't doubt it. When I returned to the kitchen table with a bottle of honey and jar of walnuts, I found Spencer still focused on the big book.

"What is this exactly?"

"It's an advance copy of a fancy art book that celebrates the history of American book covers. We're hosting a launch party for the authors. It's going to be a very big deal."

"Is that why you and Aunt Sadie have been talking for days about artists I never heard of? And our shop was on TV yesterday morning? Because of this book?"

"I knew you had a high IQ. You make me so proud." I mussed his hair—copper, like mine and my late father's.

"Quit kidding." He pulled away.

"You're a kid who's fun to kid."

"Ha-ha," he said dryly. Then he shifted, uncomfortably I thought, though his freckled face was earnest. "Mom, why don't you sell those books?"

"What books?"

"The ones I was telling Amy about. Books like *Spicy Mystery*? I've never seen them in the store."

"That's because those aren't books, Spencer. They're pulp magazines, and they were published a long time ago, before modern mass market paperback books, which is the kind we sell."

"Are the magazines you're talking about like the ones in the attic? Those old magazines that belonged to Grandpa?"

"Yes, those were pulps he collected. *Black Mask*, mostly."

"They smell funny."

"That's because the acetone in the paper is making them rot . . ." (I did my best to preserve what I could with acid-free bags, but some of the magazines were already too far gone.) "Pretty soon, nothing will be left but dust."

Spencer fell silent, thinking about that. "So this new art book is a way to keep people from forgetting how cool those pulp covers were?"

"That's the idea."

"And the art show downstairs will have pictures from *Spicy Mystery*?"

"Maybe. Why?'

"I think they're cool. Scary and weird, but really cool, too. I want Amy to see them."

"Oh, no, you don't. The last thing I need is a call from Amy's mother, accusing *my* son of showing *her* daughter *adult* things."

"Those old pulps were for adults only, then?"

"They sure were, Spence."

Now, that's a truckload of baloney, and you know it.

I gritted my teeth, relieved my son couldn't hear the ghost in my head. *Stay out of this, Jack,* I silently warned.

Why? You know I'm right. Lots of boys his age read pulps. They were sold in every drug and dime store, not to mention every penny-ante newsstand in the country.

That was another time, I told the ghost. *And times have changed.*

Change ain't always for the better. From my perspective, the march of time has trampled sanity and nearly all common sense.

Your perspective isn't relevant.

Why not?

Because you're not alive.

So? You don't have to be a part of time to have an opinion about it.

Yes, you do.

No, you don't.

While the ping-pong match went down inside my head, Spencer's stubborn Thornton streak rose up. Sitting straight in his chair, he declared—

"You can stop me from showing Amy the covers, but *I'm* going to see them!"

I wasn't in the mood for another debate, and thanks to Aunt Sadie, there was no need.

"See what?" she asked, breezing into the kitchen.

I tapped the table. "I found Spencer in here, looking at the book that arrived last night."

"The one Salient House sent you?" Sadie raised an eyebrow as she dished up her own bowl of oatmeal. "I'll bet some of those Robert McGinnis cover girls caught his eye."

"He didn't get that far. Mr. Curious got stuck in the *Spicy Mystery* section."

Sadie laughed. "Well, those old magazines were naughty, but no naughtier than what's on cable these days."

I told you, Jack gloated. *You should listen to your auntie. She's a wise old bird.*

I got the smug treatment from Spencer, too. "See, Mom!"

"I'll tell you what I see. A boy who's already not allowed to watch certain channels without my say-so, and"—I pointed at the wall clock—"one who's going to be late for his school bus if he doesn't get a move on."

"I'm going. Bye, Mom! Bye, Aunt Sadie!"

A minute later, we heard my son's sneakers hitting the stairs.

Sadie sat down. "Are you all set with the babysitter tonight?"

"Bonnie Franzetti can't make it, so I'm using her friend Tracy."

"Tracy?" Sadie thought for a moment. "You mean that girl with the blue hair?"

"Don't look so worried. Tracy Mahoney is a very nice young woman. She's in one of our new book groups, and she likes the same video games as Spencer, so they should have a good time."

Aunt Sadie touched my hand. "I'm sorry I can't go to Blackstone Falls in your place. I just couldn't let Bud go to the Retail Hardware Association dinner stag. Not after he asked me so sweetly to be his date."

"You and Bud deserve a night out. Spencer will be fine. And I'm happy to pick up those paintings. After all, it's part of my job, not yours . . ."

And so it was, because I was the shop's "events manager," a position I'd created after setting up our first-ever event space. The multipurpose room, which we also rented to community groups, was just one part of our grand store makeover, a plan I'd launched after moving back to Quindicott from New York.

With a bank account full of my late husband's insurance money, I'd convinced my aunt to trust my ideas on saving her failing bookstore. Together we overhauled the inventory

as I spearheaded restoration of the interior and exterior, replaced the old metal displays with beautiful oak book-
shelves, added comfy reading chairs and floor lamps, and
expanded the business into the adjoining storefront.

Newly christened Buy the Book, thanks to my preco-
cious son, the Thornton family's tired "We Buy and Sell
Books" soon became a hot regional store and vital online
business. We blew up Sadie's customer base to a worldwide
collectors' market. We formed reading groups, reached out
to local authors for signings, coordinated events with St.
Francis University, and booked big-name writers on national
tours. To wit—

This coming weekend, we were hosting a launch party
for *By Its Cover: A History of Modern Book and Magazine
Illustration.* Writers, artists, and academic critics were coming, along with the press. And it wasn't just because this
gorgeous, full-color book presented a celebration of cover
artists though time.

The authors, Liam and Sally Palantine, were a renowned
and highly respected power couple of New York publishing.
After decades in the business, they'd retired to their summer
home in nearby Newport, which was lucky for us. As loyal
customers of our shop, they were only too pleased to entrust
our store with their launch-party plans.

Given their publicity savvy, the Palantines were the ones to
suggest we stage an art exhibit to go with their launch, featur-
ing some of the original cover paintings included in their book.
The publisher guaranteed national coverage, and they delivered. A CBS news producer sent out a crew for B-roll footage
of our shop, which Sadie, Spencer, and I watched excitedly on
yesterday's *Sunday Morning* profile of the Palantines.

As for the art show, it would be another feather in our
bookshop's cap. But it meant I had to oversee the details—
and *not* screw anything up.

The Palantines had arranged shipments of a few paintings, which were coming by delivery service. But a local
collector would agree to let our store borrow his works only
if we picked them up in person.

That collector's name was Walt Waverly, a passing acquaintance of Sadie's from the rare books world. Unfortunately, he asked that we pick up the works this evening, and since my aunt was already committed to an important date with her longtime beau, I'd be the one making the trip to Walt's, along with two of my oldest friends.

"I know they're your friends," Aunt Sadie said, "not to mention excellent store customers, but the truth is, I doubt I could stand two hours in the same car with that pair."

"Why not?"

"You know why not. Those boys are constantly bickering!"

"They're not boys anymore, Aunt Sadie, and they're not that bad . . ."

I couldn't help defending them. I'd known Seymour and Brainert since we were nerdy kids, sharing our favorite books and running around Prescott Woods in search of Tolkien's hobbits and Narnia's fauns.

"You know they're avid readers," I pointed out. "Which means they have contemplative sides, too."

"When they're alone, sure. But they won't be alone on your trip. They'll be packed into the same van, driving and *bickering.*"

The Thornton in me stubbornly disagreed. "The ride through Blackstone Valley is beautiful, especially at this time of year. Once those two settle in, I'm sure they'll sit back and enjoy the scenery. I have no doubt our trip will be quiet, peaceful, and completely uneventful."

CHAPTER 3

Road Trip

I intend to live forever, or die trying.

—Groucho Marx

"MAN, OH, MAN," Seymour said, his big foot heavy on the gas pedal. "I cannot wait to see this guy's collection!"

With excitement animating his round face, Seymour Tarnish hurled his rattletrap of a Volkswagen bus headlong into another billowing fog bank. In the back seat, I grabbed for the shoulder harness I should have put on an hour earlier and advised Seymour to—

"Slow down! We'll get to Blackstone Falls soon enough, and I'd rather arrive in one piece."

Outside the van windows, beyond the borders of the state highway, gorgeous scenery whizzed by—majestic trees in all their autumn glory, harvest gold fields with bright red barns, and quaint little towns crowned with white church steeples.

We couldn't see any of it. Between our late start, spotty showers, and the rolling Atlantic fog, we might as well have been speeding through the Lincoln Tunnel.

"I wonder if we'll see any Mike Shayne art from the 1960s," Seymour mused aloud. "Those mysteries had the greatest paperback covers ever!"

From the passenger seat came an exasperated groan. Professor J. Brainert Parker was oblivious to the capricious coastal weather and Seymour's distracted driving. The slender academic was far more concerned with making his point than trifles like traffic accidents.

"Five minutes ago you said the Edgar Rice Burroughs paperbacks had the 'greatest covers ever.' Perhaps you should make up your mind, Mailman."

The term *mailman* isn't usually applied as an insult, and delivering the mail is exactly what Seymour did for a living. But Brainert uttered the simple noun with the same withering condescension he used on students who dared to allow their phones to vibrate during his literary lectures.

On Seymour, however, the professor's disapproving tone had zero effect. And I knew why. As one of the most voracious readers I'd ever met (and a brimming font of superficially useless facts), Seymour had channeled his hobbies and intellect into becoming a *Jeopardy!* champion. The game-show win not only made him a local star in our little town; it gave him the means to fulfill his lifelong dream of buying (of all things) an ice cream truck. Now Seymour was not only everyone's favorite mailman; he was also the town's only ice cream man, making him a beloved figure to every kid, mom, and Dove bar lover in the wider Quindicott area.

All this notoriety gave my socially awkward friend one more thing, an impenetrable shell of confidence that no one stood a chance of piercing, let alone his longtime frenemy.

"This Waverly guy we're going to see has all sorts of original stuff from the old magazines, too. Right, Pen?"

"Yes, he does, Seymour. You'll see it when we get there."

If we get there, I silently added. With our driver at the wheel, I had my doubts. On the other hand, Seymour did possess one of the most extensive collections of pulp magazines I'd ever seen, and nothing (not rain nor snow nor professorial put-downs) would diminish this postal worker's determination to view a private collection of vintage pulp paintings.

"Man! I hope he has a few *Spicy Mystery* covers. Those artists were masters."

"At what?" Brainert sniffed. "Paint by numbers?"

"At portraying the feminine form in all its glory!"

"Sans clothing, and in outrageous and exploitative situations, no doubt."

"There was no nudity on pulp covers," Seymour pointed out. "It was all suggestive. The women of the *Spicy* magazines were scantily yet tastefully clad. And who cares if the women were nude, anyway? The greatest artists in the world painted nudes. I never heard you beef about Botticelli and his Venus on the Half Shell, or Michelangelo or Carpaccio."

Once again, the professor groaned. "You do mean *Caravaggio*, don't you? Because *carpaccio* is an appetizer at Olive Garden."

"Yeah, I know." Seymour snickered. "I was just trying to get a rise out of you."

"And you've been succeeding nonstop for the last hour," I muttered.

"You must understand, I am not talking about nudity, per se," the professor now argued. "I am referring to the lurid nature of the illustrations: a mad scientist menacing a poor girl with a giant hypodermic needle, a hunchback monster slavering over one of your 'tastefully clad' victims."

Seymour released the steering wheel to throw up his hands. "Now you're talking about the fiction!"

"So?"

"So a pulp artist's job is to *illustrate* the story," Seymour went on as the bus began to drift into the oncoming lane.

"Seymour, watch the road!" I cried.

Our driver remained oblivious. "You can't condemn the artist for that. Besides, not all the pulps had shocking covers. *Black Mask* had really classy art. Did you say something, Pen?"

Both men turned away from the road to stare at me. I saw them only in silhouette, illuminated by the headlights of an onrushing truck. Between my shouting and pointing and the truck's blasting horn, Seymour righted the bus, narrowly avoiding a head-on collision, and I faced the possibility that my life could end over a pulp-art show!

Don't worry, doll, I got your back. Hell, I'll even steer

this jalopy out of harm's way, if need be. The only one who's a goner in this piece of junk went a long time ago—and that would be me.

Jack Shepard had been quiet most of the day, and I'd been too busy at the shop to notice. Now he was awake. And annoyed.

Sure, I caught lead poisoning in my prime, but there are worse fates—like listening to this pair of numbskulls bump gums for what feels like eternity!

The complaint was accompanied by a sharp decrease in the van's temperature. *Listen, Jack, I know you're upset about the chatter, but could you turn down the frost? This old Volkswagen is already draftier than a medieval castle.*

As suddenly as it came, the frigid blast dissipated.

So, Penny? What takes us out of Cornpone-cott? And in the company of these two clucking loons?

It's just work. This is a business trip.

Yeah, with all that birdbrain chatter, how could it possibly be a pleasure trip?

Had I known Brainert and Seymour would get so worked up over cover art, I would have spared you the agony and left your old Buffalo nickel at home.

That coin, which had once served as Jack's lucky charm in life, was now (for lack of a better term) my mobile connection to the dead detective. The physical talisman allowed me to take the ghost beyond the prison of our shop's fieldstone walls.

Don't let it ruffle your skirt. It's a kick to get out of that hick town once in a while, even if it's only to go to another hick town. But why with this pair of rutabagas?

Seymour volunteered to haul the paintings we need for our art show so I wouldn't have to rent a van. And Brainert came out of academic curiosity—and at my request since he's helping me arrange a second book signing on his university's campus.

It's a crying shame your work never takes you to more interesting places. Why can't your business trips ever involve a hoppin' gin joint or saucy burlesque review? I'd even prefer the track—as long as you placed a few bets on the bobtails for me.

That is a tragedy. Sorry, Jack.

Aw, forget it. You never have to apologize to me, though you might have some explaining to do to your slack-jawed pals.

I suddenly realized the nonstop bickering in the van had halted. Brainert was now openly staring at me over the back of his seat, and Seymour was eyeing me through the rear-view mirror.

"What is it?" I asked. "What's wrong?"

Seymour's expression was full of concern. "Are you okay, Pen? You completely zoned out, for like a full minute."

"It was quite disconcerting." Brainert nodded. "We spoke to you, but you didn't appear to hear us."

Having a ghost inside one's head can do that to a person.

Okay, that's the answer I wanted to give. But I wasn't up for a lecture on the benefits of modern psychiatry. Fortunately, I was spared the effort of making up a lame excuse by a sign suddenly revealed in our van's headlights.

"Eyes front, Seymour," I commanded. "The turn for Blackstone Falls is dead ahead!"

Are you trying to insult me, doll?

I said "dead ahead," Jack, not "deadhead."

I know. The ghost snickered. *I was just trying to get a rise out of you.*

CHAPTER 4

One Man's Treasures

I'm the oldest antique in town.

—Norman Rockwell

WALTER WAVERLY INSISTED we call him "Old Walt." Pushing seventy and heavyset, he clearly enjoyed the "nice old guy" persona. He even wore a long beard that was so snowy white he could have doubled as a department store Santa—but only if that Santa was a seasoned salesman, looking to unload the entire contents of his North Pole toy shop on three unsuspecting visitors.

"Everything inside is for sale!" Old Walt announced as we entered his sprawling mock Tudor home. Leading us to the library, he invited us to enjoy the spread of coffee, tea, and cookies he'd laid out in front of the roaring fire, which nicely dispelled the chill from our dark and stormy drive.

"This library is where I display a lot of my art," Walt informed us. "What I don't have stored in the attic, anyway."

The expansive room occupied nearly half the ground floor of the two-story home. The decor was original, and I suspected much of the furniture was, too, because it looked antique—but not in a good way. The chairs were ratty, the upholstery on the love seat torn and crudely mended. The doorknobs and a standing lamp were forged copper yet covered with a patina of green from age and neglect.

The house itself also needed repairs. Paint and gold leaf flaked from the ornate ceiling, dust dulled the chandelier, and smoke stains blackened the marble hearth.

By contrast, Old Walt's pristine collection of rare books appeared to be in perfect condition. As I helped myself to tea and butter cookies, Brainert pointed out one of the many gems in the old man's glass-enclosed bookcases. "Is that a first edition of *To Kill a Mockingbird*?"

"Yes, it is, Professor Parker." Walt grinned with pride. "That shelf is all first editions."

Brainert's eyes went wide as he read the spines. "*Tender Is the Night, The Old Man and the Sea, The Grapes of Wrath, East of Eden*—and here's a copy of *The Disappearance* by Philip Wylie! That novel is a forgotten classic."

"If you're interested, Professor, in any of those titles, or the entire shelf for that matter, we could agree on a price."

"Oh, my. The entire shelf?" Brainert's eyebrows rose. "I doubt I could afford—"

Hearing the start of that sentence, Walt didn't waste time listening to the rest. Abruptly, he turned to me.

"Mrs. McClure, the truth is, after I spoke to you about our appointment, I made the decision to offer your store my entire collection. All of it, including the paintings, if you'll give me a fair price. What do you think?"

I was more taken aback than Brainert. I'd come here to borrow some cover art, not negotiate a major purchase. Furthermore, I was not the partner with decades of experience in the rare books market, yet even I knew, with a collection this large, a consignment deal made more sense than one large outlay of cash.

Would Walt reject consignment?

I didn't want to commit to anything (certainly not without my aunt's input), but I didn't want to lose the opportunity, either.

"I have to admit, you're taking me by surprise," I said carefully. "Why are you in such a hurry to sell everything? I hope it's not your health."

"No, ma'am, I'm hearty as an ox. It's something else . . ." An awkward pause followed. "I need to get out of here." He shook his head, white beard swaying. "And I'm not taking any of this with me. I'm done with it. This stuff—all of it—has got to go."

How odd, I thought. Why would a man so devoted to a lifetime of collection suddenly be "done with it"? I tried to ask (gently, of course), but Walt cut me off. And then the salesman was back.

"One fair offer for the whole collection, Mrs. McClure, what do you say? It would certainly save me time."

"I understand," I said, feeling the pressure, "and I'd *like* us to make a deal. But Sadie would have to inventory everything first, before we could even estimate an offer."

"Oh, sure, of course!" Walt nodded, appearing relieved I hadn't rejected him outright. "Sadie can come up anytime, and I'll take her through everything. It's a fine collection, let me tell you!"

And he did.

While Old Walt continued chatting me up, I helped myself to more tea and cookies. Brainert joined me. Only Seymour (uncharacteristically) ignored the treats, including the treasure trove of rare books. Instead, he eagerly took in the library's gallery, ogling the paintings hung there as if he were a pilgrim, marveling in reverent awe at an enshrined collection of cathedral relics.

Every minute or so, he would point to a picture and cry out with excitement—less like a pilgrim (come to think of it) and more like a kid in Santa's Toyland.

"Look! A Doc Savage paperback cover by James Bama! Did you know that Bantam Books was launched on the backs of these pulp reprints? Doc Savage kept that company in business for decades . . . Oh wow, an actual Margaret Brundage *Weird Tales* cover. I didn't think any of her delicate chalk art survived!"

Finally Seymour made such a racket we couldn't ignore him any longer. "You guys have *got* to see this! It's the Nathan Brock cover painting for the June 1948 issue of *Spicy High Society*! His work is super rare!"

To my surprise, the ghost abruptly sounded off in my head. *Nathan Brock. Yeah. Like a stopped clock, the mailman is right twice a day.*

About what? I asked (silently, of course).

About Nathan Brock's stuff being rare. And I know why.

You do?

I waited for an answer, but the ghost went quiet.

Jack? Are you still there?

I'm here, doll. The fact is . . . I got history with Nathan Brock. But it's a long story, and you're busy.

I'd like to know, I pressed, but the ghost wasn't talking. He spoke only two words before going silent.

Another time.

I tried to refocus on Walt's never-ending sales pitch, but I couldn't stop wondering about Jack's "history" with an obscure pulp cover artist.

The name Nathan Brock rang no bells for me, but if Jack knew the man, I wanted to check out his work. Excusing myself with Walt, I hurried to Seymour's side.

CHAPTER 5

Picture This

Too many times naked women and death walked side
by side.

—Mickey Spillane, *Survival Zero*

THE MAN HAD talent. That was clear. With one glimpse
of Brock's vivid canvas, I was riveted into silence.

Using brilliant brushstrokes, the artist sensuously defined a
nude woman, seated backward in an ornate chair with her more
intimate parts discretely hidden behind the chair's back. Her
golden blond hair was bobbed short and sassy, her blue eyes
were sparkling, and her apple red lips were curled into a come-
hither smile as she flung her pink arms wide for the viewer.

Being a cover for a pulp mystery magazine, Nathan
Brock's painting included one final element. Behind the unsuspecting woman, between the fluttering folds of saffron
yellow curtains, a big, rough-looking man with pockmarked
cheeks had slipped into the room. His gloved hands gripped
a long dagger. The picture froze the action of the killer holding the blade aloft, right before his deadly strike.

I actually shivered.

Though I'd seen thousands of cover illustrations over the
years, few had the shocking power of this one. Seymour

praised the artist, and I did, too, but I wondered if the impact was partly due to the woman who'd modeled for him.

This one didn't look like the generic flappers who typically graced the *Spicy* covers, pretty girls with bland faces. For one thing, this young woman displayed an actual personality. Her dynamic energy was evident in her sapphire blue eyes and vivacious expression, so skillfully captured.

Jack said he knew the artist. Did he know this model, too?

I guess there's no point in asking you, right? I quietly pressed the ghost. *I'm sorry . . . is it your memory, Jack? Is that it? Past events aren't quite as clear as they used to be?*

They're clear enough, Jack answered. His tone was even clearer. The ghost was irritated that I'd goaded him into talking.

So you do *remember?*

I remember, all right. You don't forget a dame like that.

"Then you two were involved? Romantically?"

Wrong adverb. I was involved—professionally. Someone hired me to investigate the crime behind her picture. The story's a whopper, too, though no scribbler ever put it in True Confessions. *Come to think of it, the truth never made the legit news, either . . .*

Okay, now that you're talking again, you have to tell me about it.

Why? It's just a dusty old criminal case.

So? You've dusted off plenty of old cases and opened them for me. Why not this one?

I didn't have many cases like this one.

I'm listening.

I told you already. Not now. You're distracted.

And once again, the ghost went silent. I tried to poke him, several times—with no luck.

Fine, I told the ghost. *Then you know what? I'll start my own investigation.* "Excuse me, Mr. Waverly—"

"Just call me Walt, Mrs. McClure, plain old Walt."

"Okay, Walt—and please call me Penelope or Pen; I'll answer to either. Now I have a question for you. What can you tell me about this particular painting?"

"Funny you should ask, because there is an interesting story attached to it."

"What sort of story?"

"A crime story."

"Crime story?" Brainert cut in with a frown. "Sir, are you sure you're not talking about the pulp fiction this painting illustrates?"

"No, Professor, I'm talking about a real crime. If you're interested, perhaps we can agree on a price. Although, like your enthusiastic friend said, original paintings by Nathan Brock are scarce, and this one won't be cheap."

I knew Brainert would have no interest in such lurid fare, but he was too polite to say so. Instead, he simply shook his head and muttered, "Not on a university salary, I'm afraid."

Walt turned. "Maybe Mr. Tarnish is interested."

He wasn't.

By now, Seymour had wandered off to stare at a large portrait hanging in a secluded alcove at the far end of the library.

"About this Brock painting," I pressed, "can you share any more details concerning the crime surrounding it?"

Old Walt scratched his head. "Not offhand. I heard the story way back when I acquired it, maybe twenty-five years ago. Wrote it down in one of my notebooks. I'd have to locate it in my archives. I keep them in the attic . . ."

As our host launched into a rambling sales pitch on the contents of his attic, Brainert nudged me and whispered, "I really do think Mr. Waverly is confusing the *story* that Brock's painting illustrates with an actual event. Don't badger the old man. It will only add to his confusion."

I certainly didn't want to cause Mr. Waverly any distress. "Maybe Seymour can sort it out for me," I whispered back. "He's an expert on that sort of thing."

But Seymour was paying no attention to our conversation. He was still standing in the alcove, distracted by that large portrait. Actually, *distracted* was too weak a word. *Mesmerized* would have been more accurate.

"Earth to Seymour!" I called.

Oblivious, he just kept gazing at the picture.

"Oh, for Pete's sake," Brainert muttered. "Tarnish, what are you gawking at?!"

The professor's sharp classroom voice finally broke the painting's spell. Reluctantly, Seymour tore his gaze away from the canvas. Blinking as if awakened from a dream, he stared at us both.

"What am I looking at?" he rasped in a thoroughly un-Seymour-like tone. "Only the most beautiful woman I've ever seen."

"Please," the professor scoffed. "Not another lurid pulp cover."

"It's not a cover," Seymour said, his gaze returning to the picture. "This is the real thing."

"Let me guess. You've fallen for yet another femme fatale in a vintage James Bond movie poster?"

Seymour not only failed to register his friend's sarcasm; he didn't even muster a snarky comeback.

Here we go again, I thought, my curiosity propelling me across the library to view yet another painting. A moment later, Brainert threw up his hands and fell into step behind me.

CHAPTER 6

Portrait of a Woman Unhinged

I saw at once . . . the peculiarities of the design . . .

         —Edgar Allan Poe, *The Oval Portrait*

SEYMOUR WAS RIGHT—THIS was no pulp cover.

The skillfully rendered portrait depicted a young woman standing on a rocky beach. As the ocean wind buffeted her slender form, cascades of mahogany hair swirled around her ethereal features. The woman's complexion was pale, her expression difficult to describe yet central to the painting's magnetism.

While she wasn't openly crying, the woman's delicate features were painted in a clear expression of distress. The aspect of anxiety was rendered so poignantly and powerfully it both captivated and disturbed.

Why was the young woman so upset? The viewer couldn't help asking, and this was obviously by design. Her sea green eyes appeared almost fearful as they stared out of the painting, directly at you. Yet there was nothing in the picture that explained what she should be afraid of—or why she should be so unhappy—only her figure and the dramatic landscape.

With the female subject positioned left of center on the rectangular canvas, the background was given plenty of room for display, but the colors the painter chose made little sense (at least to me).

The woman's dress was drab gray and more than a century out of fashion, while the world around her glowed with vivid, psychedelic hues, colors bizarre enough to suggest the painter was either recalling an acid trip or expressing a vision detached from reality.

Over the woman's shoulders, a preternaturally purple sky dominated the horizon, while frothy lime green waves with yellow foam battered against a shore covered with garish blue and pink rocks not found in nature, at least not in my neck of Rhode Island—and I *knew* it was my neck of the state for a simple reason. I recognized a structure in the distance.

Apparently, so did Brainert. "That's the Finch Inn!"

In reality, the renowned inn was located too far inland to be seen from the Atlantic shoreline, but this was, after all, the painter's vision. And there was no mistaking that inn.

The grand Queen Anne, rendered in classic Victorian colors, looked exactly like the one owned by my good friends Barney and Fiona Finch. They'd operated the place as a B and B for years, though it was originally the private home of a wealthy spinster.

"So who is the artist?" I asked. "Is he from around here?"

"She," Walt corrected. "The painting is a self-portrait of the woman who first owned that Victorian mansion."

"I knew it!" Seymour cried. "It's an original Harriet McClure!"

Walt smiled. "You have sharp little eyes, Mr. Tarnish."

My sharp little ears perked up at that, along with my hackles—as they tended to do when I heard a reference to anyone in the McClure family. My late husband had been related to Harriet McClure, which meant my son shared her DNA. And that concerned me.

Since moving back to Quindicott, I'd tried to put the past behind me, for my son's sake as well as my own. That difficult past was born from a tragic truth. My husband had taken his own life. He'd suffered from depression, and I couldn't help wondering if Harriet had been similarly afflicted.

"As a young woman, the artist became estranged from her rich and influential family," Walt explained. "That Victorian mansion was built to exile her from their Newport world."

"I know her story," I said. "Harriet McClure was given that huge Queen Anne, along with the acres of grounds around it, including swatches that reached the ocean. With no husband or children, high society shunning her, and Quindicott townspeople keeping their distance, Harriet became a recluse. She spent her days wandering the woods and shoreline of her property. At night she painted hundreds of canvases, each one a self-portrait."

Brainert nodded. "A century ago, because of her wealth and name, Harriet would have been called *eccentric*, at least in polite circles. More modern mentions aren't so kind."

I sighed at this unfortunate truth. Despite the apparent progress society had made toward understanding mental illness (and the social media generation's own celebration of "selfies") Harriet was still commonly referred to as the "Madwoman of Quindicott."

Of course, I'd seen examples of her work before. Almost everyone in Quindicott had. A Harriet McClure original hung in the lobby of the Finch Inn, another in city hall, and a third in the town library. Some paintings occasionally popped up at local flea markets, or even at Gilder's Antiques on Cranberry Street—the paintings that survived, anyway.

According to local lore, most of Harriet's work did not. Legend had it the bulk of her portraits were burned for firewood during a particularly brutal winter . . . or so said Barney Finch, whose grandparents had served Harriet for decades, his grandfather as her groundskeeper, his grandmother as her housekeeper and cook.

Though the Quindicott townspeople believed the Finch family *bought* the estate from the McClures after Harriet's death, that wasn't actually true.

Fiona Finch once privately confessed to my aunt that Barney's grandparents were too poor to buy anything. Harriet McClure willed her property to the sweet married couple who'd taken care of her. After their lifetime of service, she wanted to make sure they would always have a home.

Despite her reputation as the "Madwoman of Quindicott," that decision did not appear "crazy and irrational" to me—though it was the prevailing opinion in my late husband's family.

The younger McClures knew the truth and seemed especially bitter about the Finch family's "windfall," as they referred to it, maybe because they were a trust-fund generation. For them, the McClure legacy was nothing more than a periodic check sent to them by a firm that had grown fat from the interest on the McClure family fortune.

Barney and Fiona, on the other hand, never received easy money. They'd toiled for years, using their own ingenuity, spending their own earned incomes, and making many personal sacrifices to polish Harriet's run-down Queen Anne into the gem it now was—*and* build a thriving, enviable business out of her property.

"Some say she's still around," Walt added, gesturing to the painting. "A haunted hermit in life, still haunting after death."

"I never believed those ghost stories about Harriet," Seymour said.

"You mean those bizarre reports of people seeing her roaming the grounds around her old home? I'm relieved to hear it," Brainert sniffed. "While I always appreciate a fine ghost story, believing they actually exist is lunacy."

"But the stories persist, even today," I pointed out, somewhat defensively (for obvious reasons). "Last month the *Quindicott Bulletin* reported a new Harriet sighting. A married couple, both of them respectable Realtors from Providence, claimed they saw her while hiking trails around the inn."

"How did they know it was Harriet's ghost?" Brainert asked.

"Come on, Brainpan," Seymour replied, "you don't know the local lore? Harriet's ghost is easily identified by the long lacy shawl she wore in life."

"That's right," I said. "The couple swore Harriet was floating because she was too high off the ground and moving too fast to be walking—according to the *Bulletin*, anyway."

"Oh, please." Brainert practically rolled his eyes. "Pen, you're the one who describes the *Bulletin* as a supermarket circular with a few pages of local gossip thrown in. You know we can never believe anything we read in that glorified penny saver."

"Funny," Seymour murmured, distracted again by the painting. "I wonder why there's no lace shawl in this picture."

"Probably because of her young age," I reasoned. "In all the other self-portraits I've seen, Harriet is middle-aged or older. I doubt she's even twenty-five in this picture."

The doll's easy on the eyes, too, Jack observed.

Looks like my friend agrees, I silently acknowledged. *Seymour has yet to stop gaping at her.*

Yeah, your mailman pal's gone off the deep end, all right, but who wouldn't take the plunge for a looker like her? The real mystery is how a rich young dame ended up a spinster. Were the local gigolos on strike?

I doubt Quindicott ever had gigolos, Jack.

Sorry, honey, no town on earth is devoid of a few gold-bricking gold diggers—of both sexes.

Seymour turned to Old Walt. "How did you come by this painting, Mr. Waverly? Did you know Harriet McClure?"

"Goodness, no! She lived and died before my time. But I've had this painting of hers for half my own lifetime."

"Where did you get it?"

"From a restaurant owner, a very long time ago, at least forty years."

"It's been hanging there that long?!" Seymour asked.

"No, I had a Roy Krenkel illustration of Tarzan in that alcove forever. Finally sold it three years ago and replaced it with Harriet. I remember because my wife helped me move it down from the attic to the library. That was the last good day I remember . . . before she got sick."

"Sorry to hear that," Seymour said. Brainert and I echoed his concern.

Frowning, Walt admitted, "She passed a few months ago. The cancer took its time killing her."

We all went silent for a moment, and Walt looked at the portrait again. "When I first saw this painting, I wasn't a big art collector. Back then, I was only dabbling as I traveled around the region, selling insurance. Harriet here caught my eye when I stopped to have lunch one day. I was surprised to learn the owner of the restaurant was going out of business and eager to liquidate what he could. Got her picture for practically nothing, too, because the guy already took it down and set it by the back door, near the garbage."

"Why?" I asked.

"He came to believe her self-portrait was cursed."

"Cursed?!" all three of us cried.

"What do you mean *cursed*?" Seymour demanded.

"*Malocchio* was the word he used," Walt went on. "It's Eye-talian for 'the evil eye.' I remember because that was the first time I'd heard the word, and I had to look it up!"

"Well, I don't believe in curses or evil eyes." Seymour folded his arms. "I believe we make our own luck, good or bad . . ." As his voice trailed off, his expression brightened. "You know what, Walt?"

"What?"

"This is *your* lucky day."

"And why is that?"

"Because I have got to own this painting."

CHAPTER 7

A Bid Too Far

See, how she leans her cheek upon her hand!
O, that I were a glove upon that hand,
That I might touch that cheek!

—William Shakespeare

BRAINERT AND I exchanged surprised glances at Seymour's sudden declaration, but nothing astonished us more than the mailman's next words—

"You said everything was for sale. Well, Walt, more than anything, I want to take Harriet home. You name the price."

Seymour Tarnish, long known as a headstrong haggler and the terror of the dealers' room at the annual New England Pulp Convention, was now practically inviting Walt Waverly to fleece him!

Stranger still, the man who'd been hard selling me for the past twenty minutes suddenly seemed reluctant to close a deal.

"Son, I'm sorry to tell you, this painting may be sold already."

Seymour blinked. "Excuse me? What do you mean *may*?"

"I put it online a few weeks ago, and a buyer contacted me with an offer. Seven hundred dollars—with one caveat.

The buyer insisted on coming here first to examine the painting, just to make sure it's genuine."

"I see," Seymour said. "So where is this mysterious buyer?"

Walt scratched his head. "I was expecting a visit this week but haven't heard back."

Seymour's eyes narrowed. "Look, Walt, you don't have to play me." He flashed him the I-am-wise-to-your-cheap-ploy smirk. "Even if this mysterious buyer existed, I'm the one who's here tonight. And I'll take this painting off your hands right now for *one thousand* bucks."

Old Walt frowned uncertainly.

"Your bird in the hand is right in front of you," Seymour pressed. "Snatch it while you have the chance!"

Walt stroked his beard. "I don't know. I already said yes to the other buyer. Some people can get very upset when they lose a done deal."

"It isn't done if you're not paid and the painting's still in your possession," Seymour fired back. "I'll give you twelve hundred!"

Walt shot Seymour a funny look. "Why do you want it so bad?"

With heart-tugging awe, the mailman locked his gaze on the portrait again. "She's beautiful," he whispered.

Walt went quiet a moment. "Okay, Mr. Tarnish, make it thirteen hundred and you got a deal. You obviously appreciate Harriet's work. That may make a difference."

"Difference?" I said. "What do you mean? Difference how?"

Walt shrugged. "With the curse thing and that bad luck and all . . ."

"Don't try to scare me out of it," Seymour said. "I want this painting, and I'll count myself lucky to get it. Will you take a check?"

"How about a digital bank transfer?"

Walt raised his smartphone. It was nestled in a sky blue phone case displaying tiny World War I biplanes.

When he saw it, Seymour grinned for two reasons. He recognized the phone case art as a reproduction of a cover from the Dare-Devil Aces pulp series (one of his favorites). And he had just enough money in his checking account to fund his purchase.

After their high-tech transaction, Walt handed Seymour a low-tech pen and steered him to a dark blue notebook on the cookie table.

"Just write your name, address, phone number, and to-day's date in my record book here. I always keep track of what I sell, who I sell it to, and what I sold it for."

"I'm surprised you haven't digitized your archives," Seymour remarked, taking the pen.

Walt shrugged. "Some of us old dogs get tired of learning new tricks."

CHAPTER 8

Buyer Beware

There is no trap so deadly as the trap you set for
yourself.

—Raymond Chandler, *The Long Goodbye*

WITH ITS THICK glass and solid frame, Harriet Mc-
Clure's strange self-portrait turned out to be quite heavy.
Walt and Seymour had to work together to wrestle the rect-
angle off the wall.

Despite his age, Walt climbed up and down his library
ladder like a nimble squirrel gathering nuts, while Seymour—
who could never be described as light on his feet—nearly
lost his balance on a footstool.

With Brainert giving outspoken directions, the two men
lowered the painting onto a side table. Immediately, the professor took a closer look at the canvas. After a long string of
hems and haws, he spoke.

"There's something wrong with this picture."

"What do you mean wrong?" Seymour demanded.

"I believe this might be a forgery," Brainert declared.

"You're crazy. What's your evidence?"

"Let me instruct you," Brainert replied in such a patronizing tone that he might as well have added the word *knuck-*

lehead. He then pulled a sterling silver pen from his lapel pocket, wiped a thin coating of dust off the picture glass, and tapped on a section of purple sky.

"Look along the edges of this cloud bank. Do you see the series of letters and numbers written in a very fine, spidery script?"

Seymour folded his arms. "Yeah, I see them."

"And here, on the beach. Is that supposed to be a two-headed baby carved into that red rock?"

"Sure looks like one baby with two heads. Could be two babies. It could go either way."

"Right here is a bar of music, running along the sand, while a bird hieroglyphic hovers over the house. And see that pink fish jumping out of the water? Something is written on its scales, but the script is so tiny I can't read it without a magnifying glass."

Seymour squinted. "Okay."

"And finally this bird above the house—"

"The seagull?"

"It's an albatross," Brainert corrected.

Seymour squinted again. "Looks like a seagull to me."

Old Walt stepped forward. "No, the professor is right—not about the forgery. I honestly can't say he's right or wrong about that. But he is right about the bird." Walt raised a finger and recited: *"What evil looks / Had I from old and young! / Instead of the cross, the Albatross / About my neck was hung."*

"Samuel Taylor Coleridge!" Brainert exclaimed. "I knew it!"

"Knew what?" Seymour said. "What are you talking about?"

Brainert smugly tapped the bird with his pen. "See the tiny M under the albatross? Clearly, that stands for *Mariner*, as in Coleridge's epic poem *Rime of the Ancient Mariner*—in which, of course, the careless killing of an innocent albatross is profoundly mythologized."

With a victory flourish, Brainert tucked the pen back into his lapel. "I concede that the woman in the picture *looks* like

Harriet, but she's far too young. No other existing self-portrait depicts her that age. Furthermore, there are no surreal elements in any of Harriet McClure's other paintings, so why would she indulge in such a technique here? Thus, I conclude this painting is a fake."

Seymour smirked. "Are you finished?"

Brainert raised an index finger. "There is one more detail I should point out, since you failed to notice it."

Seymour studied the portrait and finally shrugged. "Okay. I give."

"Ask yourself, Mailman, where is the signature? Because I don't see it. Yet Harriet always signed her work, in big flamboyant letters, which once again supports my theory that this work is a forgery."

"All right, Professor, I've been patient. Now it's your turn to make like a student and listen up."

Seymour counted down with his fingers.

"*First*, you have to be nuts to forge a virtually unknown painter's work. For what reason? To make a killing at the church flea market? Think, Brainiac, we are not talking Picasso here. Crazy Harriet is part of Quindicott folklore, not the international arts scene.

"*Second*. You obviously need to wear your glasses because I noticed those peculiar elements *before* we hauled the painting down. And you know what? They don't bother me in the least. Plenty of painters have put codes on their canvases—even your precious Caravaggio snuck a picture of himself into his *Bacchus* masterwork. In Harriet's case, this is an early painting, maybe her very first self-portrait, and it's clear to me she's desperate to communicate something. What it is, I don't know yet. But I feel as if she wants me to find out. That she's chosen me."

Brainert pursed his lips at Seymour's lovesick tone but said nothing. I had to admit that Seymour's statement did sound absurd. But he spoke with such passion—and (honestly) who was I to discount the legacy of a haunting spirit from another time communicating what few could appreciate or even see?

Abruptly, Seymour yanked the silver pen out of Brainert's pocket.

"Finally, there is something you failed to point out with this fancy pointy-pointer, so let me point it out for your pointy head."

With the tip of the pen, Seymour touched the lower right-hand portion of the glass, where the canvas met the dark wooden frame.

"Like I said, I know you have them, and you're too vain to wear them, but if you actually used your glasses, you would see the top of each cursive letter of Harriet's signature peeking out from under the wood. She signed this work. This frame is hiding her signature, that's all."

"Don't let that frame upset you," Walt put in. "I'm throwing it in for free."

"Great!" Seymour replied. "Then all we have to do is wrap her up and get her out to my van. Let's get this done, shall we? I have a good feeling about this."

Seymour used his smartphone to snap a few photos of Harriet McClure before he and Walt carefully wrapped Seymour's new pride and joy in protective crating and waterproof bubble wrap.

MINUTES LATER, WALT was all smiles as he returned to the house. When he did, he noticed me going through his blue notebook on the cookie table.

"What are you doing there, Pen?" He sounded upset. "Those transactions are meant to be private."

"Sorry, I was just checking to see if that story behind the Nathan Brock painting was in here."

"Oh, is that all!" Walt shook his head. "It wouldn't be in my blue book. The sale was too long ago. Like I mentioned earlier, that notebook is in my attic archives. Light's bad up there at night. I'll track it down for you in the morning."

"Thanks, I didn't mean to invade your privacy."

"It's just my policy. *All* my sales are *confidential*. I've had problems in the past."

"Problems? What sort of problems?"

Walt shrugged. "Collectors are funny birds. They can get very upset about losing a bidding war. I made the mistake of telling one bidder that he lost my Hannes Bok signed illustration to another bidder. Boy, oh, boy, was he angry. Went and tracked down the nice lady who bought the illustration for her son's birthday. When she refused to sell at double the price, he started harassing her. She had to get a restraining order, and I felt like a heel. Never again, never again . . ."

After Walt wound up his story, we loaded the rest of his loaner paintings into Seymour's VW. Walt even lent us some of his display easels. Luckily, the storm had let up, and we were able to get the work done without ducking raindrops.

At the last minute, Walt informed me that he'd placed prices on all the cover art paintings we were borrowing for the Palantines' event.

"If they sell, your shop takes fifteen percent, and I get the rest. How does that sound?"

It sounded good to me. Better than good. It was a step in the direction of that consignment arrangement I was hoping to reach with him.

I shook his hand. "We'll do our best for you, Walt."

"I know you will."

"And we'll take good care of the paintings, too."

"They're all insured, Pen. I've been doing this a lot of years, so don't worry."

"Thanks again." Before turning to go, I had another thought. "Is it all right if I take the Nathan Brock, too?" (With Jack's connection to the picture, I didn't want to part with it just yet.)

Walt was more than happy to oblige. "Let me put a price on it and wrap it up. It'll just take a minute."

"I appreciate it."

"You know, Pen, now that I think about it, I've got a few more pieces in my attic that should be perfect for the Palantines' audience. I'll bet they get snapped right up. Tell you what, I'll put prices on those, too, and drop them off at your shop this weekend. Then maybe you and Sadie and I can

discuss my entire collection, art and books, the whole treasure trove. I'll bring an inventory list."

I agreed and thought we were finally through.

Not Walt. Like an antique machine, stuck in one gear, he
couldn't stop pitching. Thank goodness Brainert came to my
rescue, interrupting with a quick offer on that Philip Wylie
first edition.

While the two worked out their transaction, I bolted for
the exit.

On the narrow front porch, I found Seymour staring into
the still-cloudy night sky. The phone in his hand displayed
Harriet's digital image. Seymour had converted her pixels
into a screensaver.

"Our luck is changing," he declared, grinning down at
me. "The storm seems to be passing. I should have my Harriet home by midnight!"

CHAPTER 9

Midnight at the Stumbull Inn

That's life. Whichever way you turn, fate sticks out a
foot to trip you.

—Detour (1945 film)

SEYMOUR WAS RIGHT. Our luck was changing—for the
worse.

Misfortune came in the form of a bottomless pothole
craftily disguised as a shallow puddle. The front tire blew
apart, and the old VW bus skidded onto the muddy shoulder.

Thank goodness nobody was injured. The paintings were
well packed and secured, with no harm there. But Seymour,
still shaking from the accident, ran off to chase down the
"vintage" hubcap that had rolled into a ditch on the opposite
side of the road.

"Look out, bonehead!" Brainert screamed as Seymour
almost walked into the path of a speeding semi.

Huffing and puffing, Seymour tossed the hubcap beside
the flat and ordered "Professor Pip-squeak" to help him get
out the spare.

When Brainert saw the extra tire, he flipped. "That spare
is in worse shape than the tire you blew!"

"I had it patched last year. So it's a little bald. So what?"

"And bald is good on wet, slick highways, right?"

"Well, it's not raining now, is it?"

As if in answer to Seymour's question, the night clouds opened up, drenching them both. Brainert dived back into the passenger seat, and our dedicated driver gamely jacked up the van to change the tire.

Then high winds began to rock our ride, turning raindrops into horizontal torpedoes that splattered loudly against the windows. Fretting in the back seat, I noticed Seymour's dashboard-mounted phone spring to life. The glowing image of Harriet McClure seemed to mock us.

"Ready to go?" Seymour asked when he finally climbed behind the wheel.

"Yes, we're ready," Brainert said. "Ready to turn around and drive to that motel we passed before we got a flat, because we're not going to survive the ride home on your questionable tires. Not in this weather!"

"Fine," Seymour said. "But I'm only agreeing because I'm wet and starving, and there's an all-night truck stop back there, too."

THE STUMBULL INN had reasonable rates. Unfortunately, the only vacancies were adjoining, so despite closing and locking the flimsy connecting door, I could still hear the bickering bunkmates in the next room. Not even juicy takeout burgers, hand-cut fries, and old-fashioned milk shakes could keep them quiet for long.

To tune out the racket, I called home and explained why I would not be back until morning. My son yawned his good night and went off to bed. My aunt, however, was in the mood to talk. She was back from her big dinner date (a little tipsy, too) and sanguinely assured me that everything went smooth as glass with our "blue-haired" babysitter, Tracy Mahoney.

"Such a delightful young woman," she said (surprising the heck out of me). Apparently, over a shared pot of tea, they'd had a lively discussion about Tracy's favorite childhood fantasy novels. This came about after Aunt Sadie learned the girl had persuaded Spencer to resume reading the Narnia series.

"Did you know she's an artist, too?" Sadie gushed. "She showed me her sketchbook. The girl is quite talented!"

"I didn't know."

"Oh! And I answered a call from a charming man who saw our bookshop featured on that CBS *Sunday Morning* profile of the Palantines. I agreed to rent him our event space. He's sending his digital contract in the morning for an open date next week . . ."

Pleased at the new business and my aunt's complete one-eighty on Tracy (being slightly tipsy didn't hurt), I finished the call, crawled into bed, and opened the book I'd brought with me—the advance copy of the Palantines' work.

The oversize volume was a beauty and quite informative. But I was disappointed to find nothing in it about artist Nathan Brock. Plenty of *Spicy* pulp covers were included, but not the one in Seymour's VW.

Try as I might, I couldn't stop thinking about that menacing pockmarked killer, holding his dagger above the luminous blond beauty. Her lifelike expression and brilliant blue eyes left a haunting impression.

Was it the artistry of Brock's image that struck me? Or simply my curiosity about the so-called crime behind the lurid painting?

Whatever the reason, I felt as though that girl were haunting me, maybe not as powerfully as Harriet haunted Seymour, but I couldn't shake my curiosity about the naked blonde.

Who was she? How did she come to model for Nathan Brock? And what was the crime associated with the picture? Did that rough-looking man with the dagger kill her in real life? Or was she some kind of femme fatale? And how did Jack get involved?

As I searched the Palantines' index, to no avail, the thunderstorm kicked up again with a low rumbling in the distance. The hollow, far-off sound made me feel vulnerable in the empty room, and more than a little lonely.

The ghost of Jack Shepard seemed to sense it.

Cozy little flophouse you found here, doll.

I shivered slightly as the temperature around me suddenly dropped. For the first time today, I didn't mind.

"Is that you, Jack?"

Well, it ain't Cary Grant.

"I prefer you."

Ditto. And I hope you know I was pulling your leg about this flophouse being cozy. This is a pretty cheap crib you've rented—and I should know 'cause I passed out in plenty.

"It may be cheap, but it's clean. And the view from the window is supposed to be lovely—not that I can see it right now. When we checked in, Mr. Stumbull told us our windows look out over the river."

Unless it's the East River, I'm less than impressed.

"Then let's talk about something more interesting." I set aside the Palantines' book. "There! I'm no longer 'distracted' with business. You have my full attention, it's only ten o'clock, and we have all night here alone. *Now* will you tell me how you got involved with that Nathan Brock painting?" I snuggled under the covers. "Are you sure that blue-eyed model wasn't an old flame?"

I swear. But she did get burned.

"Burned or extinguished?"

Both.

A sudden boom of thunder, much louder this time, gave me a start. Pulling the covers closer, I heard Jack say—

Few people know what really happened.

"And you do?"

I should. I was there, working the case.

"All right, then. Who was that beautiful blonde? What was she like? How did she die? Who attacked her? And why?"

Whoa, honey, slow the train down!

I took a breath and waited.

Listen, I could talk your ear off with answers, but I have a better idea. Instead of telling you, why don't I show you?

"You mean with one of your memories?"

Yeah, how about it? You and me on the town. You hungry? We can start with dinner for two—

"I'm already stuffed."

After-dinner drinks, then? I know just the place.

"Drinks would be nice . . ." I said on a yawn, which surprised me. A minute ago I was wide-awake. Suddenly I was feeling sleepy. "And you'll tell me about the girl?" I yawned again. "The girl in the picture?"

Like I said, I'll do more than tell you. Now, relax and close your eyes . . .

CHAPTER 10

The Albatross

Her lips were red, her looks were free,
Her locks were yellow as gold:
Her skin was as white as leprosy,
The Nightmare Life-in-Death was she . . .

—Samuel Taylor Coleridge, *The Rime of the Ancient Mariner*

"WAKE UP, PENNY. We've arrived."

I opened my eyes to a new world of old Manhattan.

Night had descended on the city, but the tall buildings around us buzzed with the primitive bulbs of electric daylight. The sidewalks were teeming with men in suits and hats, and women wearing elegant dresses with snow-white gloves.

Me? I was sitting in a big yellow taxi, the heavy door open. Standing next to me on the sidewalk was Jack Shepard, looking sturdy as a skyscraper.

Exiting the cab wasn't so easy in a black silk-and-brocade gown and heels taller than the Empire State Building. Fortunately I had the help of a courteous private detective. He offered his hand, and I took it. Jack's grip was strong, warm, and so alive I could almost feel his heartbeat.

The air was summer hot, but not insufferable, even in this

getup. I struggled to adjust the floor-length frock and shrugged, only then realizing I was wearing a set of pearls wound close around my neck. Me? Pearls? Really?

As I glanced up to complain, I got a better look at my date—

Jack had gone all out. The black-tie evening wear, cut in the style of the day, flattered the detective's powerful frame. His gunmetal gray eyes were animated, his iron jaw clean-shaven, and above the dagger-shaped scar on his chin, his mouth tossed me a little smile, rare but familiar and (like his attitude) smart and challenging. All that was missing was Jack's signature fedora, propped at an angle on his head, though the sight of him was striking enough to make at least one female passerby turn hers.

Instead of complaining, I ended up staring.

"You look good, Jack."

He winked. "You're not so bad yourself."

Our little moment was interrupted by a newsboy hawking his wares.

"Extra! Extra! Howard Hughes subpoenaed by Senate. Read all about it!"

I stopped the boy to check the newsprint in his ink-stained hand—*New York World-Telegram*, August 8, 1947.

"Hey, lady! This ain't a lie-berry."

"Here, kid," Jack flipped a coin, and the boy snapped it out of the air.

Grinning wide enough to display a missing tooth, the kid tucked the nickel into his shirt and continued down Fifty-Third Street.

"Looks like I'm all dressed up with nowhere to go."

"I promised you a drink." He pulled my arm through the crook of his. "Where we're going is just down the block."

Soon we joined a cluster of the smart set—loud men with cigars and quiet women with cigarette holders. The night-club's elaborate Vegas-like facade was fashioned to resemble the widespread wings of a giant white bird. As the tony crowd entered, the bird's wings appeared ready to enfold them.

"What's with the seagull?" I asked.

"It's an albatross, Penny."

"I've heard *this* argument before."

"You know about the albatross, don't you?" Jack said. "It's the bird a guy finds hanging around his neck."

"I didn't know you were a fan of Coleridge."

"I'm not. But I can hum a few bars of Cole Porter."

The *Ancient Mariner* theme continued as we entered the club's lobby, a plush waiting area with a white-cloud ceiling, ocean-wave wallpaper, and cushioned benches with backs resembling the sort of wooden posts you'd find in shipyard docks.

"Hello, Jack."

The man who greeted us had thin lips, oiled hair, and a face like stretched canvas. His hand slipped in and out of Jack's faster than a Whac-A-Mole bobbing its head—and I'm fairly sure a dead president was exchanged in the process.

"Hugo," Jack said, his smile wary. "Long time no see."

"Yeah, almost like you planned it that way." The oily man turned his gaze in my direction. "Who's the doll?"

"Penny, I want you to meet Hugo Box. He owns this joint."

"Charmed." He actually kissed my hand. (Well, he put his lips to my black cotton glove anyway.)

"You want a table, Jack? I've got a front-row seat with your name on it."

"A booth up by the bar."

Hugo chuckled. "Always the peeper, eh?"

What did that mean? I wondered. And soon found out.

The royal blue booth was luxurious, the lighting low and romantic. But knowing the detective as I did, I understood why Jack picked this spot, and it had little to do with ambience. To reach the bar area, we had to climb ten carpeted steps, which gave us a spectacular view of the stage *and* the customers. From this mezzanine, we could spy on the entire dining floor.

"I'll have champagne sent over," Hugo said. "It's the real French stuff, too. Since the war ended, we're drowning in it."

The waitress arrived a minute later, with a pair of crystal glasses and a bottle in a silver bucket of ice. Her uniform was navy blue, with a white sailor's collar. Her décolleté was daring, her hemline scandalously short, and her heels were higher than mine.

"Cute outfit," Jack said as he watched her leave.

"Amazing she can walk in those shoes. Maybe she should audition for the Rockettes."

Jack poured, then lifted his glass. "To you, Penny."

The champagne was sweetly refreshing. The bubbles tickled my nose as I watched the stage show, which featured a handsome young guy who looked and sang an awful lot like Dean Martin.

Jack seemed more interested in the customers.

"What are you looking at, Detective?"

"See that dame standing at the corner table?"

"The brunette chatting up those men?"

"That's the one."

I watched the table. One of the middle-aged men in the group tried to coax the woman to sit with them. He even stood and offered her his chair. She declined in a way that made the men grateful she paid attention to them at all.

"Notice anything?"

"Her dress is the same navy blue shade that the waitress was wearing—only instead of a miniskirt and white sailor's collar, it's an elegant full-length strapless gown with white gloves."

Jack nodded. "That dame works here, too. She's one of Hugo's girls—*hostesses* he calls them. Their job is to look classy and make everyone feel they're part of the party, including encouraging guests to lap up Hugo's stock, preferably the most expensive bottles."

Jack refilled my glass. "Drink up. The show's not over yet."

Jack was right. After the Dean Martin look-alike finished, next onstage was a woman who did an amazing impression of Carmen Miranda. Her colorful wardrobe featured an elaborate headdress, puffy sleeves, and a bare midriff. She could dance, too, maybe too much like—

"Wait a minute! That *is* Carmen Miranda."

Jack shrugged. "She and Dean Martin are the headliners tonight."

"You mean that really was Dean Martin?!"

"Look, there's our girl," Jack interrupted, directing my attention to a table less than twenty feet away.

A young woman with short, sassy golden blond hair and a figure to die for laughed as she helped three men stack champagne glasses into a pyramid. Her back was turned, so I couldn't see her face, but she was wearing Hugo's favorite shade of strapless navy blue.

Once the glasses were stacked, the laughing blonde deftly uncorked the champagne while she moved around the table.

"That's the girl from the Nathan Brock painting!"

"In the flesh," Jack said. "Her name is Ruby Tyler."

"So you weren't pulling my leg. You really did know her?"

"Everybody knew Ruby. She got off the bus from West Virginia at the tender age of sixteen. By the time she was legal, she had half of Hell's Kitchen at her feet."

Jack frowned at me for the first time. "I know that pinched look."

"What pinched look?"

"The one that tells me what you're thinking about the girl, but you're wrong. Ruby was never a lady of the evening. She started out a waitress, then became a model and a hostess here. Believe me, I've known plenty of good-time girls, but Ruby only played the part. At heart, she was a sweet soul and a real Robin Hood."

"What do you mean?"

"Ruby grew up in a hardscrabble mining town. See that choker around her neck?"

"Is that a cameo?"

"It's Ruby's mother, carved out of West Virginia sandstone by her pop. He was a coal miner who died underground. Six months later, her mother laid herself next to him, by her own hand."

Jack took a long gulp of champagne.

"Most dames come to New York with big dreams. Ruby came because she had nowhere else to go. That kind of background can make you mean. Not Ruby. Those years made her more sympathetic. Whenever she met a girl who was new to the city, one who really needed a friend or a hand, Ruby gave it to them. Of course, that sweet southern twang also attracted a lot of male attention, as you can see."

Jack tipped his head and we both watched Ruby entertain her table of admirers. With laughing ease, she poured champagne into the top glass in her crystal pyramid until the bubbly liquid flowed down into the rest of the cups.

"Like a lot of Hugo's girls, Ruby sometimes got pursued by the wrong type of guy."

"Married guys?"

"Not necessarily," Jack said. "Not unless they're the kind who don't take *no* for an answer. See, Hugo protected his girls. That's why they liked working for him. He even hired me a few times to get his girls out of jams."

"Jams?"

"Stalkers, mashers, worse. I'd track 'em down, have little talk. Make sure they got the message to leave the girl alone."

When Ruby's bottle was empty and all the men's glasses full, cheers rocked the room. Ruby hugged every one of the guys as she passed out the glasses.

"And Ruby ended up dead?"

"That's right, because of that Brock painting."

"So she was murdered by Nathan Brock?"

"No."

"Then who killed her?"

"The man responsible for Ruby's death was the man behind that painting."

I was baffled by Jack's reply. "But Nathan Brock is the artist who painted Ruby. She obviously modeled for him. Isn't Brock 'the man behind the painting'? Or . . . wait! I've got it! You're talking about that rough-looking guy in the picture, aren't you? The pockmarked man lurking behind Ruby, holding up the dagger?"

Jack was speaking, trying to explain, but I couldn't hear

him. His voice was drowned out by the most annoying microphone feedback ever.

I looked toward the stage, where the band was playing, but I heard no music, not even a voice. Just that loud, awful buzzing.

I put my hands over my ears.

"Jack, what is that? Make it stop! Jack? Jack?!"

I OPENED MY eyes.

The nightclub was gone. So was Jack Shepard.

I was back in my own time, in a lonely, chilly motel bedroom, and the ghost was no longer with me. But that annoying buzzing was!

My smartphone was vibrating the entire flimsy nightstand. I grabbed for it, knocking my glasses to the carpet as I wondered who could be calling so late.

"Hey, Penelope, Walt Waverly here."

As Walt greeted me, I glanced at the clock radio. Okay, it wasn't *that* late, ten minutes to eleven. The dream with Jack had taken less than an hour.

"Is anything wrong?" I asked.

"Not at all," Walt said, "and I'm sorry to bother you. I didn't think you'd pick up. I was going to leave a message—"

"It's all right. Go on."

"I wanted to let you know that I gathered together those additional paintings we talked about for the Palantines' publication party, but I'm not sure I'll be able to get them to you by this weekend—"

"Actually, you're in luck. We're only a few miles away . . ."

I told Walt about our flat tire and promised I'd return to his house in the morning.

"That's perfect!" he gushed. "Unlucky for you and your friends, but a break for me. The truth is, Pen, my online sales aren't what they used to be. But I'm sure we'll make a nice profit through your store event. The art will sell itself. The right people just have to see it."

"I agree. And when we see each other in the morning, I'd

like to know more about that Nathan Brock painting—the one with the real crime story behind it?"

"Sure thing, Pen. In fact, I already took a battery lantern into the attic and found my black and red notebooks. I color-code them, you see?"

"Yes, you mentioned that."

"My latest one is blue," Walt went on. "That's the one your friend signed. Anyway, I've got all three sitting right here on my library table now." He paused, apologizing for munching a cookie. "My notes about the Nathan Brock are either in my red book or my black one."

I sat up in bed. "Since you have them in front of you, would you mind reading me what you wrote, right now?"

"I don't mind at all, if you don't mind waiting. I'll have to flip through both notebooks to locate the Brock entry—"

Just then, I heard what sounded like a doorbell chime.

Walt groaned. "Now, who could that be at this hour? Sorry, Pen, I'll need a minute to check my front door peephole . . ." I heard shifting sounds and footsteps, and then Walt cursed.

"It's that buyer!"

"What buyer?"

"The one who wanted the Harriet McClure portrait. Shoot. I can't get out of this one. I'll have to break the bad news that I sold it. Unless . . ."

"Unless what?"

"Right after you left my house, I updated my online listing for the Harriet as sold. I hope the buyer didn't see the update and come here to give me a hard time."

"That seems extreme, doesn't it?"

"I hate causing anyone disappointment or upset. Heaven knows, I've already done enough of that in my life."

"What do you mean?"

"Forget about it."

The doorbell chimed again. And again.

"Listen, Walt," I said, "if you think the buyer will be angry, you should keep the door locked and talk it over through text messages."

"Oh, no! Now that they're here, I'm sure I can interest them in something else from my collection. I've got plenty left to sell."

"Well, if it makes you feel any better, you made my friend Seymour a happy man."

"That's the best part of this business. Making a collector happy. And your friend has nothing to worry about. There will be no harassment from this buyer. I learned my lesson years ago. These days, the information on all of my sales stays *private*!"

Again the doorbell chimed, followed by the dong of the grandfather clock striking eleven. Next I heard a loud pounding.

"I'd better answer," Walt said. "See you tomorrow, Pen."

And then the line went dead.

C H A P T E R   1 1

Slip and Fall

If I have to climb into heaven on a ladder, I shall have
to decline the invitation.

—Mercedes McCambridge, actress, *CBS Radio Mystery Theater*

I HEARD A pounding.

For a moment, I thought I was back in that Manhattan
nightclub, listening to Carmen Miranda's drummer taking
the spotlight. Then the drumming stopped and the band's
crooner began singing my name.

"Pen! Oh, Pen!"

I opened my eyes. Bright daylight streamed through a
crack in the bedroom curtains, but they weren't my bedroom
curtains. While my groggy mind searched for the reason
why, the pounding resumed.

"Pen! Are you there?!"

At last, I realized the "crooner" was J. Brainert Parker,
and I was still at the Stumbull Inn. Yawning, I approached
the closed door between our rooms.

"What is it, Brainert?"

"Can you spare an extra towel? Seymour came out of the
bathroom dressed like he was going to a toga party!"

"Why did you bother her, Brainiac?" Seymour snapped.
"I said you can have this towel. I didn't dry myself with it. I just wrapped it around my hips."

"Please, Pen, you have to help me!"

"Calm down. I'll check my bathroom."

AN HOUR LATER, we left the Stumbull Inn for the same little roadside eatery where we'd bought those juicy burgers and hand-cut fries. All three of us doubted our breakfast would be as good as our dinner.

"Hey, never judge a book till you've read it!" Seymour reminded us.

He was right.

We stuffed ourselves with the best blueberry flapjacks we'd ever eaten. By ten A.M., we were climbing into Seymour's VW bus and heading back to Blackstone Falls.

The road to Old Walt's was nearly empty, the sky clear and sunny after the tempestuous night. Best of all, Seymour was still flying high from his purchase (not to mention the carb-loaded meal). He was feeling so good he even refused to be goaded by Brainert's nonstop jibes.

Finally, we arrived at Walt Waverly's home.

"The front door is open," Seymour noted. "Walt must be ready to bring out the new paintings."

Seymour and Brainert climbed into the back of the Volkswagen and began to shuffle the old cargo aside to make room for the new. Meanwhile I followed the long sidewalk to Walt's open front door, only to stop abruptly at the edge of the porch. For some reason, water was puddled on the hardwood floor inside the foyer.

"Hello," I called tentatively. "Are you in there, Walt?"

Nothing but silence came from the house. As opposed to the inside of my head.

Cool your heels, doll.

My ghost was awake and he sounded worried.

There's something hinky here.

"You mean the rainwater inside the house? It is odd, isn't it? The storm stopped hours ago."

But I'll bet a five-spot against a plugged nickel it was raining when Walt's visitor showed up last night.

"Perhaps we're being paranoid," I said, eager to dispel my anxieties. "Maybe Walt is upstairs or in the basement and can't hear me."

I called "Hello!" again, a little louder this time. The only response was the echo of my own voice. Brushing aside my misgivings, I crossed the narrow porch in three quick steps and knocked on the open door.

"Walt, it's Pen!" (Now I was yelling at the top of my lungs.) "I'm here to pick up the paintings—" Just then, I noticed something poking out from behind the door, and the sight of it sent a stab to the pit of my stomach.

"Look, Jack!"

It's a Longfellow.

I tensed. The "Longfellow" in question was a size-twelve loafer lying on the hardwood just inside the foyer, and it didn't take long to discover the leg attached to the shoe. Whoever owned that leg was sprawled on the floor behind the half-open door.

Gingerly, I stepped across the threshold.

Don't disturb anything, Jack warned.

I didn't. I even took care to avoid the rain puddles on the hardwood.

My eyes needed a few seconds to adjust to the dark. Then I spied the same ladder Walt used in his library, only now it was tilted at a crazy angle, leaning against a partially shattered grandfather clock.

A broken picture frame with a torn canvas lay on the floor, surrounded by glass shards. I steeled myself and peeked behind the door.

My anguished cry brought Seymour and Brainert running.

"Pen! What's wrong?" Brainert asked, eyes wide.

"Behind the door," I rasped. "It's . . ."

Seymour moved past me and into the foyer.

"It's Walt," he proclaimed.

Who else would it be? the ghost asked. *Glenn Miller?*

"It looks like the poor guy fell off the ladder. I don't think he's breathing."

"Check for a pulse," Brainert said. "Walt may only require first aid."

Seymour vanished behind the door. He emerged a few moments later, shaking his head.

I swallowed hard. "Are you sure he's—"

"Yeah, Pen. Dead as rock and roll."

"You should try anyway," Brainert insisted.

Seymour gawked. "Try what?"

"Anything!" Brainert cried in a tone so hysterically high-pitched it threatened to attract stray dogs. "You know, lifesaving measures! Don't they teach government employees CPR?"

"CPR? Sure. But the United States Postal Service doesn't teach forensics—or reanimation." Seymour sighed. "I'm really sorry, but Walt isn't just gone. He's long gone."

"I have to call 911," I said, fumbling for my phone.

The operator answered immediately. I identified myself and reported what I'd found and where. I was informed that an ambulance would be dispatched. The operator also told me not to leave the location until Sheriff Gus Taft arrived to take my statement.

"Don't disturb the scene," the operator added. "Or try to move the body."

"What now?" Brainert asked after the call ended.

Seymour shrugged. "Unless you want to make like Dr. Frankenstein and harness a lightning bolt, we wait in the van."

CHAPTER 12

Grim Discoveries

When I die, I'm leaving my body to science fiction.

—Steven Wright, comedian

SEYMOUR AND BRAINERT returned to the van, perfectly willing to wait outside Walt's house. I was, too, until my gumshoe spirit refused to let me rest in peace.

Turn around, he ordered. *Now's our chance to case the scene.*

"But, Jack, the dispatcher warned us to stay out of the house."

She ordered you *to stay out. Not me.*

"But you can't go anywhere unless I take you!"

Exactly, honey. I'm so proud of you. You catch on real quick.

"Don't tease me. This is serious."

Yeah, serious as murder. And that's my business.

"You mean it *was* your business, past tense. When you expired, so did your license."

I still got the know-how. Just not the body. So get yours moving!

"Do you really think we should—"

GET IN THERE NOW! BEFORE THE COPPERS GET HERE!

"All right, all right, calm down . . ."

I approached the house again.

"Pen, where are you going!" Brainert cried.

"I'll be right back!" I sang, trying to calm his fears—and mine.

As I crossed the porch and peered into the house's shadowy interior, the ghost piped up again—

It's as quiet as a tomb in there.

"I'll excuse your tasteless pun, but only because it's as dark as a tomb, too."

Which should make you wonder: Who turned out the lights?

"You're right, of course. I doubt Walt's thoughts were on energy efficiency as he plunged to his death." Pausing at the doorway, I felt unease mounting. "I'm nervous, Jack. I don't want to disturb any evidence. And I feel terrible snooping around with Walt just lying there."

All you have to do is act like a professional. Look at it like I would. No emotions. Stay in your head, Penny. Think, don't feel.

"Easier said than done . . ."

Death was no stranger to me, but that didn't stop the hackles from rising as I approached Walt's corpse. With a sharp intake of breath, I took Jack's advice, pushed my feelings aside, and slipped through the door.

Remember what the mailman said about not being a forensics expert? Well you're not, either, so don't try to examine the old man's body.

"Then what are we looking for?"

The reason Walt Waverly is dead, not the cause. In the private eye profession, we call that a motive.

"There's only a motive if there's foul play."

And that's what you're looking for.

"I need something more specific."

Okay. Look at how the ladder fell. What do you notice?

I saw the obvious, of course. The top rungs struck the

antique grandfather clock and shattered its face. Following Jack's advice, I took an even closer look, peering through the damage to read the time.

"Jack, the clock stopped ticking at 11:29."

And what does that tell you?

"That's barely thirty minutes after Walt ended our call. I remember hearing the dong of this clock striking eleven. That's when the buyer showed up, pounding on his door."

Coincidence? If you believe that, I've got some real estate in Florida to sell you, and it's not entirely swamp. I promise.

"So you think he was—?"

Iced. Bumped off. Deep-sixed. Put to bed for the big sleep—

"Okay, okay, I get it, but you could be jumping the gun here. This might simply be a terrible, tragic accident."

Nuts to that. Too many things spell murder—the unexpected visit, the promised picture previously purchased, Walt's own experience with crazy buyers who lost a sale and lost their heads.

"If Walt did have some kind of argument with the buyer, would it be possible to knock the ladder aside while Walt was on it?"

Sure, why not? Walt was a beefy guy, but he was no spring chicken. Why don't we have a look around? These hayseed coppers are going to take their good old time. They're probably off goldbricking at the town fishin' hole. Might as well see if we can find any helpful evidence.

"Like what?"

Like something out of place. Something that looks wrong.

"Wrong? Is that the technical term?"

Like it or don't, it worked for guys like me. You'll know it when you see it.

"Fine."

My footsteps echoed as I crossed the hardwood foyer and entered the library. The large room was dark, the curtains still drawn. The only illumination came from the dying embers of last night's fire. The scene felt even eerier because of Walt's removal of so many paintings from the walls. The smudged squares left behind felt almost ghostly, their impressions once clear were now gone.

"I don't see any sign of struggle or disruption," I said loudly as I looked around. The sound of my own voice gave me some reassurance. "I don't see that anything was left behind—no scarf or hat or gloves."

Keep looking while we have the chance.

"To do that, I'll need more light."

I found the switch and was about to turn it on when the ghost boomed—

Fingerprints!

"Oh, right. Thanks, Jack."

After fishing in my pockets, I found my leather gloves and pulled them on before flipping the switch on the dusty chandelier. As light flooded the gloomy room, I noticed the refreshment table by the fireplace hadn't been cleared.

"The cookie plate is still there," I noted. "And I remember Walt snacked on a cookie as he spoke to me about his color-coded notebooks—the red and black ones he brought down from his archives in the attic."

And where are these notebooks?

"I don't see them."

Keep lookin', honey.

I searched the table—on top and underneath—and then the entire library. But there was no red or black notebook. There were no notebooks whatsoever!

"The blue one is missing, too. That was the newest one, and the last entry was Seymour's purchase. I remember Walt asking him to write down his name and address."

As I looked under the table one more time, I was no longer skeptical that Walt's death was an accident. I couldn't *prove* those notebooks were stolen. I *knew* it, from the tips of my toes to the top of my—

A blast of supernatural air suddenly shocked me. The frost was so cold it nearly froze the nervous sweat under my ponytail.

"What's with the warning freeze?" I blurted aloud. "You know what I'm looking for!"

"Excuse me?"

The sharp female voice startled me into stumbling backward. As I caught my balance, I saw the uniformed figure of a woman stepping through the library's doorway. I stared. I couldn't help it, even though I knew it was rude.

The diminutive, short-haired brunette had so many freckles her pale face seemed ruddy. But what really got my attention was the fact that she was wearing a badge and that one of her hands rested on a very large but thankfully holstered handgun.

"Did you come with the ambulance?" I asked. "Are you a local deputy?"

"Sheriff," she answered. "I'm Sheriff Taft."

"The operator said Sheriff *Gus* Taft was on the way."

The sheriff's intense brown eyes flashed and then narrowed. Just like that, her annoyance morphed into suspicion.

"My full name is Augusta. And it's time for *me* to ask the questions. Why are you so interested in the private property of a dead man?"

CHAPTER 13

The Freckled Face of the Law

I was constantly amazed by how many people talked me into arresting them.

—Edward Conlon, *Blue Blood*

"SHERIFF TAFT, I think we got off on the wrong foot. My name is Penelope Thornton-McClure, and—"

"I know your name. Your friends in the van told me. Why aren't you out there with them? What are you doing in here?"

"I was looking around because—"

"How well did you know Mr. Waverly?"

"Not well. I'm here on business."

"What business exactly? I understand Walt retired after his wife passed away."

"His plan may have been to retire, but he was still doing the business of selling his collection. That's why we came to see him. Do you know if Walt had children?"

"One son. But he hasn't been around since his mother died."

"Why not?"

"I can't answer that. I haven't spoken to his son yet. Why is that important?"

"Because of my dealings with Walt. If the son is the next of kin, I'll need to know his address."

"Fine. Now, let's back up and start at the beginning. What *specifically* was your business with Walt Waverly?"

I told the sheriff everything—about my bookshop and Walt loaning us art. I recounted our visit the day before, including Seymour's purchase and our night at the motel. Finally, I told her about the last person to see Walt alive.

Sheriff Taft's reply was sharp. "According to the man who owns that rolling safety violation out there, *you* were the last people to see Walt alive."

"No, no, we were long gone before this visitor arrived."

"If you weren't here, then how do you know about the visitor?"

"I was on the phone with Walt when this person came to see him. Check Walt's phone records. They'll show he called me close to eleven last evening. But that conversation is only important because I heard the visitor arriving."

"You heard this person talking to Walt?"

"No. The visitor was ringing the doorbell and then pounding on the door."

"So how could you know who this person was?"

"Walt told me—not the name, only that he was upset. He assumed this person would be angry over losing the sale of a painting to my friend. That's why you need to find out the identity of this jilted buyer. This person should be questioned. And you should also know that Walt's notebooks are missing. I was searching for them when you came in."

"Why?"

"I was hoping to uncover any evidence of wrongdoing—other than Walt's body, of course. And I believe I found it. Walt's visitor stole Walt's notebooks. I'm sure of it."

Sheriff Taft took a breath. "And what *value* would there be in a few old notebooks exactly?"

"I don't know. Walt's past sales were recorded in them, including the sale of that painting the buyer wanted—"

"Slow down, now. How do you know Walt didn't just

move the notebooks out of this room? Maybe we'll find them somewhere else in this big, cluttered closet of a house."

"No, listen. When I was speaking on the phone to Walt last night, we were talking about those notebooks. I heard him drop the notebook on this table here. I know it was that table because he was munching cookies—"

"Cookies?"

"Yes, the cookies were sitting beside Walt's blue notebook. I remember that from our visit yesterday, and I remember that Walt made Seymour sign that book, and—"

"Right. Okay, Mrs. McClure, I get it. Calm down, now—"

"But you need to hear *all* the details. Walt was sure this visitor was going to be angry with him over a lost sale, and . . ."

"Uh-huh . . ." Sheriff Taft kept nodding as I talked, but I could tell from her change in expression and tone that she no longer thought I was a threat. Clearly, I'd been demoted from "suspicious character" to "neurotic busybody" (or rambling idiot).

"Tell you what, Mrs. McClure," the sheriff said in a humor-the-crazy-lady tone, "I'll try to track down this 'visitor' and get a statement. Or the state police will. Either way, I honestly doubt it will make a difference."

"Why not?"

"Because what happened here is pretty straightforward. You told me Mr. Waverly was removing paintings from the walls. Seems obvious enough from the scene that last night's storm blew open the door. It struck the ladder and Walter Waverly lost his footing. Sad, tragic, bad luck even, but . . . end of story."

"I understand it looks that way, but from my perspective, if you had *heard* that call from Walt, you would be highly concerned about finding that visitor—and those notebooks."

"Like I said, it's not up to me. The state police will handle the autopsy, so cause of death is their call." Finally, with the faux-polite shrug of an overworked civil servant, Sheriff Taft added, "I'll be sure to include your statement in the case file, Mrs. McClure. You'll just need to write down everything you told me—"

"But—"

"That's the way we handle things here in Blackstone Falls. Come on outside. I have the forms for you and your friends to fill out. It's best you start now, while your memory's fresh."

AS I STEPPED out of the sad shadows of the old house and into the brilliant noonday sun, my eyes teared, but not from daylight.

While I was inside those cluttered rooms, I'd pushed thoughts of mortality aside as I observed the scene the way Jack had schooled me to—analytically, logically. But now reality dropped its depressing curtain, reminding me of all the ways the Grim Reaper and I were acquainted, though I'd never call him a friend.

Death and I first met when my mother passed. I was just a child, but on those days I visited her grave, I was certain I overheard the voice of a drowned girl interred a few rows away.

A few years later, I lost my older brother. I was a teenager for this second visit, but the Reaper stuck around for encore performances—first with my father, next with the suicide of my husband, and lately with the ghostly soul of a dead private eye occupying a large portion of my brain.

Walt Waverly's story was no different. A harmless human being with a lively spirit, a man who just twelve hours ago was making plans for the future, was now gone. Walt's demise, however it happened, was a grim reminder of that dreaded visitor who, one day, comes for us all.

"We live in a world of walking dead."

Ease up on the morbid musings, sweetheart. It's pointless to carry all that heavy stuff around. Baggage like that sinks your wagon wheels.

"Too late, Jack. I've been carrying this baggage long before you entered my head."

The ghost went quiet after that. I wasn't surprised. For one thing, I had to focus on filling out the witness statement forms, and Jack always said he detested the paperwork part of the gumshoe game.

As I finished up, the ambulance arrived and Sheriff Taft approached the driver. "Sorry, Doug. You can't move the body. The state police are sending a crime scene unit."

That got my attention.

"Excuse me, Sheriff? I'm more than willing to wait around and give my statement personally to the state police."

Sheriff Taft took my form, along with a less-than-patient breath.

"I told you, Mrs. McClure, I'll be conveying your written statement to the assigned investigators. I suggest you and your friends go back to Quindicott. If the Rhode Island State Police require anything more, they'll know where to find you."

CHAPTER 14

The Long Ride Home

Dead men are heavier than broken hearts.

—Raymond Chandler, *The Big Sleep*

THE RETURN TRIP to Quindicott started out in the strangest silence.

Numbed by Old Walt's death, Brainert and Seymour actually stopped sparring. Instead, the two stared at the road ahead, lost in their own thoughts.

I was alone in the back seat, but there was no privacy for me.

Another cornpone cop buying a flimsy frame job, griped the ghost.

Maybe not, Jack. You heard Sheriff Taft. The state police are going to investigate.

Yeah, that sure gives me hope.

Why the sarcasm? Don't you believe they care?

Care? Doll, smarten up. After a few long, hard years on the job, what most coppers care about ain't a mystery. If they can't close a case quick, they'll use a big broom to sweep it under the rug.

I refuse to think the worst. We should at least give them a chance.

Just then, Brainert cleared his throat and turned to Seymour. "I noticed you took a rather long time to fill out that police report. What were you writing, the sequel to *War and Peace*?"

Behind the wheel, Seymour shrugged. "I was only doing what Ilsa, the she-wolf of the Blackstone jackboots, ordered me to. I wrote down everything that I witnessed inside that house this morning."

"But you barely stepped through the door. What could you possibly have 'witnessed'?"

"More than you, Brainiac. You wouldn't even cross Walt's porch, yet I watched you scribbling away for ten solid minutes."

Brainert grew somber. "Along with accurate testimony, I provided my extemporaneous thoughts on Mr. Waverly's demise. And in deference to the occasion, I felt the statement should include a few stanzas of Dickinson's posthumously published 'Because I could not stop for Death.'"

"Oh, that should go over big." Seymour caught my eye in the rearview. "So, Pen. You were in that house a long time with the sheriff. What did you find in there?"

"Enough to get me thinking . . ."

For the first time, I told my friends about Walt's late-night phone call and his unexpected visitor, the same person who had wanted to buy Harriet's painting.

Brainert turned in his seat. "So you think Walt and this buyer quarreled over that deranged self-portrait? And because of that, Walt ended up dead?"

"I honestly don't know. I wish Walt could tell us . . ." Silently, I even asked Jack if he could find a way to contact him (on the other side). The ghost was not amused.

I'm a spirit, not a psychic, Jack reminded me. It wasn't the first time.

Whatever cosmic purgatory Jack was confined to, he was there with no companionship. Except for me, apparently.

"I don't understand the value of Walt's notebooks," Brainert argued. "Why would anybody want them?"

"I'll bet I know," Seymour said. "You saw how pushy

Walt was yesterday, trying to sell us everything in the place. He probably did the same thing with this disappointed buyer, applied pressured to buy a substitute item. And then I'll bet Walt and this buyer started arguing. The buyer could have caused the accident in anger and then panicked and took the notebooks because by then, Walt had already made the buyer sign their name and address inside the book, right next to the painting that Walt was taking down. Get it? You see? The buyer's name would have been linked to that painting. Bingo! Culpability! I'll bet this person was trying to cover up any evidence they'd been there!"

Brainert turned around again. "Pen, is that what the sheriff thinks?"

"No. In fact, I could tell she thought I was making too much of the missing notebooks. And the late-night visitor, for that matter. In her view, Walt's death was no more than a tragic accident."

"And you believe that, too?" Seymour asked.

"Not after last night's phone call," I admitted. "The most logical motive I can see is based on what Walt told me. He was adamant that his sales stay *private*."

Brainert raised an eyebrow. "Over his dead body?"

"It certainly looks that way to me. And *my* bet is the visitor didn't take Walt's *no* for an answer. I think those notebooks were taken for one reason—to discover what Walt refused to reveal. Who bought the Harriet McClure painting."

"That makes sense for the blue notebook," Brainert agreed. "But why take the others, too?"

"I'm not sure . . ."

All of us in the van fell silent at that mystery. All but one.

The answer's there, honey, if you ask the right questions.

What do you mean?

Ask yourself, what's inside those notebooks? And then ask why a person so interested in one particular painting would want all that information. Take your answers. Add them up, and—

"You're right, Jack!"

"Who's Jack?" Brainert asked.

"And what's he right about?" Seymour added.

I thought fast. "*Jack* is a kind of expression, that's all."

"It is?" Brainert's eyes narrowed skeptically. "Since when?"

"Don't let him bait you, Pen," Seymour replied smugly. "The professor's rarified circles don't use urban slang. In other words, he don't know jackshi—"

"That's not what I meant," I quickly clarified. "I was just excited about a possible theory on Walt's missing notebooks."

"So tell us," Brainert pressed. "What's your theory?"

"It makes sense if you think it through. The red and black notebooks were packed with information about Walt's past sales over the years. The person visiting Walt was very interested in Harriet's painting. Those older notebooks of Walt's might have been taken to trace back who owned that painting before Walt did."

To my surprise, Seymour laughed. "Come on, Pen. Why would anyone be so obsessed about an obscure self-portrait? Or want to trace who owned it in the past? Harriet isn't famous. The painting isn't worth all that much."

"*And* it's supposed to be cursed," Brainert pointed out.

Seymour waved his hand. "I don't believe any of that crap."

"I don't either. Not as a rule. But it is rather coincidental that within hours of Walt Waverly selling it, he ended up dead."

"Oh, come on, Brainpan," Seymour scoffed. "You can't pin Walt's death on Harriet. If that painting were cursed, then answer me this: Why didn't anything bad happen to the man during all those years he owned it, huh?"

"Something bad *did* happen," I pointed out.

"What?" Brainert and Seymour asked in duet.

"Don't you remember? Walt told us himself. Three years ago, his wife helped him move Harriet McClure's self-portrait out of their attic and into their library. He said it was 'the last good day' before she got sick."

For a long minute, we all sat in tense silence.

Finally, Seymour shrugged. "Well, I'm not worried. Harriet and me, we're completely simpatico."

"Or completely unhinged," Brainert muttered.

There's one more thing you amateurs are forgetting, Jack said.

Since I was the only one who could hear him, I had to be the one who asked. *What?*

If last night's visitor has the old man's blue notebook, then it means our murder suspect knows where your mailman lives.

The ghost was right.

"Seymour, listen to me. This is important. You need to be careful from now on—"

"I'm watching the road!"

"No, I mean, about the painting."

"What? The curse again? I told you, I don't believe—"

"Not the curse. If anyone contacts you with an offer for that painting, you need to alert the state police."

"Aw, don't worry about me, Pen. I have no intention of selling Harriet. And anyone who comes to my place looking to take her from me is going to meet my little friend."

"Who?" Brainert smirked. "Your parrot?"

"No, the Louisville Slugger leaning next to my front door."

CHAPTER 15

Curses

If it wasn't for bad luck, I wouldn't have no luck at all!

—Albert King, *Born Under a Bad Sign*

IT WAS THREE o'clock before we turned onto Cranberry Street and pulled into the alleyway behind my bookshop. Stiff from the drive, the three of us were happy to put our muscles to work moving Walt's paintings and easels from the van to the bookshop's stockroom.

Finally, it was time for us to part, and Seymour and Brainert climbed back into the van. But when Seymour slammed his door, the driver's side mirror slipped out of its frame and shattered on the concrete.

"Great! Now I've got fourteen years of bad luck!"

Brainert rolled his eyes. "That's seven years, you clown."

"Not when you break two mirrors in one week it isn't. I cracked my bathroom mirror last Thursday."

"Forget that silly superstition and get this heap of rusty tin moving."

"It's no use," Seymour declared after continually twisting the key. "The engine won't turn over. This VW is deader than a Triassic dinosaur."

"This Volkswagen *is* a dinosaur. You should have donated it to a natural history museum back in the twentieth century."

Ignoring the professor, Seymour exited the van and pocketed his keys. "Man, this is going to set me back a chunk of change. I'll need a tow truck, plus I'll have to replace that blown tire, and who knows how much the engine repairs will cost!"

"You're broke because you overpaid for that ridiculous painting. Maybe that's the curse."

Seymour's eyes narrowed. "There is no curse!"

Brainert just tapped his cheek and pretended to ponder the sky. "Now, what is it they say about a fool and his money?"

"Hey, this fool got us home in one piece, didn't he?"

"You got us as far as Pen's bookstore. But I'm due to teach an afternoon class, at the *university*."

"Can't you catch the school's shuttle bus?"

"I just missed it. And there won't be another for at least two hours."

"Then I guess you better start walking, because my Magic Bus is going nowhere."

The professor looked ready to take Seymour's head off.

You better call the coppers, doll, before there's another dead body.

My friends don't need a cop, Jack, just a referee.

Then get in there and stop the sparring.

"Don't worry, Brainert!" I called from the shop's back door. "I'll get you to your class on time."

We were all hot and sweaty, and tempers were frayed. Thank goodness our shop assistant was cool and collected. When Bonnie Franzetti came out to help me clean up the broken glass, she offered to drive Brainert to the campus for me.

As the two sped away, Seymour called for a tow truck. Then he waved me back over to his van to ask a favor.

"I'd like to leave my Harriet in your shop until I get my van back. I hate to part with her, but I don't want this beauty hauled off to a smelly garage where a bunch of grease-soaked Neanderthals will drool all over her. You don't mind, do you?"

I hesitated, not sure if I should mind or not.

Like Seymour, I'd initially dismissed Walt's talk about the so-called cursed portrait bringing bad luck, but ever since the painting entered Seymour's life—and, by extension, my own—things had been taking a freakish turn.

Don't tell me you're letting your fears make decisions for you, Jack challenged. *You never used to be the superstitious kind. Didn't you once say there's no such thing as curses?*

I once said there's no such thing as ghosts, either.

Jack's chuckle came with a chilly breeze that sent goose bumps over my skin.

"Earth to Pen!" Seymour called. "Did you hear what I said?"

"I heard you. And, *yes*, you can keep your picture here. Let's move it into the stockroom with the rest of the art."

"Great!"

Though Seymour was relieved, I couldn't help feeling a stab of dread. At least it wouldn't be here long, I reasoned, so where was the harm?

Exactly, Jack agreed. *And better here than your friend's house, that's for sure.*

Why?

Because you didn't write an address in that missing notebook. He did.

I tensed, remembering Walt's late-night visitor. *I don't want Seymour to end up like Walt.*

Then maybe your pal should get his hands on a gat.

A what?

A burner. A roscoe. A heater—

You mean a gun?

Yeah, Seymour should be strapping.

That's a very bad idea. I can hardly trust Seymour behind the wheel of this VW, let alone with a lethal weapon . . .

As my head continued to argue with Jack, my arms helped Seymour carry his carefully wrapped painting out of the van and into our stockroom. Then Seymour strode onto our shop's selling floor to wait for his tow truck. I followed, lagging behind to check the aisles.

The air-conditioned interior of Buy the Book felt heavenly after the unseasonable warmth of the fall afternoon, and I was happy to see all was well. Our shelves were neat and well stocked with this week's delivery of new releases. The comfy mismatched chairs were set in place, the lamps and tables had been dusted, and our newest displays were looking good, including our cozy mystery book group's monthly reader recommendations (*Meat Your Maker* and *Bone Yard*, the first two titles in the new Butcher Block culinary series).

Animated voices brought my attention to the cash register, where Seymour was now regaling my aunt with the details of his purchase. "Wait until you see the weird elements in my Harriet original—and how hauntingly unhinged it is. She looks young in this self-portrait, too, and I have to say, she's pretty hot for a madwoman."

Sadie folded her arms. "I've always been skeptical about those 'Crazy Harriet' stories. Maybe the woman was simply shy or reclusive. Seems to me when you're the least bit different, people talk. And people can say cruel things."

"Well, if she wasn't crazy, she put on a good act," Seymour countered. "Living alone all those years? Spending day after day painting nothing but images of herself—"

"Have you told Fiona Finch about the painting?" Sadie raised an eyebrow at Seymour. "You know she and Barney have a proprietary interest in acquiring Harriet's work. After all, their Finch Inn was originally Harriet's home."

"Sorry, but it's not her home anymore. It's a posh bed-and-breakfast, and the Finches already have several of Harriet's paintings. They can't have mine. Not for any price. They'd have to pry it from my cold, dead hands, which actually isn't a stretch from how I got the thing, now that I think about it."

"What does that mean?" Sadie asked with a frown. "Did someone die?"

I tensed, fearing Seymour was about to tactlessly blurt out the story of Old Walt's demise, but this wasn't the time or place to do it.

Thank goodness my son came to the rescue.

CHAPTER 16

A Breeze from Beyond

With boys, you always know where you stand. Right
in the path of a hurricane.

—Erma Bombeck

BOUNDING OFF THE school bus, Spencer whooped with
excitement when he saw me through the shop window. He
burst through the front door, tossed his backpack behind the
counter, and faced me.

"Are the pictures here?!"

"Nice to see you, too. Can I have a hug, please?"

He obliged. "Glad you're back, Mom."

"That makes two of us." Sadie smiled. "We missed you."

"I missed you both, too." I mussed my son's copper hair,
and he tilted up his freckled face.

"So?" he pressed, wasting no time. "Do you have them?"

"Yes, Mr. One-Track Mind. We have the pictures."

Through the store's window, I noticed Seymour's tow
truck arriving. So did he. "My ride is here!" With a wave
good-bye, he hurried out—a huge relief.

I no longer had to worry about Seymour blurting anything, and I could break the bad news about Walt to Sadie

this evening, when we had the time to talk it over and she had the privacy upstairs to react.

Right now, the shop was open and there was work to be done.

As Sadie went back to ringing up customers, I headed for the stockroom to process special orders, my son on my heels.

"What kind of pictures did you get, Mom? Are there any monsters? How about gorillas? Are there any gorillas? When can I see them?"

"I'll be setting up the art show in the event space tomorrow. You can see the pictures after you get home from school."

Spencer tugged my arm. I stopped to face him.

"But you promised I could see the pictures yesterday. Then you didn't even come home. Now I have to wait until tomorrow? It's not fair, Mom."

The pint-size Perry Mason wore me down. "Follow me . . ."

Entering the stockroom, which doubled as our store office, I skirted the desk and file cabinets and gestured to the many pieces of art leaning against the walls and shelves, their details still masked.

"You can pick one. Just one. And I'll unwrap it for you now. A private showing, just for you."

Eyes wide with excitement, Spencer raised his arm, finger extended. Without warning, I felt a sudden, *highly suspicious* draft flow through the room, gusting just strong enough to stir my son's hair. With a little shiver, Spencer suddenly swung his arm in the opposite direction and jabbed his finger.

"That one!"

The canvas and frame felt surprisingly light as I set them on an easel. I tore at the tape for a moment, and the brown paper fell away to reveal Nathan Brock's painting of the nude Ruby Tyler.

Spencer's eyes went wide. "Wow, Mom!"

I jumped in front of the canvas and quickly re-covered it

with paper. "That one might be a little *too adult* for you," I announced with pointed emphasis for any *spirited* eavesdropper who might be listening. To my son I gently said, "Let's try again."

"Okay!" Spencer grinned, pleased at this bonus reveal. "How about that one?"

The picture was large and weighty, and Spencer had to help me place it on a second easel. I didn't do more than tear at the corner before I recognized the heavy antique frame of Harriet McClure's portrait. I tried to cover the painting again, but the tape refused to stick and the paper fell away.

"Hey, that's not a cover, Mom," Spencer said, disappointed. "And it's really weird."

Apparently, my son was immune to Harriet's supernatural charms.

"Last time," I said.

Spencer rubbed his hands together like a game-show contestant contemplating which door to open. Once again, he raised his arm, finger extended toward one of the wrapped paintings. And again I felt a sudden, highly suspicious draft gust through the room. With a swing of his arm, my son abruptly changed his choice—

"That one!"

This time Spencer selected a picture that would satisfy any boy's imagination. The full-color rendering depicted a big, tough-looking blond cowboy blazing away at a rampaging dinosaur using a pair of six-shooters.

"Whoa! That is awesome!" Spencer cried.

It was more than that. There was something about the cowboy and the painting that struck me as vaguely familiar.

"Is this picture in the book?" Spencer asked excitedly, pulling me away from my thoughts.

"Let's see." I grabbed my copy of the Palantines' *By Its Cover* and flipped through the pages.

"Found it! This was the cover for *Fantastic Western Adventure*, June 1948."

Spencer cocked his head. "What else does it say?"

"Artist Roland Prince, a skilled painter and illustrator,

was quite prolific. In his short career, Prince produced more than five hundred covers and interior illustrations in wildly differing artistic styles."

"Five hundred? Wow, that's a lot! Roland must have been rolling in dough if he sold that many paintings."

"I suppose so."

Spencer's attention returned to the image. "That's a pretty cool T. rex, Mom, don't you think? It's just like the one in *Jurassic Park*. I can't wait to show this picture to Amy!"

Which was fine with me. I doubted even Amy's helicopter mother would find fault with a vintage fantasy image of a cowboy and dinosaur, though when it came to parental objections these days, one could only feel safe with a blank canvas.

"Okay, honey, that's all for tonight—"

"Hey, what's this?"

"What's what?"

Spencer pointed to a notation in the lower right corner. Beneath the Roland Prince signature, there was a small circle with the letter B drawn inside it.

"I think it must be a special mark for the painter," I said, voicing my assumption.

"But why would Roland Prince use a letter B? Wouldn't you think he'd use a P for Prince or RP for Roland Prince?"

"Maybe it's not a signature."

"What else would it be?"

I shrugged. "Maybe it was a notation for the printer or the magazine that bought the rights. This could have been the second in a series of illustrations they commissioned—A, B, C, and so on."

Spencer's eyes widened again. "I'd sure like to see A and C, wouldn't you?"

"Not at the moment, honey. It's getting late. You can see the rest of the pictures tomorrow. Now, go upstairs and do your homework. I'll be up to make dinner soon."

CHAPTER 17

A Quiet Place

The place is very well and quiet and the children only scream in a low voice.

—Lord Byron

HOURS LATER, I was back in our stockroom, surrounded by Walt's paintings and work I *should* have been doing. Instead I sat back in my desk chair, half listening to the girlish laughter echoing from the event space.

The day had been long and harrowing, and despite the fact that Buy the Book closed its doors at nine P.M., my work would not end for another hour, though, to be honest, I was already slacking off. Usually, I sat in on Tracy Mahoney's book-group meetings.

Ever since Bonnie Franzetti convinced me to include young adult fiction in our store, Tracy's gatherings had become a handy resource to learn about the appeal of new authors and hear about emerging trends. And ever since the coming of crossover hits like *The Hunger Games*, *Twilight*, *The Fault in Our Stars*, and *Thirteen Reasons Why*, plenty of adults were now enjoying young adult and "new adult" fiction, which is why adding select titles and series proved profitable for our store.

Tonight, however, after two straight days of the postman and the professor, I needed a peaceful break from humanity. I was nearly caught up on processing our online special orders when I was jarred by what sounded like the anguished outcry of a young woman.

"No! Oh, noooo!"

The plaintive howl came from the event space, where Tracy Mahoney's reading group was meeting.

Careful not to stumble over all the borrowed artwork and easels, I moved to the open stockroom door in time to see five members of Tracy's group moving toward the store's exit. Next came a pair of student members from St. Francis University. Shoulders slumped and faces grim, they kept their eyes locked on their phone screens as they departed.

It was clear the gathering had broken up, but not on its usual cheery, high-spirited note. I found Tracy sitting alone in the event space, the circle of chairs now empty.

"You guys broke up early. Is something wrong?"

Staring with a tormented expression at her smartphone, Tracy swiped tears from her cheeks. "It's nothing, Mrs. Mc-Clure. Just some ugly comments on our Facebook page about my fantasy art, that's all."

"Can I help?"

She quickly shook her head. "It's probably just an Internet troll."

I could tell the poor girl was rattled. "Why don't you come upstairs for some tea? You'll feel better if you talk things out."

She just shook her head. "Thanks. That's nice of you, but I need to get going. Good night."

I followed Tracy to the door and stood watching as she pulled on her motorcycle helmet, threw a leg over her blue Yamaha, and sped down Cranberry Street. For the space of a breath, I wanted to join her.

Youth was exhilarating, but it was a lot of other things, too.

When you're still struggling to discover who you are and what your place is in this world, every barb, every slight (real or imagined), feels like a cut to the bone, and every unkind voice takes the volume of a deafening chorus, echoing through your head with reverberating ridicule.

On a sigh of regret (and relief) I turned the key in the shop's front door. With everyone gone, I was finally off duty. I dimmed the lights. But before I could head upstairs, I had to perform one last task—the nightly hide-and-seek ritual of catching Bookmark and carrying the complaining kitty upstairs.

I sympathized with our grumpy marmalade-striped feline, who was used to roaming the store in search of the occasional unsuspecting mouse. But I had no choice. With our recent security upgrade—including motion detectors in our event space and stockroom—our cat's nocturnal wanderings had to be curtailed. We'd learned this after one too many sleep-depriving false alarms in the wee hours of the night.

I appeased the disgruntled furball in our upstairs kitchen with a tasty bowl of gourmet cat food. As she licked her little cat lips, I heard the sound of the evening news going on, and I knew my aunt was still awake.

Steeling myself for an unhappy but necessary duty, I brewed us a pot of chamomile-honey tea and opened a fresh box of shortbread cookies. I loaded a tray and brought it to the living room.

"Pen! I didn't hear you come in," Sadie said, making room for me on the couch. "Sit, and you can tell me about your trip."

As gently as I could, I finally broke the news of her colleague's death to my aunt. She took Walter Waverly's demise harder than I'd anticipated.

She asked how it happened, of course, and I decided not to complicate an already terrible situation, telling her what Sheriff Taft came to believe—that Old Walt's death was a tragic accident.

The next thirty minutes were tearful enough to bring out the sympathetic side of the usually indifferent Bookmark. Hearing Sadie's distress, the cat curled up on my aunt's lap to purr comfortingly.

"Walt is going to be missed." Sadie sniffed, stroking Bookmark's marmalade fur. "He was a memorable fixture on the convention circuit."

"Which one?"

"You name it. Antiquarian fairs, antiques conventions, rare book shows, art sales, he went to them all. Walt was always on the go."

"Did he have many competitors?"

"No more than anyone else at those events. Walt was a big, jovial teddy bear who would drop everything to help a customer, or even a fellow vendor."

"No serious rivals that you know of? No enemies?"

"Of course not, Pen. Everybody loved him. Why would you ask such a thing? Did Walt mention a threat of some kind?"

I shook my head, deliberately holding my tongue on Walt's late-night mystery visitor. I didn't want to upset Sadie, but I did need to fill in more blanks on Walt's background.

"Did you ever meet Walt's wife?"

"No, never did," Sadie said. "God rest her soul. Walt said she had no interest in traveling. Only his son, Neil, came with him on the road—until he moved."

"His son moved?"

"Yes, Walt was grooming Neil to take over his business. The last time I saw Walt, I asked where his son was. He said Neil was living in Los Angeles. This wasn't long after Mrs. Waverly died, so I assumed the two of them were dealing with their grief by throwing themselves into their work and expanding to cover both coasts."

That seemed wrong to me, and I said so. "If there was a West Coast contingent to Walt's business, then why was he trying to push his entire collection on us in one rushed deal?"

"Maybe he wanted to move to Los Angeles to be with his son, and he didn't want to move the collection."

"Walt only said he wanted out. He never once mentioned Los Angeles or his son."

"How odd. Do you think they had a falling-out?"

"Maybe."

We both fell silent after that, drinking our tea and watching the news. Finally, my aunt excused herself, heading off to bed with a drowsy Bookmark in her arms.

As for me, I was far too agitated to sleep. I felt as though I'd learned a bit of useful background information for Sheriff Taft. It was late, but I didn't see any harm in leaving a message.

Turned out I didn't have to. Augusta Taft answered on the first ring.

"Hello, Sheriff. This is Penelope McClure. I didn't know you were on duty."

"I'm always on duty, Mrs. McClure. What can I do for you?"

"It's more what I can do for you, Sheriff."

I informed her that Walt's son, Neil Waverly, had moved to Los Angeles. "If the man's whereabouts prove elusive, you might check with the contemporary art galleries in the LA area. He sold collectable art before; maybe he still does."

"That's very helpful," Taft admitted. "Not even Walt's semiretired lawyer knew Neil's current whereabouts."

"That's odd."

"Isn't it, though?"

After a pause, I took a chance. "May I ask: What did you learn from Walt's notebooks?"

"Nothing. I couldn't find the notebooks you described, even after a thorough search of the premises. There's so much junk, it's possible they're in the house, somewhere, but there are other factors that lead me to believe—"

"That they were taken?" I sat up straighter.

"I believe so," said the sheriff. "The state police—"

The buzz of another phone drowned out her words. Then I was put on hold, and after a short silence, Augusta Taft ended our conversation.

"I apologize, Mrs. McClure, but I have to go now. Duty calls. Thanks for the tip. We'll speak again."

CHAPTER 18

Nocturnal Wanderings

My mind goes sleepwalking while I'm putting the world right.

—Elvis Costello

IF I WAS searching for some sort of closure, I certainly didn't get it from my conversation with Augusta Taft. The sheriff of Blackstone Falls left me with as many questions as answers, and frustrated enough to throw in the towel and go to bed.

After that fitful night at the Stumbull Inn, I had a new appreciation for the comfort of my own crisp, clean sheets and thick comforter. As I snuggled under the covers, I tried to relax, but sleep wouldn't come.

Behind my eyelids a medley of colors flashed and danced like fireworks—saffron yellow, ice blue, rich dark red, and deep, shadowy black. Soon those colors coalesced into a single image—Nathan Brock's painting of Ruby Tyler.

With that depiction of frozen violence burned into my imagination, I fell into a kind of half sleep. I imagined myself getting out of bed and walking with bare feet in my long, flannel nightgown to the front door of the apartment.

As if from far away, I saw myself open the console and tap into the security system.

It was the quiet chirp of deactivation that snapped me back to consciousness, and I discovered I hadn't imagined a thing. I was actually there, at the front door, poised to go down the staircase—and with no question about where I was headed.

I decided to consciously follow the commands of my unconscious mind.

With an undetermined draft billowing the folds of my nightgown, I descended the stairs and entered the bookshop. I couldn't tell you the time, only that the world outside was dark and silent. Fog had crept in from the ocean and blanketed our little town with a thick gray mist that rolled past our store windows like waves of ghostly smoke.

I made my way back to the stockroom, certain I'd turned off the lights earlier. Yet now they were on, and the Nathan Brock painting of Ruby was the first thing I saw.

Taking my time, I took in every detail. Ruby's exuberant expression, the saffron yellow curtains, the knife-wielding killer—

"Wait," I whispered, my gaze freezing on the killer's image.

Something about that big, scary pockmarked man drew me closer. I'd seen that man somewhere else. But where?

"Jack? Are you there?"

Another chilly draft lifted my hair, but there was no voice, only a shivery, electric feeling through my body and a sudden urge to turn. When I did, I found myself staring at that cowboy-and-dinosaur painting, the one my son had gushed about.

This Roland Prince pulp illustration was expertly rendered, bold and striking, and a little unsettling in its utterly realistic portrayal of the cowboy shooting at the T. rex.

"The cowboy," I realized. "That's it!"

He had the exact same hulking build and rough-looking face as the killer in the Nathan Brock painting of beautiful Ruby Tyler.

There were some minor differences: Ruby's killer had dark hair and pockmarked cheeks. The cowboy's hair was blond and his cheeks were smooth. So either Roland Prince had brushed clean the pockmarks for his painting's cowboy, or Nathan Brock had painted in those pockmarks for his knife-wielding killer.

Regardless of the hair color and skin condition, the shape of the face and the wide brow and large hawklike nose were identical. The same man had served as the model for both paintings.

As I compared the two pictures, I realized the menacing man wasn't the only thing familiar. The saffron yellow of the curtains in Nathan Brock's painting appeared to be the same shade as the desert sun in Roland Price's cowboy-shoots-dinosaur painting. I compared the reds and blues and realized the color palettes were almost identical.

Perhaps the pulp magazines suggested these colors to their painters. Did they suggest models too? Did Roland Prince ever paint Ruby Tyler?

After staring for a long while at Ruby's sapphire blue eyes, I began to wonder what I was doing down here. If anyone saw me, they'd probably think I was acting as obsessed as Seymour—or as crazy as Harriet. That's when I turned off the stockroom's lights, went back upstairs, and reactivated the security system.

CHAPTER 19

Mortal Dreams

Deep into that darkness peering, long I stood there, wondering, fearing, doubting, dreaming dreams no mortal ever dared to dream before.

—Edgar Allan Poe

UPSTAIRS, THE CHILL of the night got to me, and I practically dived under the covers. The warmth of my thick comforter brought me no comfort, however, and no rest.

Maybe I can help, the ghost whispered.

"Finally!" I told the ghost. "I've been waiting for answers from you. I've got two mysterious women downstairs, one haunting Seymour and the other me—"

Hold your horses, honey. The answers I've got don't start with Ruby Tyler.

"But when I close my eyes, her image is all I see."

Oh, Ruby's a feature player in this drama, but the case didn't begin with her. It started with a dame who showed up at my office one morning wrapped in misery, cigarette smoke, and an oversize raincoat.

"And she was?"

A classy brunette named Shirley Powell.

My eyelids felt heavy. "Go on, Jack. Tell me about her."

You know I can do better than that.

"Another dream?"

A memory, but I'll tuck you into it real nice. Now, close those peepers, and I'll take you back to a day when I was dead tired but still very much alive, you get me?

"I get you . . ."

Once upon a time, I'd been pounding the pavement for a couple of worried parents on a missing kid case—their teenage daughter, Millicent. I'd been at it for forty-eight hours straight, following leads, staking out joints.

"Did you find her?"

Yeah, a little worse for the wear, but I got Millie home safe and sound. Her parents were thrilled enough to line my pockets. I shook their hands, hit the street, and was more than ready to pass out on some bedsheets. But my secretary was out, sunning herself in Myrtle Beach, so I swung by my office to check the mail.

"And Miss Shirley Powell was waiting for you?"

Found her leaning against my locked door.

"I'm all caught up, Jack," I murmured, drifting off. "Go on with your story. What happened next?"

THE DREAM JUMP (for lack of a better term) was abrupt. One moment I was under my bedcovers in a flannel night-gown, barely awake. A split second later I was smartly dressed in low heels and a fitted brown suit with one white-gloved hand on a grimy brass doorknob. In front of me was a door with four words on its beveled glass window—

JACK SHEPARD, PRIVATE INVESTIGATOR

I turned the knob and pushed. A secretary's battered wooden desk stood empty beside a wall of ancient metal file cabinets, the morning light barely slanting in through the window's half-closed venetian blinds. Beyond another door marked PRIVATE, I heard a woman's voice—

"You're a hard man, aren't you, Mr. Shepard?"

The answer came in a deep, gruff voice, the one I usually heard in my head—

"I've taken a few punches. Generally I roll with them."

"You don't talk much, either."

"I'm not here to talk, miss, and I can't promise I'll take your case. Have you hired a lawyer?"

"Yes, over the phone. He's the one who told me to see you."

Jack sighed. "Okay, then. Since you're here, I'll explain the rules to this game. It's simple. You spill. I'll listen—"

That spurred me forward. (If a client was about to "spill" for Jack Shepard, I wanted to hear it.) Without bothering to knock, I barged into the inner sanctum. And there he stood, in the flesh.

It was always a bit jarring to see Jack alive. He stood like a steel tower in the little room, tall and imposing and impossible to ignore. Though he was aloof, almost indolent in the way he spoke and moved, energy seemed to be simmering perpetually beneath his surface.

On this particular morning, however, that pulsing vitality was subdued. He looked tired, dead tired, just as he'd said. His suit's gray jacket was tossed haphazardly over a chair; his pants looked wrinkled; his white dress shirt bunched like an accordion beneath the leather straps of his shoulder holster. His eyes were bloodshot, and the five-o'clock shadow on his iron jaw had sprouted into cactus needles.

When I entered the room, he'd been in the middle of a chat with an attractive brunette who'd wrapped herself in an over-size raincoat. The young woman stared up at me with big, expectant eyes, mascara slightly running, as if she'd been crying. My tongue suddenly froze. I wasn't sure what to say.

Jack took care of it.

"Here's my secretary now. You're just in time to take notes, Penny. Meet Miss Shirley Powell."

"Please call me Shirley," she said. "When anyone calls me 'Miss Powell,' I feel like I'm back at boarding school."

She looked like she'd gone to boarding school, an elite one; sounded that way, too. The quasi-English accent reminded me of Katharine Hepburn or Lauren Bacall—which meant it was either an organic affectation of the upper crust or a studious attempt to mimic it. She did display poise and a touch of haughtiness, which I'd seen often among my Mc-Clure in-laws, though it was clear she'd fallen on hard times.

When she loosened her raincoat, she revealed a dress of faded yellow, with a big pink bow.

I took a seat in the empty chair *after* moving Jack's abandoned suit jacket—first I draped it neatly across the chair's back; then I carefully smoothed the shoulders and lapels. Jack's eyes were on me as I did this. Then his gaze slipped over my fitted suit and lingered on my upswept auburn hair.

Was something out of place? Why was he staring?

I met his eyes with a questioning expression. Jack said nothing, just slipped me a wink as he folded his tall frame into the creaky desk chair. Then he slid me a notepad and yellow pencil before prompting his client—

"You say your boyfriend's in a bind?"

"My fiancé," Shirley corrected, flashing the pinprick of a diamond on a wire-thin ring. "And yes, Mr. Shepard, if you call being arrested on suspicion of homicide a 'bind,' then I guess Nathan is in one."

"I'd say he was in deep. Who's the victim?"

"One of his female models. A woman named Ruby Tyler."

Hearing Ruby's name as the victim knocked the wisecracks out of Jack. I understood why. He'd known Ruby and clearly thought she was a swell gal.

For a moment he fell into a long silence, his expression grim.

I made eye contact with Shirley. I spotted a flicker of pain and maybe betrayal, but she looked down at her coffee cup before I could glean more.

Finally, Jack spoke.

"I'll take the case. Go on with your story."

CHAPTER 20

The Painter's Case

Now it seems to me the place to start is at the beginning.

—Perry Mason

"NATHAN IS A fine artist," Shirley said, still staring into
the cup. "He's sold a number of pieces around town. None
of the important galleries will accept him as a client—not
yet. But Nathan is extremely talented, and he's starting to get
noticed. It won't be long before he'll have his own gallery
shows, and—"

"What's all this got to do with murder?"

"Nathan does his painting at a tiny studio in Greenwich
Village. Twice last week I decided to drop in on him—"

"Drop in?" Jack interrupted. "You mean unannounced?"

"Nathan doesn't have a phone at his studio. He says it's
too distracting, and the line would be an added expense.
Anyway, Nathan wasn't there. The first time, I thought
maybe he was scouting."

"Scouting?" Jack lifted an eyebrow. "I take it you don't
mean building campfires and tying square knots."

"No, of course not. Nathan sometimes walks the streets
with that camera of his, scouting for interesting faces—"

"And did Nathan find Ruby Tyler *interesting*?"

Shirley sighed. "All I know is . . . a few days ago, I arrived at his studio just as he jumped into a cab. He didn't see me, so I followed him. Nathan met this Ruby woman at a diner. The Pluto, I think it's called."

Jack nodded. "On Eighth Avenue, near the Greyhound bus terminal?"

"That's right, Mr. Shepard. They met there, but they didn't stay long. Nathan and Ruby then crossed town in a taxi and went into a Park Avenue residential building with a doorman. They stayed up there quite some time."

Jack's eyes narrowed. "And you know this how?"

"Because after two hours waiting for them to reappear, I gave up."

Shirley glanced at Jack. Then she fixed her stare on me.

"Don't give me that look, girlie. I'm not proud of what I did, but you'll find out what it's like when you fall for a guy someday."

I was about to answer when Jack cleared his throat (loudly) and asked, "Didn't Nathan bring along 'that camera of his'? Or any of his gear? Paint? Canvas? An easel?"

Looking down at her coffee again, Shirley shook her head. "He keeps all of those things at his studio. That's where he does his painting."

"So your fiancé was having a fling with Ruby Tyler?"

"What else?" I saw tears. "I confronted Nathan that night, but he denied everything. He was furious that I'd followed him and stormed out. When he came back, I could tell he'd been drinking, but he didn't clear out. He made up with me, swore he'd been faithful. He said he still loved me, said I was the only one for him, and he wanted nothing more than to take care of me. He even started crying. Then last night Ruby was found dead in her apartment. Early this morning, the police came for Nathan. I'm sure they're questioning him now."

"Is he going to cave under pressure?"

She blinked. "I don't understand the question."

"Is Mr. Brock guilty?"

"Certainly not. You have to understand. Nathan may

seem a bit eccentric, a head-in-the-clouds kind of man, but he's a gentle and sensitive soul. That's one of the reasons he's such a brilliant painter. And he would *never* hurt another living thing."

"Yeah, but is he nuts enough to confess to a crime he didn't commit?"

"Why would he?"

"Oh, lots of reasons. Some of these artist types can go mental under pressure. And you never know what'll happen when the bulls decide to break out the rubber hose."

Shirley visibly shuddered. I felt for the woman, but Jack didn't let up.

"Tell me, Shirley, when Nathan denied the affair, did you buy it?"

She nodded, then looked away. "I never had any reason to question Nathan's faithfulness before."

"So despite what you saw, you believed him? I have to wonder why?"

"Because I have to, Mr. Shepard." Once again Shirley studied her cup, now nearly empty. "I invested in him—in us. We fell in love in college. I convinced him to leave Ohio and come to New York City with me. I had an inheritance. He didn't. We've been living off my savings to get his art career started. Nathan's got so much talent. One day, he'll be famous. I'm sure of it, and all of these struggles will be behind us."

Her coat still open, Shirley sat back in the chair. I took a hard look at the woman's form under that faded yellow dress and said—

"There's another reason you have to believe him, isn't there?"

Shirley shook her head weakly.

"How far along are you?" I asked.

She flushed red and touched the tiny bulge. "About four months."

"Did you tell Nathan?"

She sniffed. "He figured it out."

"Surprise pregnancies can shake up some men," I said

with a glance at Jack. He nodded for me to press on. "This thing with Ruby Tyler, was your fiancé looking for a way out?"

"I told you he's innocent."

"Innocent of murder or of an indiscretion?" I asked.

She slammed the cup on the desk. "Both."

Jack rose and stood over the woman.

"Look, Shirley. I can't guarantee I can clear him of your suspicions or the law's accusations. But if Nathan Brock is innocent of either of them, I'll prove it."

She didn't expect those words, I could tell. With tears welling, she gazed up at Jack with grateful eyes. Reaching into her pocket, she produced a plain white envelope and placed it on his desk.

"Inside you'll find the address of the doorman building where Ruby Tyler lives."

I grabbed the envelope and lifted the flap. Small bills kept company with a sheet of plain white. I saw names and addresses in flowing cursive—leads for Jack to follow.

"You'll also find one hundred dollars in there. Your advance."

Jack nodded. "I'd like to see the place where Nathan did his painting."

"As I mentioned, he has a small studio in Greenwich Village. I don't have the key with me, but I can meet you there."

"Let's put it on the back burner for now."

Jack asked more questions and I took notes. Finally, with encouraging words, he ushered the girl out.

"What do you think, Penny?" he asked when we were alone.

"Honestly? I feel for her. But Nathan Brock sounds guilty as original sin."

"I'm sure the police agree. And that's where we come in—along with one hundred little portraits of George Washington." He plucked the white envelope out of my hand.

"You didn't take this case for the money, though, did you?"

"No. I took it for Ruby."

"So if the painter didn't kill her, who did?"

"That's the question Shirley Powell's paying us to answer."

"But you already know the answer."

"Not in this memory, honey. On this day, I was just getting started."

"Fine. Where did you start?"

"With coffee," Jack said, "at the Pluto Diner. Care to join me?"

Pulling his suit jacket from the back of my chair, he slipped me another wink and grabbed his fedora. Excited to begin our gumshoeing, I rose, straightened my skirt, and led the way out of Jack's private office.

For some reason, the small reception area looked much brighter than when I'd left it. That's when a sudden noise surprised me. I listened again and realized it was a knock at the door.

"You must have a new client," I said and pulled it open.

The hallway was empty.

"Jack, what's going on? I don't see anyone. Jack?"

"I'm here, Penny," he whispered in my ear. "I'm right here with you."

But when I turned around, he was gone.

CHAPTER 21

Talk of the Town

Dreams are alive, more real than real . . . for a moment
at least . . . that long magic moment before we wake.

—George R.R. Martin

I OPENED MY eyes to bright sunlight peeking between
bedroom curtains. A little too bright, I realized with a
shock. Squinting my nearsighted eyes, I read the digital
clock. Today was Wednesday, and the time was—

"Eleven A.M.?!"

After all the drama last night, I'd forgotten to set the
alarm. Now I'd slept in. I was supposed to pick up Seymour
at half past noon so that he could be reunited with his Volkswagen, and I was already running late.

Suddenly the knocking from my dream returned, louder
than before.

"Pen?" My aunt's voice was muffled behind the door.
"Are you awake?"

"I am now. Come in! Why didn't you get me out of bed
sooner?"

Sadie pushed open the door. "You seemed exhausted
from your trip, so I let you sleep. I'm only bothering you

now because I thought you'd like to see what Spencer and I accomplished."

"You and Spencer?" My mind raced but came up with zip.

"Don't look so worried. I'm sure you'll approve. Come on down to the shop and see."

That got me moving. I threw off the covers and hit the bathroom.

Thirty minutes later, showered and presentable in a skirt, tights, and sweater, I descended the stairs, entered Buy the Book, and found our store busier than the local bank on payday!

"What is going on?" I asked no one in particular.

And one particular ghost replied.

It's like Grand Central in here. What's with the crowded aisles? How's a guy like me supposed to rest in peace?

Sorry, Jack. There's usually a lunchtime rush, but this is—

"Amazing, isn't it?" Bonnie Franzetti appeared beside me, eyes bright. "Early this morning, Spencer wanted to see more of the pictures. By the time I got here, he and Sadie had unwrapped them all. We went to work and put the whole exhibition together in less than an hour. Spencer even adjusted the track lighting in the event space before he went to school."

Sadie was now back behind the counter, checking out customers as fast as she could. And there were still people waiting in line!

"I'd better open up that second register," Bonnie said as she scurried off.

Sadie spotted me and waved.

"Go in and see, Pen!" she called. "You'll love it."

While I slept the morning away, Sadie, Spencer, and Bonnie had done a remarkable job. All the works were in place. Easels had been strategically lined up along the walls, with plenty of space between them for gawkers.

Though the place cards hadn't been printed up yet, I could see that Sadie had used the Palantine book as her guide. The art was arranged both chronologically and by type, with pulp covers on one side, book covers on the other.

A display copy of *By Its Cover* was mounted on a bookstand in the center of the room. The bookstand was actually our heavy speaker's podium. Sadie had dragged it out of storage and polished the dull maple with Murphy's oil soap, until it looked like it had just been varnished. Beside it, she'd positioned a table with stacks of shrink-wrapped copies of the just-delivered Palantine book for purchase.

I still didn't understand how the display alone had drawn so many customers. But Sadie was right. I loved it—until I didn't.

I noticed that a few of the most spectacular pieces of art were mounted on the wall. These included a fantasy cover by Frank Frazetta, a painting by Edgar Rice Burroughs, artist Allen St. John, Nathan Brock's painting of Ruby Tyler, and finally—to my shock and horror—the cursed self-portrait of Harriet McClure.

So much for keeping the location of that painting a secret, Jack cracked.

What do I do now?!

Now? Nothing. It's too late. You should have been more honest with your auntie and not played your cards so close to your vest.

What I found more shocking than anything was that despite all the great art displayed, the McClure self-portrait was getting the lion's share of customer attention.

Thanks to Spencer, who had tinkered with the track lighting, Harriet was illuminated by a powerful white glow that bounced off the wild colors, giving the work a near supernatural aura, one that clearly impressed my fellow Cranberry Street merchants.

Moving closer, I paused to eavesdrop on the co-owner of our town's bakeshop, Linda Cooper-Logan, and everyone's favorite hairdresser, Colleen, as they oohed and aahed over the surreal elements in Harriet's self-portrait.

"Whenever I see that grim, unflattering painting of Harriet at city hall, I always shudder. This is different. So alive and imaginative, and it shows Harriet to be so human." Colleen pointed at the canvas. "I love all that hair flying in the wind. The dress is great, too. I'll bet I could make a pattern."

"The dress? You're kidding. It's so severe," Linda said. "She's dressed like an undertaker. Or a killer schoolmarm."

"The Goth look is always in. Talk to Barb at the sewing shop; she'll tell you."

Linda stepped closer to the portrait, her spiky platinum pixie cut blazing whitely in the glare. "That beach looks wild, doesn't it? I had a poster with Day-Glo colors like that in my dorm room." She shook her head. "Makes me nostalgic for the trips I used to take in my college days."

"Did you travel to different countries?"

"Ah, no. By 'trip' I meant peyote," Linda replied, pointing at the lime green waves and flying pink fish. "That's the way you see the world when you're on psychotropic drugs."

"Oh!" Colleen laughed uneasily.

"Don't look so worried. Those days are far behind me. I'm a doughnut pusher now."

They both laughed.

"Well," Collen said, "I doubt Harriet dropped acid. But from the look of these crazy colors and strange symbols, I'd say the rumors of her madness are true."

"I guess," Linda said.

"Excuse me, Mrs. McClure—"

Startled, I whirled to face my own reflection in Joyce Koh's huge, scarlet-framed glasses. Eighteen and pop culture obsessed, Joyce had come directly from work at her father's store—I knew because she still wore the Kelly green Koh's Market blouse.

"I wanted to see the madwoman's picture," she said.

"Sure, but how did *you* hear about it?"

"Sandy came in for groceries last night. You know, the lady who runs the cab company? She picked up Mr. Tarnish at the garage yesterday to take him home. On the way, he mentioned the picture."

"Mentioned? You mean Seymour bragged about the picture, don't you?"

"That's right." Joyce blinked. "I guess Sandy told you all about it, too."

I wanted to smack my forehead—or Seymour's. The location of Harriet's self-portrait was supposed to be a secret, not the talk of the town!

Joyce peeked over my shoulder, itching to get that first look at the Harriet McClure. I stepped aside.

"Join the crowd," I said, which was beginning to resemble the Louvre's eternal knot of tourists around the *Mona Lisa*. As I untangled myself from Harriet's knot, I nearly collided with Wanda Clark.

The director of the church choir, Wanda seldom shopped around town without the Reverend Waterman's wife in tow, and today was no exception.

"Wanda! And Mrs. Waterman. Are you here to view the portrait?"

Mrs. Waterman nodded. "I was walking by and I saw the sign—"

"Sign?"

"The sidewalk sign about Harriet's newly discovered self-portrait," Mrs. Waterman replied. "I simply had to pop in and see it!"

I wasn't too happy about the sign, but I also noted that her "popping in" included grabbing an armful of books. And Wanda was carrying a whole basket of titles, most of them newly released hardcovers—being the wife of Stuckley Autos' top salesman came with a lot of perks.

At her first glimpse of the portrait, Mrs. Waterman sighed. "She's lovely. Like a Madonna!"

Joyce shook her head. "More like Taylor Swift . . . around the eyes."

"Oh, no!" Linda cried. "She's definitely a Pat Benatar."

"Or Aretha Franklin," said Colleen. "Definitely a soul singer."

The reverend's wife finally caught on to the joke when she saw the mischievous grins on the other women's faces. Then all of them started laughing together.

After extracting myself from the Harriet knot, I was about to head for the stockroom when I caught a whiff of La Chienne—La Chienne Number 5, that is, a scent not widely available outside of France. This I knew because it was a trigger for me. Just like the sight of rats for Winston Smith in *1984*, that cloying aroma threw me back to a place and time I preferred to forget.

I spotted her standing with folded arms at the entrance to the event space. Stylish clothes, heels, perfectly blunt-cut blond hair, and a sour expression: Georgia Gilder had finally deigned to visit my bookstore.

I'd heard my old high school classmate had returned from Boston. Up to now, I'd managed to avoid her. Georgia's parents had been the owners of Gilder's Antiques, a beloved fixture in our community for decades. A few months ago the couple retired and moved to Arizona, but not before they turned their antiques business over to their daughter.

Since then, Bud Napp (Sadie's beau and owner of Napp Hardware) reported that his friendly visit to welcome "Glamorous Georgia" had resulted in a snobbish dismissal. She'd told Bud she had "zero interest" in participating in our Quindicott Business Owners Association, known affectionately around town as "The Quibblers."

Sure, we were a rambunctious group with members who liked to speak their minds. But when we banded together, we managed to get things done and help solve one another's problems.

Bud wasn't angry as much as hurt by Georgia's insulting treatment, but her attitude wasn't new to me. I'd say we were frenemies in school, but we never even pretended to be friends. Not the way she used to put down Seymour and Brainert and roll her eyes at me. To her, we were geeks, nerds, bookworms—"losers with zero social currency" is how she once described us to her cool-kids group.

Sounds like a peach.

Sure, Jack, one that's rotten at the core. I remember her always bragging that she couldn't wait to get out of our little "nowhere" town.

So why come back to Cornpone-cott?

No idea. The last I heard, she was married to a partner in a big Boston law firm, where she worked in human re-

sources. Her parents said she was living the high life, traveling the world, hobnobbing with political big shots.

And now she's back in nowheresville.

I'm sure it's just temporary. At least I hope so. I don't know how long I can avoid her.

I'd say ten more seconds.

Jack was right. The rotten Georgia peach was heading my way.

CHAPTER 22

Bully for You

If they don't like you for being yourself, be yourself
even more.

—Taylor Swift

GEORGIA GILDER STOPPED right in front of me and
tossed her salon-glossy highlights. Index finger brushing her
pointed chin, she appraised me with critical green eyes.

"Well, Penelope, you certainly clean up well. But of
course, one is only as good as the company one keeps."

"Excuse me?"

"I understand you're still associating with the fussy
scholar and the peculiar postal carrier."

"If you mean my *good friends*, respected professor J.
Brainert Parker and *Jeopardy!* champion Seymour Tarnish,
then, yes, I am, and proud to be."

She scowled the haughty scowl I'd seen thousands of
times through my adolescent years.

"I'm surprised you and Sadie Thornton are still hanging
on. I thought by now e-books would have finished this
quaint throwback to the nineteenth century." She tilted her
head and sniffed theatrically. "Funny how quickly printed
paper mildews. I could never stand that smell."

*Tell the dame she's one to talk. She's doused herself with
enough perfume to pickle a red-light cathouse.*

For once, I didn't tell Jack to pipe down. In fact, I bit my
cheek to keep from laughing.

My barely suppressed smile clearly wasn't the response
Georgia had hoped for. As her face flushed with fury, I became suspicious. Was she *trying* to provoke me? With all
these people around, any angry or unprofessional outburst
from me (including giving in to the overwhelming knee-jerk
urge to kick her out of my store) was sure to be the talk of
the town. But why would Georgia want that? What would
she gain by making me look bad in a public scene? And putting my shop at the center of ugly gossip?

*One thing you're good at, doll, playing cards close to
your vest. Keep it up.*

Jack was right. I had no clue what Georgia was up to,
which is why I remained on guard as she pursed her peach-
glossed lips and leaned in close (so close my son would have
described it as "getting in my face"). And, wow, was Jack
right about the perfume!

*Of course I was right. That cloud of flower juice could
choke a horse.*

"So, where is this treasure?" Georgia demanded.

"And by *treasure* you're referring to . . .?"

"Don't deny it. Half the town knows about the mailman's
big find, and the other half probably married their cousins."
She rolled her eyes.

"Follow me. I'll show you the portrait."

As I led the way to our very own *Mona Lisa* mob, Georgia kept carping—

"I can't believe that schlub scored something with such
regional value, a painting that could hang in the local courthouse or a Newport museum. But what I really want to know
is why Tarnish is allowing *amateurs* like you and your aunt
to sell it."

As we crossed to the portrait, Georgia silently scanned
the other paintings on display. When she came face-to-face
with Harriet's portrait, she blinked in surprise.

"That's certainly different from the other McClures I've seen. Are you sure it's authentic?"

"Has anyone ever forged a Harriet McClure?"

"Stranger things have happened."

"Look closely," I said, pointing.

"Yes. I see the top of Harriet's signature, if it *is* her signature. But what is all this other nonsense?" She stepped back for a better look. "I can't understand any of it except that bar of music. It's Brahms' 'Lullaby.'"

"Is that so? What do you think it means? Is it a message?"

She threw up her French-tipped fingers. "It's a bar of music!"

Georgia stepped close again and appraised the portrait much the same way she'd evaluated me.

"How much money are you asking for this?"

"We're not selling it. Seymour Tarnish owns the work, and he's not willing to part with it."

As per usual, Georgia continued to speak as if I hadn't. "He'd be a fool to sell it through anyone who isn't an *experienced* broker."

With a sharp turn, she locked eyes with me. "What's really going on here, Penelope?"

"It's not hard to decipher, Georgia. This is an exhibit to promote the art history book displayed on the podium right there in the middle of the room."

"An exhibit? Really? With *price tags* on every painting? This doesn't look like an exhibit to me. It looks like *commerce*."

Before I could explain Walt's tags, she turned on her high heels. On her way to the exit, Georgia called over her shoulder.

"Stick to peddling old books and silly stories, Penelope, and stay out of my art and antiques business. Gilder's has been working that trade for decades, and I'm now cultivating a high-end clientele, which you know nothing about. *I'm* going to be the destination store for Newport, Boston, and Greenwich antiquing. If you try to compete with me, I will make sure you regret it!"

A sudden, inexplicable draft blew Georgia's skirt up to her elbows. With a yelp, she batted the material back down and ran out of the store.

"Thanks, Jack," I whispered.

Believe me, it was my pleasure.

I don't doubt it, especially with that peek at her French underwear.

As Jack and I shared a silent chuckle, Sadie hurried to my side.

"I overheard that woman's threat. What nerve!"

I shook my head. "Some people never change. Georgia was a bully in high school, and she's stayed true to form."

My aunt considered my words. Then her eyes twinkled, and she leaned close. "What do you think about a *bigger* sign? To promote the art show and the Palantines' appearance, as well as Harriet's painting?"

"I don't know . . ." The idea was a good one for our business, but I couldn't help fretting over it. Setting aside the whole Harriet curse, there was still the issue of Walt's unnatural end.

I asked the ghost what he thought.

Cat's out of the bag, no getting her back in now.

"But where will the cat lead us? That's the question."

"I don't understand," Aunt Sadie said. "What cat? Are you talking about Bookmark?"

"Uh, no . . . sorry, I was talking to myself . . . about the situation we're in."

"What situation?" Sadie replied. "Look around you! Thanks to Harriet McClure, our business has never been better. You're not going to let Georgia Gilder intimidate us, are you?"

"You know what? You're right. The cat *is* out of the bag. Harriet is already drawing customers in large numbers. And I don't give a fig about Georgia's threat. Let's make that window sign *really* big. In fact, let's put out a giant sandwich board on the sidewalk, too, so people can read it from all the way down the street—or at least as far as Georgia Gilder's antiques store."

As Sadie happily ran off to get things started, Jack laughed.

That should drive your perfume-soaked peach to distraction. And make your big-mouth blabbering pal Seymour puff up with peacock pride.

"Shoot, that reminds me—" I checked the store clock. "It's time for me to pick up Seymour and drive him to the garage."

Say hello to the art lover for me. I'll just hover here and watch the gawking rubes until you get back.

"Oh, no, you don't. I've got your lucky nickel tucked in my . . . *ahem*, let's just say close to my heart. You're coming with me, Jack Shepard. Like it or not."

CHAPTER 23

The House on Larchmont Avenue

It's like déjà vu all over again.

—Yogi Berra

I SPED ALONG a scenic route toward the lofty Victorian mansion Seymour Tarnish called home.

If there was a tony section of our little town, Larchmont was it. Located far beyond our crowded commercial area of Cranberry Street and the narrow confines of the "suburbs," with tiny yards and doll houses, Larchmont sported rolling hills and palatial homes with sprawling, manicured lawns and perfectly pruned ornamental shrubbery.

How an ordinary mailman and part-time ice cream truck vendor came to live on this luxurious avenue, in the reputedly "haunted mansion" of the late Theodora Todd, was a story in itself. I could only say that for a seemingly unremarkable man, Seymour Tarnish led a pretty remarkable life.

Jeopardy! win aside, I'd seen my unassuming friend hold his own with a drawing room of Harvard professors *and* the Phelps Tool-and-Die's crew on bowling night. For his vast knowledge of popular culture alone, Seymour deserved an honorary doctorate in American social studies. And though his outspoken nature could be off-putting at times, Quindi-

cott's one and only ice cream man was still one of a kind—
and a true friend.

Not that friendship with the guy was always easy.

Case in point: I'd placed a call to Seymour as soon as I
hit the highway, but he didn't pick up. I figured he was in the
shower and tried again ten minutes later. Still no answer!
And he was the one who wanted to be picked up "no later"
than half past twelve. I would be plenty peeved if I found
him lounging around in his Spider-Man pajamas, streaming
episodes of *Green Acres*.

Right on time, I turned onto the winding driveway that
led up to Theodora Todd's mansion. Hugged by a pair of
wind-twisted oaks and hemmed by grounds that were anything but manicured, the old Victorian looked haunted even
in broad daylight.

In truth I never much liked this place, and I would never
understand how Seymour felt comfortable enough to actually *live* here—

"Oh no."

My running thoughts stopped dead when I saw the mansion's front door standing wide open, and with no Seymour
in sight. I slammed on the brakes so hard I was thrown
against the shoulder harness.

Proceed with caution, Jack said. *Remember what you
found at Old Walt's place.*

"God, I hope not!"

Fighting panic, I pressed the gas and rolled the car forward. When I reached the house, I cut the engine and threw
off my shoulder strap.

*Hold your horses, Calamity Jane, where are you riding
off to?*

"Seymour might be hurt. I have to go in—"

First I want you to grab your Ameche.

"English, Jack!"

*Don't go in there until you use your Dick Tracy wrist
radio to call in the law.*

"You actually want me to call Chief Ciders? But you hate
the guy."

Better a dim bulb than no light at all.

Like many of the local merchants in Quindicott, I had the chief's personal phone number on speed dial, and he picked up on the first ring. I told him I believed I had stumbled across a burglary, or maybe even a robbery in progress at Seymour's place.

"That old spook house on Larchmont? Are you sure your pal's not pulling off some prank? You remember that stunt with those firecrackers, don't you?"

"That was over twenty years ago!"

"And fireworks are *still* illegal."

"Are you going to send help, or do I call the staties?"

(That got him.) "I'll dispatch Deputy Chief Franzetti. He's across town, but he can be there in ten or fifteen minutes."

"I can't wait that long. Seymour may be injured."

"Well, if this is a burglary, like you claim, he could be knocked cold, and you will be too if some opioid junkie is ransacking the place. Lock your car door and stay inside until Eddie gets there."

The chief ended the call, and I tucked my phone away. Then I opened the car door.

You're not going to wait for the coppers, are you?

"Seymour may be in trouble, Jack."

I was across the porch and over the threshold in seconds. The first thing I did was peek behind the door—and felt a rush of relief when I found nothing.

"Seymour?"

I activated the lighting Seymour had installed in the foyer. A dozen colorful canvases—framed pulp cover prints mixed with movie posters—were bathed in a soft glow. The rest of the house remained in shadow.

I walked passed the art gallery and made a left.

The noonday sun streamed through the lace-curtained windows in Seymour's living room. The place seemed undisturbed. I noted the ultraexpensive home theater unit and giant-screen television were untouched—an odd miss for a burglar.

"Jack?" I whispered.

I'm on the same party line, doll. If there's a crime, it isn't your average knockover.

I called for Seymour again—and again there was no reply.

Swallowing my fear, I decided to head for the second floor. But as I approached the staircase, I heard a loud thumping noise emanating from the walls themselves.

At the same time an eerie fluttering sound, not at all human, echoed down the windowless hallway that led to the kitchen.

I was about to call out again, when I heard the blood-curdling screech.

"DANGER, WILL ROBINSON! DANGER! DANGER!"

What looked like a rabid bat to my fevered imagination zoomed out of the dark hallway. I ducked and covered, flattening myself on the worn Persian rug as the winged creature swooped over me.

I heard the fluttering thing settle on the mantel behind me. Then another scream, this one straight out of Seymour's favorite *Star Trek* movie.

"KHAAAAANNNNNNNNN!"

That's when I realized I'd been assaulted by Seymour's talking parrot.

"Waldo, calm down!"

In response, the parrot took a short flight from the mantel to Seymour's life-size Mr. Spock standee, where it cocked its head and promptly took a dump.

"Shame on you."

"DANGER! DANGER!" the parrot squawked back.

I heard another thump, followed by a muffled but most definitely human cry.

Scanning the room, I saw the sound was coming from the walk-in coat closet—"saw" because the double doors vibrated with each thump!

"Seymour? Is that you?!"

The pounding redoubled in intensity, but the doors remained shut tight. I soon discovered why. The twin brass doorknobs had been tied together with a curtain rope, effectively trapping the victim inside.

"Hold on, Seymour! I'll get you out."

It took a full minute of frantic striving and two broken fingernails before I managed to untangle the decorative rope. The closet doors burst open immediately.

With a horrified shout, I jumped backward.

Bound and gagged and wearing wrinkled Superman pajamas, Seymour plunged through the gap. He let out a muffled howl as his already bloody head rebounded off the hardwood floor.

CHAPTER 24

Violations

"You always have . . . a smooth explanation ready."
"What do you want me to do? Learn to stutter?"

—Dashiell Hammett, *The Maltese Falcon*

DEPUTY CHIEF FRANZETTI frowned.

Now, I'd known Eddie Franzetti since I was a gawky adolescent with a major crush on my older brother's best friend, which is why I recognized that particular pinched face. Eddie was seriously skeptical of Seymour's story, and almost certainly the reason he asked the mailman to recount it again, from the top.

When Seymour was finished, Eddie began firing off questions.

"You're saying someone broke in, hit you over the head, tied you up, and locked you in the closet?"

"Yeah."

"Hmm," the deputy chief muttered.

"What?!" Seymour replied. "You think I gave myself ten stitches and a concussion?"

"Four stitches," Dr. Rubino corrected. "And no sign of a concussion. Though you really should go to the emergency room—"

"Not until I find out what happened here, and what's missing," Seymour snapped.

Dr. Rubino cleaned and stitched Seymour's wound. Then he wrapped his head in a gauze turban. Despite the fact that he'd been knocked cold, and in the face of the physician's recommendation, my friend adamantly refused to go to the hospital.

Out of sheer bullheaded stubbornness, Seymour wouldn't allow Eddie to call an ambulance, either. Lucky for him, Dr. Rubino lived in the neighborhood. When he saw Eddie's police car roll up, he stopped by with his doctor's bag to see if everything was all right.

Obviously, it wasn't.

While the doc ministered to his reluctant patient, Eddie Franzetti searched Seymour's house. I attempted to join him, only to get scolded for disobeying Chief Ciders' order and entering the house before he arrived.

"In my defense, I did free Seymour."

Eddie ordered me to turn around and go back to the living room.

I can't believe it, Jack. Eddie is peeved at me for helping.

He's peeved because you might have gotten your scrawny neck broken.

But what was I supposed to do? Seymour needed help—and I don't have a scrawny neck.

Your mailman chum needs help, all right. He's completely bing and I don't mean Crosby.

Bing?

He's a bunny—attracts trouble the way a serge suit gathers lint. And I think we both know what the burglar was looking for.

Yes, we do. And when he gets back, I'm going to tell Eddie about my suspicions—

Fat lot of good that will do you. You're going to sound just as daffy as your lug-nut pal.

Eddie was gone for a surprisingly long time. When he finally did return, he seemed more dubious of Seymour's story than ever.

"Someone came in through your back porch door," Eddie said. "Appears you left it unlocked, because it wasn't messed with. The screen door lock was flimsy, and it looks broken. As far as I can determine, nothing was taken. Your entertainment system is untouched. There's a jar full of loose bills and change on the kitchen table, along with your very expensive smartphone, which is still in its charging dock. And all your valuable books are behind lock and key, like you told me they were."

The deputy chief paused. "So, Seymour, tell me what really happened. A Tinder date gone wild maybe?"

"No! You said it yourself. Someone broke in through my back porch screen door—"

"A burglar who didn't steal anything and you can't identify?"

"I can't ID them because I never saw a thing," Seymour said. "When I heard Waldo squawking, I went to the bottom of the steps to see why, and someone hit me from behind. That's all I know, until I came to in the closet, tied up like an extra in *The Perils of Pauline*!"

"Do you think this was personal?" Eddie asked.

"What do you mean?"

"A gripe, a grudge, revenge. Did you piss off someone on your mail route or peddle some bad ice cream?"

"Certainly not." Seymour squared his shoulders. "I'm a consummate professional at both of my vocations."

"Okay, maybe this was a stunt one of your friends pulled, like that guy Henry Gilman. Aren't you two always arguing?"

"It's *Harlan* Gilman. And he'd never expend the energy for a stunt like this."

"Brainert always argues with Seymour, too," I pointed out. "But Professor Parker wouldn't do a thing like this, either."

"I'll concede we've had some burglaries, in and around Larchmont," Eddie said. "I suspect one of a half-dozen opioid junkies who took up residence at Wentworth Arms—"

"That mobile home park out near Phelps Tool-and-Die?"

The deputy chief nodded. "We're no different than any other small town as far as drugs and crime go."

Seymour cocked an eyebrow under his gauze turban, giving a fair impression of Omar Sharif in *Lawrence of Arabia*. "I sense a 'but' coming."

"But nothing has been taken, Seymour, so I can't even file a burglary report. We can go with assault, but since you didn't see the assailant and you have no security cameras, there's not much the police can do other than canvas the area. You know, ask your neighbors if they saw anything suspicious."

"You do that," Seymour shot back. "And don't be so sure nothing is gone. I have a lot of valuable stuff around here. Let me have a look-see before you run off to buy doughnuts."

Seymour's "look-see" commenced with an outraged cry.

"Waldo! Bad bird! You crapped on Leonard Nimoy's shoulder."

I heard wings fluttering in the kitchen, followed by the parrot's reply.

"Bad bird, bad bird, what you gonna do? What you gonna do when they come for you?" The bird whistled.

Eddie smirked. "Why do you keep that parrot, Seymour?"

"Waldo is a companion I can talk to at night, though I'm rethinking our relationship now that he defiled my favorite Vulcan."

Seymour circled the room, checking shelves and tables for any missing items. He moved to the hall, the dining room, and finally the kitchen.

Watching Seymour, I silently consulted my own companion: *It looks like nothing was stolen, Jack.*

That's because what the thief came for wasn't here. Harriet's portrait is hanging back at your shop.

You're probably right, but Eddie won't see it that way. We need a way to prove the portrait and this break-in are connected.

"Ah-HAH!" Seymour cried. "There *is* something missing. That creep stole my mirror."

"Mirror? Off the wall?" Eddie asked.

"No. Last week, I broke the big mirror in my master bath. A few days ago, I picked up a replacement at Napp Hardware, and I left it right here." Seymour shrugged. "I was going to mount it tonight, but I guess my evening is suddenly free."

"Seymour, what did the mirror look like?" I asked.

"It was a nice bathroom mirror. Had a thick wooden frame." Seymour shrugged again. "I didn't even unpack it—"

"What?"

"It was wrapped in cardboard and taped shut—I mean really taped. Bud Napp is one thorough packer."

"Any labels?"

"Just my name. Bud wrote it with a Magic Marker."

"What was this package shaped like? How big was it?" I hammered.

A puzzled Seymour demonstrated the size with his hands. "About this big. And rectangular . . . Maybe this wide."

"In other words, around the same size and shape of the Harriet McClure painting!"

Seymour's jaw dropped, and I faced Eddie.

"I think the thief came here to steal a painting that Seymour bought. When this person saw a wrapped package of a similar size and shape, they grabbed it without realizing there was a mirror inside instead of the painting they came for."

Deputy Chief Franzetti scratched the dark stubble on his chin. "I need more . . . Maybe you'd like to explain, Penelope?"

"I'll be happy to—in detail."

Good luck with that.

CHAPTER 25

What, Me Worry?

Deny, deny, deny.

—*A Guide for the Married Man* (1967 film)

"OF COURSE EDDIE Franzetti didn't believe your theory, Pen. I don't believe it either, and I'm the guy who got clobbered." Slouched in the passenger seat, Seymour folded his arms and stared at the road ahead.

"You're also the guy who was with me when we found Old Walt's corpse," I reminded him.

"Walt's death was an accident."

"I got a better look at the scene than you did." I argued.

"Sheriff Taft declared it an accident. Who are we to dispute the verdict of the she-wolf of Blackstone Falls?"

"I talked with Sheriff Taft last night. I get the feeling she's rethinking her 'verdict.'"

Before we left his house, Seymour grabbed a knit cap to hide his gauze turban. Now he was intermittently scratching and yelping when he accidentally prodded the wound.

"You should take that hat off," I told him. "It's too warm to wear it."

"No way, Pen. Until the bandages come off, I'm going full Mike Nesmith."

Seymour pulled his hand away from his head and held it in his lap.

"At least you didn't tell Eddie the portrait was cursed. That's just crazy talk," he said.

"You're right about Eddie not believing in curses, but I'm not so sure it's crazy talk—"

"I might have believed your theory that a thief was looking for Harriet's portrait *if* Eddie hadn't told me about the junkies from the Wentworth knocking off homes on Larchmont."

"Seymour, face reality. Someone wanted that painting bad enough to assault you and leave you for dead."

"Maybe. Maybe not. But either way, from now on, I'll take precautions."

"Precautions may not be enough, not against—"

"A curse?" He shook his head. "Pen, someone trying to steal the portrait doesn't make it cursed."

"No, but it does make owning it dangerous."

He folded his arms to keep from scratching his head. "Well, Harriet's mine, and I intend to keep her."

"How about a compromise? Leave Harriet at my bookstore for a few more days—"

"But I want her with me!"

"Just temporarily, Seymour. We have a security alarm with cameras, something your house lacks."

"Okay," he agreed. "But only until I upgrade. Clearly, Waldo is an inadequate warning system. But once I get my place squared away, my Harriet is coming home with me."

I didn't want to argue, but I was still worried about Seymour. Even with modern security installed, he'd still be all alone in that giant house. What more could I do to protect him?

Wait for the genius to figure out he's in a jam, Jack replied. *A few more dents in his bowling ball should do the trick—*

I'll do no such thing, I told the ghost. *But I'll tell you what we are going to do. We're going to protect my friend by finding out who killed Walt.*

Just then Seymour yelped and pulled his hand away from his sore head.

"That's it," I said as I made a sharp turn.

"Hey, this isn't the road to the garage."

"We're not going to the garage. I'm taking you to the ER to have that hard head of yours examined."

TWO HOURS LATER, we were on our way back to my bookstore. Seymour had submitted to an evaluation at the hospital and came away with a cleanish bill of health and a prescription for painkillers.

I asked Seymour if he wanted me to stop at a pharmacy, but he shook his head.

"I'm a postal worker, Pen. Pain is my middle name."

He demanded I go right to the bookstore. He wanted to see his "girl" on display before he headed to the garage for his VW. I gently reminded Seymour that his *girl* was really an *it*, but my words fell on deaf ears.

When we arrived at Buy the Book, I noticed a strange vehicle parked in front, a pristine white van emblazoned with a CC COMMUNICATIONS logo in bold scarlet letters.

Inside the shop, we found Bonnie alone at the register.

"Professor Parker called," she told me. "He's coming over with a guest. Some visiting professor wants to see Harriet's portrait."

Seymour grinned. "Finally! Harriet is going to get the critical attention she deserves."

I scanned the busy aisles and noted that most of the customers were either entering or leaving the art exhibit. "I think that portrait is getting plenty of attention already. And where's Sadie, by the way?" I asked Bonnie.

"She's showing the art exhibit to our client."

"Client? What client?"

"Sadie said you know all about it."

"I do?"

As Bonnie shrugged and turned her attention back to the

customers in line, Seymour charged toward the event space. I caught up with him at the door, and we entered together.

Sadie and a tall man in a tweedy suit had their backs to us as they gazed at the McClure portrait. Suddenly the stranger extended his long arms and spoke in a voice so deep it reverberated like a bass guitar and so loud it boomed off the walls of the hollow space.

"That's it! *That's* the art I've been searching for!"

The next words the stranger spoke sent a chill through me.

"Why, I would *kill* to own that painting!"

CHAPTER 26

The Price of Publishing

The cheaper the crook, the gaudier the patter.

—Dashiell Hammett, *The Maltese Falcon*

SEYMOUR HEARD THE chilling declaration, same as I. But his reaction was not at all what I expected.

Grinning, he hurried toward the lanky stranger.

"I'd know that voice anywhere," Seymour cried. "You're the spokes guy for Conway Communications. I hear you on the radio all the time!"

Seymour lowered his voice to an intimate announcer's murmur.

"You've written a book, but how will you get it published? Clifford Conway Communications has been a friend to authors for twenty years. Let Clifford Conway be your friend, too!"

Eyes sparkling, the newcomer flashed a toothy smile on his closely shaved face. "Bravo, sir. You have me pegged." He clicked the heels of his oxblood oxfords, bowed curtly, and extended his hand. "Cliff Conway, at your service. And you are?"

"Seymour Tarnish." He puffed his chest like a strutting rooster. "I am the proud owner of this masterpiece."

"And a magnificent work it is," Conway replied. "The woman is beautiful, haunting, and just a little bit disturbing. It's the sort of image just begging to be used for a book cover."

Conway shifted his gaze to me. "And this auburn-haired siren must be Mrs. Penelope McClure."

Mother Machree! Jack cried in my head. *This guy's as oily as a leaky Hudson sedan!*

"Silly me!" Sadie pulled me closer. "I should have made introductions. I told you about Mr. Conway, Pen. He saw our shop on the CBS *Sunday Morning* profile of the Palantines and called to arrange the renting of our event space . . ."

As Sadie reminded me of these facts, I couldn't miss the excited gleam in her gaze: *Look! A romantic prospect for you!*

Jack didn't miss it, either.

While the ghost brought an irritated deep freeze to the room, Conway nodded cordially, shook my hand, and scanned the area.

"Yes, I believe this is the perfect venue to launch my new project. A little drafty, but we can deal with that."

"Excuse me?" I said. "What is your project exactly?"

"I'll be taping an infomercial, Mrs. McClure. I wanted an authentic and, to be frank, a respectable location to shoot it. Buy the Book is both. There is enough room for a good-sized audience, yet the space feels intimate. It has an old-fashioned charm, but with all the modern amenities."

"You'll have a live audience, then?" Sadie asked, clearly excited.

"Paid actors, actually. I've already booked two dozen through an agency. I'll coach the performers to be suitably enthusiastic. I'll shoot close-ups of attractive faces and staged reaction shots before my talk even begins. Then I'll layer them in during postproduction where they are most effective."

Conway faced the McClure portrait again. His eyes narrowed like a hunter getting a bead on his prey.

"Who is the artist, Mr. Tarnish?" Conway asked.

Seymour explained that the painting was a century-old

self-portrait and that the woman who painted it was long dead. He then offered a truncated version of Harriet's life.

Conway's toothy grin grew even wider.

"Why, this is perfect. More than seventy years have passed since the creator's death, and this work was never copyrighted. So, as the owner of this painting, you also own the image. Did you realize that, Mr. Tarnish?"

Seymour shrugged. "I do now."

"How would you like to license this striking image to me? Exclusive publication rights for five years? All for a generous fee, of course."

"I don't know."

"It's a beautiful painting of a lovely woman," Conway coaxed. "Shouldn't the world see it? Shouldn't this beautiful and striking image grace the cover of someone's life work, a novel they worked on for years, published for the very first time?"

"I'm not sure if I *should* license Harriet's image," Seymour confided. "It makes me feel sort of like . . . Well, like a pimp."

Conway laughed. "Don't be silly, Mr. Tarnish. Just think of the proud possibilities for Harriet McClure's legacy. What if her stunning image were to grace the cover of a future bestseller by a talented new literary voice? Imagine the attention—perhaps even the worldwide fame this picture would garner on the cover of a twenty-first century novelist who just may be the next F. Scott Fitzgerald or Sylvia Plath."

Will you listen to this pushy patter? Jack declared. *Sounds like the too-good-to-be-true pitch of a door-to-door tonic salesman. Which makes me suspect he's selling snake oil.*

I hope you're wrong, Jack.

As for Seymour, he appeared to remain skeptical. But the more Conway talked, the less resistant Seymour seemed, until it was clear his defenses were cracking.

"If I agree to do it—and I didn't say that I would. But *if* I did, just what would it entail?"

Cliff Conway scanned the event space with a critical eye.

"The light here is nearly perfect. With a little enhancement, I can photograph the portrait with the high-definition camera I have in my van. I can do it right now, here in this space—after I clear the public out. The painting will never leave your presence. In fact, you can stay and help."

"Well . . ."

"If you orally agree to accept my licensing fee, I can give you a down payment right now by check. I have our standard contract in my van. Sign it today, and I'll have my assistant send the second half of the payment tomorrow."

Seymour's mouth gaped. "The second half?"

"Another fifteen hundred dollars, for a total of three thousand. How does that sound?"

Seymour grabbed the man's hand and pumped it. "Like you've got yourself a deal, Mr. Conway."

With a theatrical flourish, Clifford Conway whipped out a leather-bound checkbook and began to scribble. After handing the check over to Seymour, Conway grinned.

"Now, let me collect my camera, and we'll get started."

"Follow me, Mr. Conway." Sadie escorted the founder of Clifford Conway Communications to the front of the store. When they were out of earshot, Seymour whooped.

"Three grand and I won't even have to part with my Harriet!"

He kissed the check in his hands. "That's more than twice what I paid for her. With this windfall, I can easily get my Volkswagen out of hock without eating ramen noodles for a month. Plus, I can buy another bathroom mirror and install that new security system."

"And you're not worried about the curse?"

He waved the check. "Pen, if this is what a curse looks like, I'll take it. Wait until I tell the Brainiac!"

After listening to Seymour gloat for five solid minutes, I left him in the event space to gaze with adoration at his newfound money machine.

Jack's laughter echoed in my head.

It looks like the mailman fell for Harriet's dough after all. And you said there were no gigolos in Cornpone-cott.

I reached the front counter a few minutes later and noticed Sadie staring out the window so intently that she didn't notice my approach.

"What's up?"

My aunt whirled, her face pale, her expression troubled.

"Sadie, what's wrong?"

"Take a look," she whispered.

On the sidewalk in front of our bookshop, Conway stood at the rear doors of his open van, a tripod on the pavement beside him. But he'd stopped unloading equipment and was now locked in a heated argument with our blue-haired babysitter, Tracy Mahoney.

I couldn't hear their words through the window, so I moved to the front entrance—too late, it turned out. Just as I got to the door, Tracy whirled on her motorcycle boots and ran down the sidewalk, her blue plaid skirt fluttering in the wind.

Conway shook off the encounter and began to unload his van.

I pushed through our front door.

"Pen, where are you going?" my aunt called.

There was no time to reply. I had to catch up with Tracy.

I hit the sidewalk and breezed past Conway while his head—along with his attention—was inside the van.

The sidewalk was moderately busy, and I soon lost sight of Tracy. I headed off in the direction she took and hoped for the best. A few blocks later, I spied her in front of Gilder's Antiques.

"Tracy!" I called.

My voice was drowned out by the roar of a powerful engine. A large motorcycle—likely a Harley-Davidson—rolled up to the curb right in front of Tracy, and the biker cut the engine.

The tall, powerfully built young driver was swathed in black leather from boots to jacket—which stood out in stark contrast to the flowing blond hair streaming out from under his helmet. The man braced the bike with his knees but did not dismount. He simply reached out his hand.

"Come on, let's go home, Tracy."

"I just wanted to tell him, Dennis!" she cried. "Tell him that I hate what he's doing! It's not right."

"No, it's not," the biker's deep voice replied. "And Mr. Conway will get what's coming to him. You can be certain of that. But not here. Not now."

He stretched his hand a little farther.

With a resigned sob, the girl took it. He deftly swung Tracy onto the bike behind him. She donned the extra helmet that hung from the seat. The biker revved his engine in a blast of smoky exhaust. With Tracy clutching him tightly, they sped down Cranberry Street, around the bend, and out of sight.

CHAPTER 27

Art History 101

It takes . . . real heart to make beauty out of the stuff that makes us weep.

—Clive Barker

AT MY RETURN to Buy the Book, I faced a barrage of questions from Aunt Sadie and Bonnie about the public fight in front of our store.

I had no answers, of course. But I intended to get some.

I headed back to the event space, pondering how to breach the subject of Tracy Mahoney with Clifford Conway. Instead of barging in, I paused at the doorway to watch the man in action.

Already, Conway had cleared the public out of our event space and back into the bookstore. He was now in the process of setting up a pair of fan lights, along with a complex tripod topped by a large camera with a special wide-angle lens. While he explained to Seymour how the device was used, Conway seemed composed, calm, and professional, as if the ugly confrontation on the sidewalk had never happened. Nor did it appear to matter to him whether or not anyone had seen the incident.

In short, Clifford Conway was shameless.

Beware the cold fish, Jack warned. *They're usually sharks.*

Even sharks are warm-blooded. As for Cliff here, I'm wondering who he's going to bite—or may have already bitten.

Got anyone in mind?

Tracy, of course. She's not the type of person to pick a fight on the street with a stranger.

Sounds like Mr. Silver Tongue and the blue-haired baby-sitter have a history.

That's a safe bet. And I'm going to find out what it is.

I crossed the room. "Excuse me, Mr. Conway. I couldn't help noticing the altercation outside."

"Oh." Conway frowned. "I'm sorry you had to see that."

"Yes, please explain. What did I see, exactly?"

"Well, Mrs. McClure. I'm a public figure. I sponsor seminars all over the country. I encourage artists and writers to submit their work for publication. It's very rewarding to find new voices, new artistic visions. But sometimes even a person's best work is not good enough."

"You're talking about the young woman outside?"

Conway shrugged. "Her fantasy art was . . . substandard. Amateurish. My staff decided against offering her creation to the public. I'm afraid she took our professional rejection personally. You saw the result."

Conway's answers sounded reasonable, and I didn't know enough to question his assertions. Until I talked to Tracy, I'd have to take his words at face value. Still, I would have pressed Conway for more, but Seymour grew impatient—

"So, are you going to start snapping away, or what? My Harriet's waiting."

"Excuse me, Mrs. McClure, I have work to do."

Conway fiddled with his lights and then with his tripod, while stopping to peer through the camera after every tiny adjustment. Finally he frowned.

"Unfortunately we have a problem, Mr. Tarnish. Light is reflecting off the glass no matter how I angle the camera. The glass itself is old and slightly filmed from age. The more light I throw on it, the fuzzier the image becomes."

"So what do we do?" Seymour asked.

"I'm afraid we are going to have to remove the painting from its frame for maximum effect."

Just then, I heard my name being called from the bookstore. Brainert had arrived with his academic colleague.

"Ah, Pen, there you are! This is Violet Brooks, a visiting adjunct professor and valued contributor to the *Contemporary Arts Journal*. Ms. Brooks was last year's first prize winner at the International Awards for Art Criticism."

"I didn't even know they gave out awards for outstanding art criticism, and here I am meeting a winner." I smiled a welcome and she nodded in return.

Tall enough to be a model, even wearing flats, Violet Brooks nevertheless slouched a little, as if self-conscious of her height. Her short, form-fitting dress was slippery black, like wet sealskin, with slashes of purple that resembled a painter's brushstrokes.

High cheekbones hinted at Ms. Brooks' refined features, though she did her level best to hide herself behind a large mop of unruly dark hair and bangs long enough to cover the top half of her large, purple-framed glasses, which perfectly matched the mock brushstrokes on her dress.

Of course, Jack popped into my head and offered his two cents.

Seems to me the young Miss Brooks should have a vat of hooch strapped around her neck.

Excuse me?

With hair like that, she has a lot in common with a St. Bernard.

If you're going to be rude, then I'm going to ignore you, I warned the ghost.

"Ms. Brooks is a guest lecturer at the university," Brainert explained. "We were chatting in the faculty lounge, and I happened to mention the McClure painting that my friend recently acquired. She was only too eager to see it."

"I hope you don't mind, Mrs. McClure," Violet Brooks said. "I have a particular interest in feminist art and women painters who've been overlooked by art historians."

"Your field of study sounds quite worthwhile, and I'm delighted you stopped by. Unfortunately, the painting is the subject of a photo shoot at the moment." When Brainert and Violet appeared disappointed, I suggested we go into the event space anyway. "I'm sure the photographer won't mind if we take a look."

After introductions all around, Violet approached the picture. With both hands, she pushed aside her bangs and studied the work.

"Before Professor Parker mentioned Harriet McClure to me, I'd never heard of her. The name didn't come up in any of the academic sources I searched on the way over." She waved her tablet computer. "And I don't see a signature on this work."

"It's partially hidden by the frame," Brainert replied.

Ms. Brooks nodded. "Can anyone tell me more about this artist?"

To Conway's impatient dismay, Seymour paused from removing the painting from the wall to give the art critic an abbreviated version of Harriet McClure's biography.

Violet's eyes grew wider as Seymour spoke. When he finished, she couldn't wait to share her thoughts.

"This appears to be a remarkable discovery, Mr. Tarnish! From this portrait alone, I can see this woman was a pioneer. I believe she should be celebrated. Just look at her use of those dazzling hues—colors unimaginable in her time, but which would be described as psychedelic a half century later."

Violet leaned close to the painting. "The artist's use of surreal imagery is ahead of its time, too. Salvador Dalí was just a teenager when Harriet McClure painted this, yet he's considered the father of surrealism—"

"Really?" Brainert scratched his head. "I thought her use of these outrageous shades meant she was undisciplined, as if she didn't know how to mix her colors—"

"I'm sorry, Professor, but this isn't your field, and you're quite mistaken. Harriet McClure was in total control of the medium. And this artist's background, how she was treated by her family and society, and her artistic reaction to that treatment, reminds me of another female painter from this region. Though their styles are different, Harriet McClure's story is not unlike that of Newport painter Beatrice Turner."

"You don't say." Seymour was hardly listening. He and Conway were too busy taking the portrait off the wall hooks and laying it facedown on a hastily set up folding table.

Violet launched into the story of Turner's life—a lecture I didn't need to hear. As the widow of a Newport native steeped in that town's lore, I already knew about Turner's life and legacy.

The only child of a wealthy family, Beatrice Turner had her dreams crushed when her stern Victorian father pulled her out of art school because of the scandalous behavior of the faculty (the artist models posed nude, apparently).

Beatrice's response to this act of tyrannical control was to never marry, to never move out of her childhood home, to never change in the least as she aged—even wearing Victorian-era fashion until her death in the mid-twentieth century. Like Harriet, Beatrice painted hundreds of self-portraits before passing from this earth.

"Of course, Turner painted other subjects besides herself," Violet explained. "There are portraits of Beatrice and her mother together, always in profile, and always facing opposite directions—Beatrice's way of showing the world she was at odds with her family."

After a pause, her tone became thoughtful. "Obviously pain, longing, and loss inspired Beatrice Turner's art. Her life was both a rejection of the values that destroyed her dreams and a weird sort of acceptance that she was, in her family's eyes, only a child. So a dependent child she remained until the day she died."

Violet watched as Seymour and Conway began working on the ancient screws in the back of the frame.

"It makes you wonder what pain or disappointment or even tragedy Harriet McClure must have endured. I mean, something drove her obsession to paint her own image over and over again. What was it? Will we ever know?"

Violet's eyes met mine, her gaze intense behind the dangling bangs. "You're related to Harriet, aren't you, Mrs. McClure?"

"By marriage. Her surviving family members live in Newport."

"Do you know them?"

"They're my in-laws."

Violet leaned close, until she was looming over me.

"Would it be possible for you to provide an introduction? I'm very interested in writing a piece about Harriet McClure, and it would be wise for me to interview her living descendants."

I understood her drift, though Violet either misunderstood the artist's history or misspoke. Harriet died childless, so there were no "living descendants," only relatives.

That said, the very last thing I wanted to do was deal with my in-laws. The farther away from the McClure family I stayed, the happier I was. But before I could politely but adamantly refuse Ms. Brooks' request, Seymour whooped and waved his screwdriver in triumph.

"I've got the last one loose!" he cried. "We'll have Harriet out of her prison in no time."

CHAPTER 28

Every Picture Hides a Story

A photograph is a secret about a secret. The more it tells you the less you know.

—Diane Arbus, American photographer

"GENTLY, NOW," SEYMOUR cautioned. "We don't want to damage the painting."

Clifford Conway nodded in response.

Meanwhile Violet Brooks, Professor Parker, and I watched as the two men carefully pried the canvas loose from the antique frame that had held it for more than forty years.

"Make sure the oils don't stick to the glass," Violet warned. "Time and the elements can cause that to happen. You risk tearing the canvas if you're not careful."

The men popped the painting loose and lifted it out of the frame.

For a moment they patiently held the artwork upside down just inches above the table, while Brainert wrestled the heavy wooden frame to the floor.

"On three we'll flip the painting over and lay it faceup on the table," Seymour instructed. "One . . . two . . . three."

As one, we gasped.

With the complete painting revealed, it was clear the frame had hidden more than Harriet's signature, which was now plainly visible.

Also visible were a series of cursive words, interspersed with tiny, colorful images of planets, stars, moons, and shooting stars. The curious interstellar motif ran completely around the edges of the rectangular canvas like a lace border.

And there was more.

Without the aged and filmy glass between the viewer's eye and the painting, the colors appeared even more vibrant, the details sharper. More important, the tiny words, odd symbols, and musical notes scattered throughout the painting were clearly delineated—as well as completely baffling.

"What does it all mean?" I cried.

"It's Harriet," Seymour whispered. "I told you before. She's talking to me. Trying to tell me something."

Conway snorted. "Don't be absurd."

"Perhaps he's correct, in a way," Violet countered. "This does appear to be a secret message of some kind."

"A secret message?" Conway scoffed. "That's preposterous."

"Not at all," Violet replied. "You'll find secret messages and strange, hidden images in many works of art. In this instance, on this particular work, one would need to know much more about this painter's life to decipher her secrets."

"I *have* to find out what it all means," Seymour proclaimed.

Conway offered a patronizing smile. "That's easy, Mr. Tarnish. What you're seeing are the random, nonsensical doodles of a highly disturbed woman."

Seymour bristled. "You're wrong. I believe Harriet used these symbols to speak in her artist's voice. Look at her. She painted herself in sublime distress. She wanted to share something with the world but couldn't for some reason. So she hid her secrets in plain sight, in this painting."

Conway frowned. "That's crazy."

"Not really, Mr. Conway," Violet argued. "And with publishing your trade, I'm surprised you're not aware that Leonardo da Vinci famously buried messages in his art. It was the subject of an internationally bestselling novel, as I recall. Did you know one of the more recent discoveries about the *Mona Lisa* involves symbols hidden in the eyes? It's quite fascinating. A researcher discovered a tiny L and S—and didn't even need to disturb the painting at the Louvre Museum to do it. He used high-definition scanned images from Lumière Technology in Paris. Some believe the L refers to Leonardo himself while the S is meant to help future generations identify the true subject of his masterpiece."

While Seymour listened to the conversation about an artist burying messages for future researchers to discover, he began intensely studying the brushstrokes Harriet left behind. Suddenly he groaned.

"What kind of messed-up message is this? Between the stars and space stuff, Harriet just repeats the same meaningless word over and over. She wrote it in different scripts, sometimes big, sometimes small, but it's always the same five letters."

Conway's grin was triumphant. "See? The nonsense of a madwoman's mind, just as I said, and while I hate to interrupt everyone's fascinating speculations, I need to photograph this image before we lose the afternoon light."

"Sure. Of course," Seymour said. "Let's set it up."

"Wait!" Violet pulled out her phone. "Let me get a few pictures of the—"

A scowling Conway stepped between the woman and the painting, hand raised to ward her off.

"I'm sorry, Miss Brooks, but I paid good money for the exclusive rights to this image. This is a private shop, not a public place, and I can't allow you to take your own pictures."

"But, surely, for the sake of scholarship—"

"If you require the image for your academic pursuits, you can license the rights from Conway Communications, the same as everybody else." He handed her his business card.

"Excuse me, Ms. Brooks," Brainert gently interrupted. "But we should be getting back to the university. Your guest lecture is scheduled to start soon, and there's a meet and greet beforehand."

"Of course, Professor. I'll say my good-byes, then."

But Ms. Brooks took her sweet time saying good-bye. She spoke with Seymour for a good five minutes, stealing lingering looks at the portrait while Conway aligned his equipment to shoot the canvas.

Meanwhile Brainert sidled up to me. "I'm glad I brought Violet Brooks over. She certainly appears to be interested in the McClure portrait."

That was an understatement. I caught the art critic glancing again and again at some detail on the canvas, until Conway ordered her to step back and out of the way.

I could see her frustration at not being able to photograph the work. But she finally got the message, and I escorted her and Brainert to the front door. After our good-byes, a brace of customers decided to check out at the same time, so Bonnie and I manned twin registers and cleared the line in twenty minutes.

After a short break, Sadie and Bonnie hit the aisles to restock, while I worked the counter.

When Clifford Conway finally finished his photography, he packed up his equipment and left the event space with a camera bag over his shoulder and Seymour in tow.

"Don't forget, you promised me a copy of those digital files, Mr. Conway. When will you send them?"

"No worries, Mr. Tarnish, I'll e-mail them over to you tonight. But only if you agree to sign a legal document stating that you will not distribute those images in any way, for any reason, to anyone."

Seymour blinked. "But Harriet's mine. You can't just—"

Conway cut him off. "You own the portrait, Mr. Tarnish, but as per your acceptance of my check, I have exclusive rights to the image. For the next few years, I will decide how that image is used."

CHAPTER 29

Revelations

A reputation is built on manner as much as on achievement.

—Joseph Conrad, *The Secret Agent*

AFTER A BUSY afternoon, I made dinner for Spencer and sat with him, though I couldn't eat more than a few bites. Sadie wasn't hungry, either, opting for a brisk walk to the commons "to clear out the cobwebs."

Things were slow at this hour. I knew things would pick up again in the early evening when the local movie theater and pizza place drew crowds, and older couples took after-dinner strolls down Cranberry. So I asked Bonnie to continue watching the register while I headed for our shop's stockroom to do a bit of detective work.

Since the public altercation on the street that afternoon, I couldn't stop thinking about Clifford Conway. I'd tried to phone Tracy Mahoney several times to get her side of the story. After leaving three messages, I gave up and decided to concentrate on the other participant in that confrontation.

The website for Clifford Conway Communications was slick and professional. The home page had a pitch for Conway Classics, a catalog of literary titles billed as "timeless masterpieces bound in quality faux leather, in a long-lasting hardcover format to read again and again. As seen on TV."

Despite his line of public domain "classics," it didn't take much detective work to discover that Conway's bread and butter was his vanity-press business.

According to the pitch, the "highly trained" staff of CC Communications would edit your book, design the cover, get your title into bookstores and online selling sites, and provide publicity and marketing support—all for a hefty but undisclosed fee, of course.

As a come-on dream teaser, there was a Design Your Own Book feature that allowed wannabe authors to pick from a selection of fonts and genres and cover art, to create the look of their own book.

"Okay, let's give this a try . . ."

First I made up a phony name: Penny Thoughts. And typed in a phony title: *What's the Matter with Seymour?* Then I picked a font and a genre (mystery, of course). I was about to be redirected to several pages of art to choose from (all licensed by Conway Communications) to create my sample cover when Sadie burst into the stockroom. Her face pale, she stammered in agitation.

"That man . . . he's a crook!"

Uh-oh. "You don't mean?"

"Yes, Clifford Conway!" Sadie cried. "I found complaints about his shoddy business practices through a search on the Internet."

It appeared Sadie was even busier than I was on her downtime.

Sitting on a park bench, she'd used her smartphone's browser to research Conway beyond his slick public image. What she found was his name and company discussed on a website posting for authors and artists. The site warned creators about unethical publishing practices in general—and the tactics of one Clifford Conway of Conway Communications in particular.

"Conway takes advantage of writers and artists desperate to call attention to their work. He's a predator, Pen. That man took advantage of us, too. He intends to use our space and our good name to promote his predatory practices! And goodness knows what that man did to poor Tracy Mahoney!"

"Mom?" Spencer appeared in the doorway, a frown on his little-boy face. "Are you talking about that guy with the big white van? The man Tracy argued with today?"

"Yes, we are."

"Then I should tell you something. When I got off the school bus, I saw Tracy and that man in the street. When I saw them arguing, I snuck up on them to listen."

"Do you remember what they said?" I asked excitedly.

Spencer shrugged and shook his head. "Not much. I didn't really understand what they were talking about."

My heart sunk. Meanwhile Spencer turned sheepish.

"I have something else to tell you, Mom. Please promise you won't get mad."

"About what?"

"Last year my friend Denny was at the football game in Millstone. He saw a fight break out in the bleachers. And, well . . ."

Spencer paused. I was losing patience.

"What are you getting at, Spence?"

"Denny used his phone to film that fight. Later, when the boys were arrested, Denny's recording was used in court and everything."

Spencer paused a second time. When he spoke again, it was barely above a whisper. "I know you told me it's not polite to spy on people, but . . ."

"Wait!" I cried. "Are you saying—"

"When I saw Tracy and that man fighting, I used my phone. I recorded the whole thing."

CHAPTER 30

Candid Camera

Every man is surrounded by a neighborhood of voluntary spies.

—Jane Austen, *Northanger Abbey*

SPENCER HELD UP his phone so both Sadie and I could see the screen. The recording was wobbly at first, and we had to turn the volume to maximum, but before long, we could see and hear everything.

The argument had already begun when Spencer started to record, and he wasn't the only bystander, either. I could see a number of people watching the confrontation, including (embarrassing as it was) Georgia Gilder, along with Colleen and electrician Leo Rollins. I recognized my friend Brainert, too, getting out of a compact car driven by his stylishly dressed visiting professor friend. They both noticed the argument as well.

"You have to stop," Tracy cried as angry tears ran rivulets through her Cleopatra mascara. "People are blaming me for what you did."

"And just what have I done, Miss Mahoney?" Conway replied, his tone smug.

Tracy shook a blue fingernail at the publisher.

"I don't like the way you're using my art. It's not right. I withdraw my permission for you to license my work, and I demand you remove all copies of it from your website!"

"I no longer need your permission," Conway replied. "Quite simply, it's not your art anymore because I altered it—"

"Yes, by putting word balloons on my portrait of Princess Florinda, all of them filled with lies about how wonderful your publishing services are!"

"I paid you a fair market fee for the worldwide rights to that artwork. You signed a contract."

"I didn't know you were a crook and a cheat, Mr. Conway. I'll pay you back your money. I just want the rights to my art back."

"I repeat. It's no longer your art."

"I'll sue you!" Tracy shouted.

"You don't have a legal leg to stand on, young lady—"

"I do!" she insisted. "I'll sue for damages to my character, my illustrated fantasy novel—"

"Your *unpublished* fantasy novel. You balked at paying for our premium package, so your book remains unpublished and unread. And there are no damages because I never used a word of your silly, girlish prose or the name Princess Florida—"

"It's *Florinda*!"

Tracy's fingers curled into blue claws. I thought she was going to lunge at the publisher. Conway must have thought so, too, because he quickly switched to a more conciliatory tone.

"Listen, Miss Mahoney. You brought that artwork to me hoping I would publish it, and I have. People all over the world have seen your art, admired it. Why, I could easily sell more of your work if you'd let me—"

"But I didn't want it used that way!" She sobbed. "Or in bits and pieces like that 'Reach for Your Publishing Dream' ad where you just used an arm from my painting—"

"As is my right. And your art is no exception. I just licensed a century-old self-portrait by a local artist named McClure." Conway pointed to our bookshop. "I'm about to photograph every inch of that canvas, and I will use it as I like, including its 'bits and pieces.'"

"But the way you used my art destroyed my reputation. A woman called me terrible things online and reported my 'duplicitous behavior' to the Society of Children's Book Writers and Illustrators. She said she paid for *exclusive* rights to use my fantasy art on her cover, but another author with another book had the same cover art. She was humiliated. She blamed me because *you* told her that I tricked your company. You claimed some young assistant who 'no longer works for you' was taken advantage of when I sold her the same art multiple times. Lies!"

Tracy took a breath. "After that, I did my own research and uncovered four different novels with the very same piece of art—*my* art—on their covers: *Barry Potter*, *Game of Gnomes*, a vampire story called *Sundown*, and *Her Dark Materials*, about a magic seamstress. All four of those authors bought publishing packages from you. You bought *one* copy of my original art. Then *you* photoshopped in different backgrounds. *You* changed the color schemes, and *you* tricked these authors into thinking they were getting unique cover art for their works." She shook her head. "It may be too late for me. But I feel sorry for the people who fall for your crummy crooked publishing packages—"

"That's slander, Miss Mahoney. There is nothing crooked about my business. Each of those covers may have started with your original art, but the new backgrounds and graphics legally rendered them 'transformative' and thus unique. You're just too young and inexperienced to see the truth."

"The truth! The Writer Beware website warns creators about your publishing scams. I wish I had seen it before I believed your slick advertisements."

"I have no idea what you're talking about."

"Well, SFWA, MWA, and the Authors Guild do! They warn their memberships about your predatory practices. How you charge seven hundred dollars to obtain an ISBN for an author's work—when they can get one themselves for a fraction of that! How you claim you'll put an author's book onto store shelves across the country, but you don't. Almost no bookstores sell the titles you publish, so you demand authors buy five hundred copies up front. You claim they can resell them at signings you'll arrange 'at the request of stores,' but those requests never happen because you provide no marketing. Your 'publicity package' amounts to flashy ads on content-farm websites that look slick but deliver almost no traffic—and all happen to be run by a shell company owned by *you*. Finally, when your authors complain about the heartbreakingly low number of print or e-book sales, you really twist the knife, telling them it's *their* fault as you pronounce their book a failure!"

Conway leaned close to the girl, almost looming.

"Miss Mahoney, I provide a valued service. The people who come to me aren't destitute. They have careers, lives. Sure, they can write a book, pour their thoughts and dreams into their writing, but they don't have a clue how to get their work onto the printed page or into proper digital formats for the array of e-book platforms—nor do they want to learn, because they simply don't have the time. But they do have the money, and that's where I come in."

Tracy covered her ears. "Stop trying to justify your behavior!"

"Of course, no one wants to know how the sausage is made. They only want to savor the results. So I take some of their money and do the heavy lifting for them, and my clients enjoy the results of seeing their work professionally packaged and published or uploaded to an online store."

Conway's outward demeanor was all benevolence.

"Perhaps you should reconsider the premium package, Miss Mahoney. Printing an illustrated book can be quite expensive, but we have many payment plans for clients, like yourself, who are less fortunate. We can set you up with any major credit card, or . . . do you have a PayPal account?"

"Stop talking!" Tracy screamed. "All your promises are empty! All you sell are lies! Lies!"

With that, Tracy turned and fled down the sidewalk. A moment later I saw myself on the screen as I bolted out of the store in pursuit of the girl.

That's where Spencer's recording ended.

For a moment no one spoke. I looked to Aunt Sadie. She was literally shaking with rage.

"I'm going to call Clifford Conway right now," she said through gritted teeth. "I'm going to cancel his contract with us and throw his advance right back at him."

"Are you sure that's the right way to handle this?"

Doll, you don't want to get in front of that freight train.

Jack was right. Sadie swept me aside and grabbed the phone from her purse on the stockroom desk.

"Wait!" I cried.

Sadie blinked. "Why should I?"

"Because you have to set your phone on speaker first. Spencer and I want to hear the conversation, too!"

Sadie nodded and punched in the number. Conway answered on the first ring.

"I heard what you did to poor Tracy Mahoney, Mr. Conway, and what kind of businessman you really are. I refuse to allow you to use our shop to promote your unethical business practices. So I'm returning your booking fee. Our contract is canceled."

Conway sighed audibly into the phone.

"What is it about the small-time minds in this town? Does no one read the fine print?"

"What do you mean?" Sadie demanded.

"It's simple, really. The contract you signed for me includes a damage clause, Ms. Thornton. Of course, you have the perfect right to cancel at any time. But I have an equal right to recoup any losses incurred, and those losses are considerable."

"Impossible," my aunt insisted.

"Not at all. I've already hired a cameraman. I've hired actors. I rented your place in good faith. Your unreasonable cancellation on such short notice activates that damage clause."

I could hear the triumph in his voice. "You may keep my advance, because you'll need it. You now have thirty days to pay me damages of one hundred thousand dollars, or I will see you in court."

Before Sadie could protest, Conway ended the call.

CHAPTER 31

Fish Story

When people show you who they are, believe them.

—Dr. Maya Angelou (attributed)

I GAVE UP on my fourth attempt to reach Clifford Conway and hung up. "My call's not even going to voice mail. I think Conway's blocked us."

I fell into a helpless silence, while my aunt, who blamed herself for being "easily swayed by a sweet-talking fraudster," worriedly paced the bookstore aisle.

"It's not your fault," I said. "We both trusted him."

"Then we were both fools. Tell the truth, Pen, didn't your stomach turn a little when he started describing how he was going to tape his infomercial here? Using paid actors instead of a real audience. Coaching them to be 'suitably enthusiastic.' Shooting staged reactions of attractive faces before his talk even began. That man was a sham from the beginning. He told us who he was. But we didn't want to hear it. Instead we swallowed his fish story, hook, line, and sinker."

"Calm down. I'm sure I can fix this. If he would just pick up his phone, I'll do my best to reason with him—"

"He's not a reasonable man! He's a con artist who is going to use that contract I signed as an excuse to extort money.

And if we don't fight this, if we give in to him and let him use our store, it will ruin our reputation!"

"First of all, we are not going to cave and allow that man to use our store in an infomercial. That's off the table and out of the question. Second: Contracts can be legally challenged, not that I like the idea of throwing away our hard-earned money on a legal defense—"

"Mom?" Spencer tugged the sleeve of my sweater. "We're not going to lose our home, are we?"

My son's face was etched with a weight of worry and fear I never wanted him to bear—and it was my own stupid fault. I was wrong to let him listen in on the conversation between Conway and Sadie. I never imagined the man would make threats that a boy might take even more seriously than Sadie and I did.

I bent down to meet my son's anxious gaze.

"We're not going to lose anything, Spencer. You know Sadie and I would never let that happen."

Spencer nodded, but I knew my son wasn't sure he could believe me. With a sinking heart, I sent him upstairs to finish his homework. Then I went back to work.

While Sadie remained in the stockroom to box returns, I sent Bonnie home and took her place at the register, though it didn't stop my worrying—which is why I was glad I still had someone with me to talk things over.

Jack, I have to do something about Conway. But I don't know what. He won't take my calls.

You'll figure it out, Penny. A smart doll like you always finds a way. You'll see.

I felt like Jack was blowing sunshine someplace where it didn't belong. But I also appreciated the ghost for trying to lift my spirits (pardon the pun).

As the evening wore on, a passing rain shower swept through. The faux-Victorian lamps along Cranberry Street bathed the puddled sidewalks in a yellow glow. People headed for home, umbrellas raised, and our shop emptied out.

When my phone rang, I welcomed the distraction.

"Pen? It's Seymour." I could barely make out my friend's words over a cacophony of laughing, shouting children.

"What's going on?"

"My ice cream truck is catering a kid's birthday party that's gone into extra innings—"

The rest of his sentence was drowned out by preadolescent sugar-fueled screams, followed by Seymour's shouted command for everyone to "Pipe the hell down!"

"I just checked my e-mail, and I've got nothing from Conway. When we left your store, I went to his van and signed all his legal paperwork, but he has yet to send me those promised digital copies of the pictures he took of my Harriet."

Sounds fishy, the ghost said.

"Seymour, do you think the e-mail delay was a Wi-Fi issue?" I reasoned with hope. "Because it could mean Conway is staying right here in town at the Finch Inn. Fiona Finch told me Barney installed a new Wi-Fi system himself to save money, and ever since, the signal's been buggy—"

"Conway isn't staying at the Finch Inn, Pen. He's at the Comfy-Time Motel."

"The chain that promises to keep the light on for you?"

"Nope. Comfy-Time guarantees their 'Wi-Fi is free for the whole fam-a-lee.' With a motto like that, their stuff shouldn't be buggy, right?"

"Okay, Seymour, you blinded me with science. Now I've got some news for you . . ."

I told Seymour about our run-in with Conway and the bad reputation we uncovered. I then texted him the phone number Conway gave us, and Seymour said he'd try to reach the jerk.

A moment later the phone rang again.

"The SOB won't pick up my call, either," Seymour said without even a hello.

"You know what?" I said. "There's safety in numbers. Conway's at the Comfy-Time, right? How about you meet me there, and we'll talk to him together?"

"I'm in! The rain's shutting this party down anyway. I'm

across town, so give me twenty minutes. I'll help you make an honest guy out of him—at least where you and I are concerned."

Sadie emerged from the storeroom just as I hung up the phone. She was doing her best to buck up and put on a happy face.

"The returns are done," she said. "I called Dependable Delivery, too. Vinny Nardini will be picking up those boxes tomorrow."

"That's great. May I ask a favor? Seymour needs help dealing with . . . something. So I'm going to pop out. I probably won't get back in time to close the shop."

Sadie was happy to cover for me, so I grabbed my purse and jacket from the stockroom. Then I pushed through the back door and into the damp night. Clouds were piling up, and the air was heavy with the threat of another downpour. It was a treacherous evening for a drive, but at least I wasn't alone.

Where are we headed, honey? And what's the hurry?

CHAPTER 32

A Not So Comfy Time

We'll leave the light on for you.

—Tom Bodett

THE COMFY-TIME MOTEL was located up on the highway, past the McDonald's and a hamburger's throw from the Gentleman's Oasis—a "girlie bar" with cheap beer, backroom poker games, pole-dancing entertainment, and a notorious reputation.

The roadside motel where I was heading wasn't notorious. But the economy lodgings were no great shakes, either, and the absolute antithesis of the charming, meticulously cared-for Queen Anne mansion that served our town as the Finch Inn.

These days the Comfy-Time was showing serious signs of wear. Its paint had faded under the relentless New England winters, and no matter the season, the swimming pool was always covered with canvas and a layer of dead leaves.

I pulled into a spot near the office, grabbed my purse, and dodged raindrops until I pushed through the glass doors.

Behind the Day-Glo orange desk, a young clerk looked up.

"Do you need a room?" she chirped on the uptick. "We're nearly full, so it will have to be on the ground floor."

"Actually, I'm looking for one of your guests, although he might have checked out. His name is Clifford Conway—"

Her smile revealed nearly invisible braces. "Mr. Conway has taken our executive suite for the rest of the week. He's there now."

"How do you know?"

"A little while ago he complained that his suite was too warm and asked me to turn down the heat. I told him I didn't know how, but the night manager would be here soon, and he would fix the problem."

"Where exactly can I find Mr. Conway?"

"Room 224, the corner suite on the second floor. Take the guest staircase, turn right at the top, and follow the veranda. It's the very last door before you hit the metal service stairs to the dumpsters out back."

I texted Seymour the info. After a few minutes of waiting, I got antsy and decided to stretch my legs—in the direction of Conway's room.

Outside again, I walked by the ice machine and drink dispenser. As I crossed the outdoor veranda, wind whipped the occasional blast of rain in my face (always a special treat). The spray was accompanied by the overpowering aroma of sizzling burgers and French fries from the nearby McDonald's—which only served to remind me that I hadn't eaten more than a few bites of food all day.

Through my streaky glasses, I saw that Room 224 was the last in the row, before the service stairs at the end of the veranda, just like the clerk had said. The light from that suite was reflecting strongly on the wet concrete floor. It didn't take a seasoned private eye to figure out Conway's door was ajar.

"Great." I stopped, still ten feet away. "Another open door."

Don't give yourself heartburn, sweetheart. This is a public motel, not a private home. It's no ghost town, either. The clerk already told you the place is packed. Give a shout and you'll have company fast. And don't forget the upside.

Upside?

Someone left the light on for you.

I was going to back off and wait right here for Seymour when a sudden wind blast tossed more drizzling rain across the balcony and into my face. I shivered.

"Okay, this is silly. There's no reason for me to just stand here getting wet. I'm going back to the office to call Seymour for an ETA—"

I was about to do just that when I heard a loud door slam, and I could swear the sound came from inside Conway's suite.

"Mr. Conway?" I called out. "Are you in there?"

No response. Not from Conway. My ghost, on the other hand, had plenty to say—

How long are you going to stand here treading water like an Alvin before you go in already?

I swiped at a raindrop dangling off the end of my nose and lightly pushed at the open door. As it swung wider, I saw an upholstered chair with Conway's fancy camera equipment piled on it. Beside the chair sat a cheap motel couch, a standing lamp, and a flat-screen TV mounted on the wall next to a Comfy-Time clock.

Next came a wave of air so warm it fogged the edges of my wet glasses. No wonder Conway had complained! There was a sweet smell with it, though the McDonald's odors were so strong, I couldn't trace it. My guess was that fresh flowers, maybe roses, had been in this room, though I didn't see any now—

Maybe Conway carried them into the bedroom, Jack cracked, *to combat the unsinkable scent of fast food.*

And then, through the haze, I noticed the glass-topped coffee table in front of the couch held two water tumblers with the Comfy-Time logo. Beside them sat a bottle of champagne—uncorked.

This looks pretty cozy, Jack.

Yeah, so did the Ardennes around Christmas 1944.

I mean it looks like Conway had an intimate party.

In '44 we called our intimate get-together the Battle of the Bulge.

"Mr. Conway?" I called again from the doorway. "It's Penelope McClure. Are you in there? We need to talk!"

I finally stepped over the threshold and sank in pile as deep as the Mariana Trench. Beyond the suite's rectangular living room setup, I counted three doors, all closed. They formed a little cul-de-sac.

Was it one of those doors I'd heard slam?

We're this far in, Penny. Let's make the most of it and do a little snooping.

I don't know, Jack. Maybe we shouldn't—

Stop wasting time bellyaching and LOOK AROUND! Do it while you have the chance!

Okay, okay!

On a writing table at the side of the room, I noticed a laptop glowing with a CC COMMUNICATIONS screen saver. Beside it, an appointment book was opened to today's date. Only one notation was scribbled on the page.

Barney Finch, 7:30 P.M.

"Barney? What business does Barney have with a shady character like Clifford Conway?"

The wall clock read 8:55 P.M., which meant Conway's scheduled "appointment" with our good friend Barney Finch, owner of the Finch Inn, had taken place more than an hour ago.

I reached for the appointment book, hoping to learn more—and bumped the laptop enough to wake it. The screen saver vanished, and twin images took its place. On the right side of the screen, the art page from the Conway Communications website was displayed. My blood ran cold as soon as I glanced at the selection.

Are you seeing this, Jack?

I see some pretty pictures right out of Old Walt's library.

The ghost was right. I counted four paintings from Walt's collection. Some were photoshopped with different backgrounds, and graphics and dramatic framing made them seem a little different, but they were recognizable nonetheless. One of them was even part of our exhibit at the bookshop—Nathan Brock's painting of Ruby Tyler.

For several mesmerized seconds I stared at Ruby's beautiful blue-eyed image and that frightening pockmarked killer behind her. Finally, Jack shook me out of my stupor with a blast of cold air that cut right through the uncomfortable warmth of the motel room, if not the all-pervasive scent of McDonald's French fries.

When I shook my head clear and focused on the other side of the screen, it took me a moment to realize I was looking at a close-up of the leaping fish on Harriet McClure's painting. Under digital magnification, the spidery text on its flanks was legible:

Stars like dots in the sky

What does it mean, Jack? Is that from a poem?

Hmm, let's see. "Hickory dickory dock. The mouse went up the clock." Nope, doesn't ring a bell.

Is it Shakespeare? I don't recall a phrase like that. Could it be from the Bible?

I reckon that quote is a Harriet original. After all, she had stars in her eyes and was dotty as the day is long.

You're not helping.

If you want to know what it means, knock on Conway's door and ask him.

Too dangerous. I shook my head. *Obviously, Walt licensed works to Conway, which means there's a connection between the two. It could be completely innocent, and Conway's reactions to the Harriet painting could have been a coincidence. But this focus on an obscure detail in the painting tells me there's much more going on here, certainly more than a "madwoman's" scribblings.*

After what I'd seen, the gumshoe in me hated to leave.

If we just look around some more, Penny, we might find Walt's notebooks, which means right here and now, we could crack that case.

Jack's argument was tempting. Calling Sheriff Taft to

turn Conway over as a prime suspect would certainly solve my legal problem—not just Walt's murder. But it was too risky to stay even one minute longer. If Clifford Conway did kill Walt *and* attack my friend in his own home, who knew what he'd do to me if he found me snooping among his things.

I'll tell Sheriff Taft my suspicions, but right now I'm going to wait for Seymour in the motel office.

With urgency, I headed for the front door. I was only a few steps away when I sensed a rushing movement behind me. Jack did, too.

Look out, Penny!

Before I could even turn my head, I was slammed with such force that I fell forward. As I did, a hand on the back of my head made sure I connected with the doorjamb.

After that, it was lights out.

CHAPTER 33

Hot Sheets, Cold Blood

Well, I do detective work, all right, but I'm not exactly
a detective.

—Frank Gruber, "The Sad Serbian," *Black Mask* (magazine), 1939

"PEN! PEN! ARE you okay? What happened? Did you
pass out?"

I opened my eyes to blurry shadows. Sprawled on the
suite's living room carpet, I felt rain pelting me from the
open door. I pondered where I was, how I got here, and
where in the heck my glasses went. I felt pain in a half dozen
places, starting with my throbbing head.

"Did I get hit by a truck?" I moaned.

"On the second floor of the Comfy-Time Motel? Doubtful. All I know is, I came up to meet you and found you on
the floor."

Kneeling beside me with a concerned expression, Seymour obviously hadn't changed from his moonlighting gig.
He was still wearing his vanilla white ice cream vendor
smock over white slacks and a flannel shirt.

"Sorry it took me so long, but those kids just wouldn't let
up. And then it comes time to pay the bill and daddy tries to
squeeze me for free Dove bars. Some people!" Seymour

shook his head, the wool cap still in place covering the bandage underneath.

I staggered to my feet and found my glasses. The frames weren't too messed up, considering.

"So, what were you doing on the floor?"

"Someone made sure my head hit that doorjamb. I was intentionally knocked out."

"Was it Conway? I'll murder him!"

"I don't know who it was . . ."

I didn't bother asking Jack. I already knew the answer. The bookshop where he died was his tomb and his prison. Whenever I brought him out of it, he used my senses to see the world. So if I didn't see something, neither did he.

"Do you need an ambulance, Pen?"

"No, I'll be okay." I rubbed the hot, tender lump on the top of my forehead. Suddenly, I froze.

"What is it?" Seymour asked. "What are you staring at?"

I pointed. "Those three doors at the end of the hall. They were all shut when I arrived. Now one is partially open."

This is your chance, Penny. Your sno-cone-peddling backup is here. Search the place for Old Walt's notebooks. Do it now!

"Watch my back, Seymour. I'm going to check that room. If anyone comes through the front door, give me a shout."

"I will," he said with a nod. "Right after I slug 'em."

I proceeded with caution, gently nudging the half-open door with my elbow before stepping across the threshold. The bedroom was illuminated by a single lamp on the end table, but it was enough.

I found the body of Clifford Conway sprawled across the blood-soaked bed. Fully dressed, he lay facedown, the white pillow beneath his head stained gory red.

Check the hands, doll.

Conway's dead white knuckles clutched the wrinkled bedsheets.

The first whack didn't do the trick, so more followed. The Reaper took his good old time with Conway.

My own hands were shaky as I called Chief Ciders. I got

his second-in-command instead. I told Eddie Franzetti where I was and what I'd discovered. I even had the presence of mind to give him the room number.

"Don't leave the motel," he warned, "but get out of that crime scene. Wait for me outside, and try not to touch anything on the way out."

"Got it, Eddie."

I was sweating now—and had a whole new appreciation for my gumshoe ghost. Jack's shivery presence was helping me keep my cool in more ways than one.

You're doing great, Penny, he coaxed. *Just remember, the cops will seal this place when they arrive. Survey the scene now while you have the chance.*

Okay . . .

On top of the dresser, I saw a wallet, keys for a rental car, and loose change. The phone was facedown and mostly covered by a copy of the *Quindicott Bulletin*, but I recognized the sky blue cover with the tiny biplanes on it—

"That looks like Walt Waverly's phone!"

I almost moved the newspaper to make double sure, but Jack reminded me not to touch a thing this close to the body.

If the phone and wallet were left, this couldn't be a robbery. Not your typical burglary, anyway.

Walt's phone—if it is Walt's phone—is on the dresser. But I don't see his notebooks. They might be in his van.

Or he could have tossed them.

You're right, Jack. If he grabbed all three, trying to figure out who bought the Harriet painting, then he didn't need them anymore.

With time ticking by, I returned to the front room and told Seymour how I found Conway. As his jaw dropped in shock, I realized this room looked different.

"The computer and appointment book are gone!" I blurted and saw the camera was taken, too. With hope, I looked to the coffee table. One of the water tumblers was missing, though the other glass and the bottle of champagne remained untouched.

The killer likely nipped it for a cleaner getaway, Jack said. *No fingerprint clues for the coppers.*

There may be one clue, I told Jack. *The champagne toast. It looks like Conway and his killer were celebrating something. But what? On the surface, it doesn't add up.*

Are you sure?

Back at our shop, Conway dismissed the possibility of secret messages in Harriet's work. He scoffed and called them "the random, nonsensical doodles of a highly disturbed woman." Yet before Conway's laptop was taken, he was looking at an extreme close-up of an obscure detail in that painting. Why was he suddenly so interested in studying those "nonsensical" doodles?

And why would a murdering thief leave a wallet and smartphone but take a computer and camera?

The digital copies of Harriet's painting were in that camera's memory card and the laptop's hard drive—could that be the reason?

If it is, then the creep who cracked Conway's skull may be trying to crack Harriet's secret, too.

CHAPTER 34

Deadbeat

The why of murder always fascinates me so much more
than the how.

—Ann Rule

DEPUTY CHIEF EDDIE Franzetti found me and Seymour
on the veranda. The rain had ended, and I was using my wait
time to straighten the frames of my glasses without success.

"You're a mess," Eddie declared. "There's a lump on your
head."

"I know."

"You'll need that looked at. The paramedics are on their
way. Now, tell me what happened, Pen."

"I had a dispute with the doorjamb."

My attempt at levity fell on preoccupied ears as Eddie
peered over my shoulder at the half-open door.

"The corpse is in the bedroom," Seymour informed him.
"Far end of the suite, door on the left."

"I'll take your statements after I check the scene."

Eddie was inside for a couple of minutes before the paramedics arrived. A young woman with large, serious eyes
and a name tag that read MERCY JOHNSON insisted I sit down
while she took my vitals and checked my bruises.

"How long were you out?" she asked.

"I don't know, a few minutes."

"Then you should get into the ambulance now. We'll take you right over to the ER."

"I'm declining medical attention."

She shook her head. "Well, you're not getting away before I clean and bandage that head wound."

While the paramedic worked me over, I heard Eddie inside the suite. Like Blackstone Falls, Quindicott didn't have the manpower or the resources to conduct a proper murder investigation. So Eddie was calling for reinforcements, aka the state police.

"The victim was bludgeoned to death," he said. "Struck from behind several times with a blunt object. The murder weapon doesn't appear to be at the scene."

Soon Eddie ended the call and exited the room. Hatless, his hair still damp, he swiped his dark locks to one side and frowned at me and Seymour.

"Okay, start talking."

Seymour told Eddie how he came here to speak to Conway about the promised digital files of Harriet's painting—which were never sent—and found me on the floor, knocked out cold.

Then I told him about Conway's computer—there when I arrived, stolen while I was unconscious—and how I believed it was taken to retrieve those digital files. I also informed Eddie about the missing tumbler and suggested the killer might have been "celebrating" something with Conway and took the tumbler to keep the police from lifting fingerprints.

In the middle of my explanation, the exasperated deputy chief grabbed the eyeglasses I'd been fiddling with and proceeded to straighten them properly.

"I have kids," he explained, slipping the realigned specs onto my face. "If I went to the optometrist for every twisted frame, I'd be moonlighting at the Gentleman's Oasis."

"As security or ladies' night entertainment?"

Eddie wasn't amused, so I dropped my last bombshell on him.

"I'm pretty sure Walter Waverly's phone is on Conway's dresser."

"Waverly?"

"He sold the portrait to Seymour and then ended up dead. If Conway had Walt's phone, then he's likely involved with the man's death. You better get in touch with Sheriff Augusta Taft and give her the heads-up. She and the state investigators have been looking for that phone."

I wrapped up my story by reminding Eddie about Seymour's belief that the portrait held a secret message and reiterated that the theft of the digital files was the likely motive for Conway's murder.

"Sorry, Pen," Eddie replied, scratching the five-o'clock shadow. "I'll make sure crime scene checks out that phone. But the rest of your theory sounds pretty far-fetched. This scene looks like a typical pickup gone wrong to me."

"Unless that's what Conway's killer wants you to think."

"Deputy Chief! Deputy Chief!"

The desk clerk arrived, waving a printout. "The night manager wanted me to give you this. The other list is printing out now."

Eddie snatched it and ran his finger down the page.

The young woman lingered to gaze at the policeman—no surprise. With his athletic build and thick dark hair, Eddie was even handsomer these days than he was in high school.

"Anything else I can help you with, Officer? Some bottled water?"

"No, thanks."

To the woman's disappointment, Eddie barely looked in her direction. When her offer got more personal, he lifted his left hand, which included a gold band. Finally getting the universal "I'm married" message, she shrugged and walked away.

"Excuse me, what did that desk clerk bring you?" I asked.

"It's the guest log for the second floor." He handed it to me. "Recognize any names?"

There were more than a dozen customers along the veranda, including a big family from Philly occupying several rooms, a couple from Maryland, another couple from Columbus, Ohio, and a single man with a Nashville address.

"Sorry," I said. "Don't recognize any of the names on that list."

"Do you know of any enemies Conway may have made? Did anyone clash with him while he was in town?"

I hesitated and then told Eddie about Tracy Mahoney arguing with Conway in front of our shop. Plenty of people witnessed it, so Eddie would have heard about it one way or another anyway.

He wrote down her name.

"One more thing," I said. "I got a look at Conway's appointment book before it was taken. Our friend Barney Finch was in it. They were supposed to meet today at seven thirty. So you've got to talk to Barney and see what he can tell you."

"Will do. The crime scene unit won't be here for another twenty or thirty minutes. I'm going to see the night manager about the rest of the guest list—the people on the first floor. I want you to look it over with me, so stick close."

Eddie shifted his gaze to Seymour.

"That goes for you, too, ice cream man. Don't go drifting off, or I'll have you arrested for impersonating an iceberg."

Seymour rolled his eyes and tailed me as I followed Eddie down the steps to the motel office. At the vending machines, my smartphone buzzed.

"It's my aunt. I'd better take this, Eddie."

He barely nodded, already greeting the motel manager.

Seymour hung back with me to buy a Dr Pepper from the machine. But before I could answer my phone call, I heard a familiar roar in the parking lot—*loud* and familiar.

Jack heard it too. *Where did I last notice that same rumbling beat?*

On Cranberry Street, Jack. Remember the big motorcycle Tracy Mahoney's friend was driving?

I gawked at the huge Harley rolling past the office. I was *pretty* sure the powerfully built rider in black leather was the same man who'd fetched Tracy after her confrontation with

Clifford Conway, though I didn't see that telltale long blond hair. But this biker was bundled against the weather with a heavy black scarf and gloves, and he could have tied up his hair under his helmet.

I told Jack that I was almost certain it was the same biker riding the same Harley. And I recalled what that man had said to Tracy—

"He'll get what's coming to him. But not here."

Was this really the same guy? The one Tracy called Dennis? If it was, did he mean Conway would pay tonight, at his motel? Or was that threat just a coincidence?

Coincidence? Jack scoffed. *You know me, Penny, I'm not one to make book on "coincidence." Not without proof. Can you think of another reason for him to be here except to push Conway's button?*

As the biker stopped at the motel exit, I spied the waterproof pack on his back. It was a big, bulgy thing with what appeared to be the long neck of a baseball bat sticking out of the top. I squinted to read the license plate, but he was too far away!

Conway was bludgeoned to death, Jack. And Eddie said the weapon was gone. And that muscular guy looks strong enough to knock me cold with or without the help of a doorjamb.

The biker revved his engine. He was ready to hit the highway.

Go after him, Penny!

What?! I squawked.

You need to write down the plate numbers. Do it quick before he disappears. When I hesitated, Jack blew up. *What's your alternative? Blab to the law? And while you're explaining it all to your copper pal, the biker gets lost and lands who knows where. Then your pal's got no choice but to squeeze your little blue-haired babysitter on where her boyfriend's hiding—and she may not want to give him up so easy. All the harder on her.*

Okay, okay, I'm on it. I tugged Seymour's white smock. "You're coming with me."

"Wait!" Seymour squawked, nearly choking on his Dr Pepper. "I was going to buy some French fries. Where are we going?"

"You'll see."

"But Eddie told us to stay put."

"We'll be right back. Now, come on!"

CHAPTER 35

They Drive by Night

Faster, faster, faster, until the thrill of speed overcomes the fear of death.

—Hunter S. Thompson

"YOU'RE TELLING ME that Clifford Conway got his head bashed in, and you think the biker in front of us canceled his clock—and knocked you cold on his way out?"

As Seymour spoke, he stared through the rain-slick windshield.

"That about sums it up," I replied, my eyes never leaving the twisty rural road ahead.

"If he's an actual murderer, why are we chasing him?"

"If we get this guy's license number, or better still his address, we can turn the information over to Deputy Chief Franzetti."

Seymour visibly relaxed. "You had me worried there. I thought you were planning some sort of citizen's arrest. But if all you want is a license plate number, then keep driving, McDuff—and a little faster. That Harley is getting way ahead of you."

I pressed my foot harder on the gas.

Whoa, hang back, Jack warned. *If you get too close, that biker might spot your headlights.*

Just what I don't need. Two backseat drivers.

The rear light on the big motorcycle vanished around a tree-lined bend ahead of us—too far ahead for my liking.

You better snap those beamers off, or you might get made.

And drive in the dark? I'll end up a ghost like you!

Fortunately, it didn't come to that. As we rounded the next bend, the biker hung a sharp right and rolled his motorcycle across a plank bridge spanning a rain-flushed stream. Seconds later, he vanished among the trees on the opposite side, and we heard the engine cut out.

"Looks like he reached his destination," Seymour said.

"I don't suppose you got his license?"

"He was too far away."

I didn't like the idea of turning my car onto that rickety wooden bridge, so I continued driving, very slowly, down the country path along the bubbling stream.

"Look!" Seymour said. "Through the trees, see that huge square of light?"

I hit the brakes. A large building sat beyond the rickety bridge. It stood with an open door as big as a barn's. That square of light shined brightly and then abruptly went dark, as if the big door had been closed.

"That building is pretty far back from the main road," Seymour said.

"You're a postman; don't you know the address?"

He shook his wool-capped head. "We're not in Quindicott anymore. We left that zip code miles ago. I didn't even know this glorified cow path existed." Pulling out his phone, he checked an online map. "This building isn't charted that I can see. All that's listed in this area is a fast-food restaurant, a campground, a church, and a nursing home. So what do we do now? Turn around and go over that bridge, too?"

Not a good idea, Jack advised. *If you go over that bridge with those headlights, someone may spot you. Get out of your car and walk across.*

I told Seymour the plan.

"What?" He was squawking like his parrot again.

"It'll be okay. We'll be careful."

I parked on the shoulder near a lonely streetlamp so I could find the car again fast if we had to. When I opened the door, night sounds and chilly air filled the compartment. Under the buzzing light, my partner in crime-fighting glowed like a reflective traffic cone. "You might want to lose the ice cream apron, Seymour. You look like Casper the Friendly Ghost."

"But it's cold out here."

"Look, I'm not dressed for this, either. But at least it stopped raining."

Now you know why I wore a topcoat eight months out of the year, Jack said. *You never know when you're going to follow some hooligan to his drafty hideout.*

I thought you wore that coat to hide your gun.

That, too.

Seymour tossed his white smock into the back seat and fastened the top buttons of his flannel shirt. I zipped my light jacket all the way up to my chin.

With only my keychain flashlight to guide us, Seymour and I pushed ahead along the road's narrow shoulder. Though patches of stars were visible in the night sky, the moon remained tucked behind billowing clouds. With all the trees around us, the darkness felt thick.

Finally, we reached the wooden bridge. Up close, I saw the span looked pretty dilapidated, and I was glad we didn't try to cross it with a car. We walked cautiously, avoiding gaps and broken planks. My flashlight was small, and the beam was barely bright enough to light our way, its reflection only faintly reaching the gushing waters beneath us.

Among the trees on the other side, we found a clearing. Eight motorcycles were parked there, big high-performance machines.

"Now we can get the license number and get out of here," Seymour said.

"But which Harley is it? Three of them look exactly the same to me."

"Me, too," Seymour confessed. "What should we do?"

Jack gave me a clue. *Find the one with the hot engine!*

"Of course!"

Seymour looked at me with a puzzled expression. I told him Jack's idea, and he quickly started touching metal. A moment later, he yelped.

"Found it!"

Between us, we managed to come up with a pen and paper. I scribbled down the license number while Seymour held the light.

"Okay, Pen, now let's get out of here."

I was about to agree, but I couldn't help being a little curious about that big building where the biker had disappeared. It wasn't a house, and there were no signs on the building that I could see.

"I wonder what that biker is up to inside that building."

There's only one way to answer that question.

I turned to my ice cream man backup. "Do you want to take a look?"

"Are you nuts!" Seymour cried, then checked his volume. "Have you never seen a Burt Reynolds movie on TCM? In the sticks, bootleggers do crazy things like shooting at nosy neighbors and revenuers, whatever the hell they are."

"Seymour, there are no bootleggers around here."

"What about meth labs? This is just the kind of place to set one up. Isolated. Guarded by a gang of psycho bikers."

"Come on, Seymour—"

"I have two words for you: *Breaking Bad.*"

"I'm going to take a quick peek. If you don't want to come, then wait here for a minute. I won't be long."

Seymour flinched when he heard a car pass on the road. Then he squared his shoulders. "I'll go with you. I can't just stand here like a doofus and let you go up there alone."

"Don't worry. No one will see us. It's pitch-dark out here."

"All right," Seymour griped, "let's get it over with."

The only path out of the biker's parking lot was through a long, covered grape arbor. Inside that leafy tunnel, the air was heady with the cloying sweet-sour reek of decaying fruit.

"Is it me," Seymour whispered, "or do you smell Welch's grape juice?"

More like a Bowery trash bin the morning after a wino's bender.

Charming memory, Jack, thanks.

On the other side, we found the building. The big door was closed tightly, the place so dark and quiet it seemed deserted.

"Listen!" Seymour whispered, alarmed. "Hear those engines?"

Unfortunately, I did. Two new bikers were approaching. The growl of motorcycles filled the silent night. The clatter of wooden planks came next as their tires crossed the shaky bridge.

"Trapped like rats!" Seymour whispered, while Jack bellowed—

Don't just stand there! Find a place to play hide-and-seek. You're about to have company.

CHAPTER 36

Roadhouse

Spying is waiting.

—John le Carré, *The Russia House*

"QUICK, IN HERE!"

I grabbed Seymour by his flannel shirt and dragged him into the brush growing around the arbor. Pushing through the thick, swishing branches, we were well out of sight. The vegetation was dripping wet, and it didn't take long before we were, too.

I'm freezing, I told the ghost. *I wish I had your topcoat now.*

Better if you had my snub-nosed peashooter and a couple of .38-caliber rounds to go with it.

Ignoring the rainwater trickling down my neck, I waited beside a grumpy Seymour for the arrival of the newcomers. We heard the clomp of their boots inside the arbor first. Then one of them spoke—quite loudly, too, his hearing obviously blown by the cycle's roar.

"That gig in Cincinnati went off without a hitch! If all goes well south of the Mason-Dixon Line, we're going to make a killing."

"Those southern gentlemen aren't always happy to have northerners muscling in on their turf," the other replied.

"Nothing's a sure thing," the first man agreed. "But I trust the man upstairs. He got us through a hail of bullets, right? He'll show us the way forward this time, too."

"Holy moly!" Seymour whispered. "I told you this place was trouble. It's a gang hideout, and those guys are talking about an interstate crime wave and a kingpin they call 'the man upstairs'!"

As we peered between grapevines, the pair came into view—big and brawny men in black leather. And the next words they uttered froze my already chilly spine.

"Once Dennis takes care of business at the motel, we're set to make our move."

Slapping hands, the pair exited the arbor and crossed to the building. As we watched, they slid the big door aside and entered. I tried to glimpse the interior, but they closed it too quickly.

I don't know what's going on in that place, Jack, but it sure sounds like Dennis, the blond biker, killed Conway with that bat in his backpack.

You don't say.

There's no way I'm wrong. What else could "take care of business at the motel" mean?

"We better leave," Seymour advised.

"Not yet. After what we heard, I *really* want a peek inside that building."

"I say again. Are you nuts? Eddie was right. You need to have your head examined."

"Listen to me. If you and I witness illegal activity, we can alert the authorities. Two birds with one stone."

"But curiosity killed the cat, Pen, and neither of us has nine lives."

For once Jack agreed. *The ice cream mailman is right. You don't know how many more felons are coming to this conclave—*

"Listen!" Seymour whispered. "There's another biker coming!"

I heard the sound of the motor, too, but this motorcycle

was muted and far less throaty compared to the others. The sound quickly sputtered and faded.

Seymour and I both let out the breaths we'd been holding. That's when I made up my mind. "You're both right. Let's get out of here."

"Both?" Seymour asked, glancing around. "Am I missing something? Or somebody?"

"Uh, no. Let's go . . ." With a final glance at the mystery building, I turned into the arbor—and ran right into a black-clad figure coming the other way. The stranger and I bounced off each other like balls on a billiard table. As we went down, I heard a distinctly feminine squeal.

My padded posterior saved me from much damage. In the darkness I heard a rustle of material; then a harsh flash-light beam shocked my eyes.

"Mrs. McClure?!"

The light shifted away from my face.

"Hey, you're blinding me, lady!" Seymour groused, throwing up his arms.

"I know you! You're my mailman," the young woman said. That's when I recognized her voice.

"Tracy? Tracy Mahoney?"

Seymour helped us both off the ground.

"I'm sorry I crashed into you, Mrs. McClure. I was in a hurry."

"No, Tracy, it's totally my fault."

In the indirect glow of the flashlight, I saw Tracy frown. "I've asked Dennis to string lights through here, but he's always so busy! I'll have to do it for him."

Play dumb, Penny. And keep the dame talkin'. She might spill something useful.

"Sorry? Who's Dennis?"

"My brother. He runs this place." Tracy gave me a strange look. "What are you doing here? There are no events scheduled."

Close the trap, honey. Time to press her with the truth. Squeeze her and see what flows out before she can make up a story.

"I'm not here for an event, Tracy. I was actually looking for you. I left a few messages on your phone, but you never got back to me. Now we *really* need to talk."

"Okay. But let's go inside."

With Seymour in tow, we'd just reached the door when I heard the discordant sounds of a band tuning up.

Tracy stopped and turned. "We better enter through the front door. We won't be able to hear ourselves speak otherwise."

The invisible band launched into a banging song with guitars, a keyboard, and drums, all playing loud enough for me to feel it in my chest.

"Is this place a roadhouse?" I yelled.

"No." Tracy shook her head and smiled. "It's God's house."

CHAPTER 37

Wheels on Fire

Tough as leather . . . Harder than steel.

—*Outlaw Riders* (movie tagline)

PUZZLED BY TRACY'S answer, which I barely heard, I followed her around the building, where the music faded to a dull roar. When we reached the front, I saw a paved parking lot (empty now) with easy access to a well-trafficked road, a far cry from a forgotten rural route with a rickety old bridge.

The steel building was intended for industrial use but had been transformed—figuratively as well as literally—as revealed by the sign over the door.

THE CHURCH OF LOST SOULS
REVEREND DENNIS MAHONEY, PASTOR

"Your brother is a reverend?"

"Denny finished his divinity degree after he got back from Afghanistan," Tracy explained.

"He was a soldier?"

"Three tours of duty with the Special Forces."

Tracy unlocked the double doors, and Seymour and I followed her into the church. The waiting room was spacious, but soundproofed it was not. Music again exploded from the opposite end of the building. Rowdy and raucous at first, it thankfully turned soft and melodic.

"What's the name of the group?" Seymour asked.

"Wheels on Fire," Tracy replied with a note of pride. "The members are wounded vets. If you want to check them out, Mr. Tarnish, go through that door. They'd love an audience, even if it's only one."

"Yeah, I think I will," Seymour said.

While Tracy brewed coffee from a setup in the corner, I perused the event postings, including advertisements for Wheels on Fire, who'd already played concerts in Providence, Boston, Bangor, Syracuse, Lancaster, and Dayton.

"Is Dennis also a musician?"

"Sure is. My brother carries that guitar of his almost everywhere he goes. Calls it his 'spirit rifle.'"

Jack, did you hear that? That bulge in the backpack was a guitar, not a baseball bat!

You don't say.

"Next month, Wheels is going to Atlanta to open for Make a Joyful Noise," Tracy continued. "Dennis arranged a gig in Nashville, too. He met with the promoter tonight at the Comfy-Time Motel."

Hey, remember the guest list at that fleabag motel?

I did. And I knew that single male visitor from Nashville could give Dennis an alibi—if it was even needed. I also realized the "hail of bullets" those bikers faced came from their military service, and the "man upstairs" really was the Man Upstairs!

Tracy grinned. "I was so excited I swung by the motel to see if the meeting was over. It wasn't, but Dennis just called to say he signed the contract. Wheels will tour the South next summer, ten cities, and I'll be going as a roadie!"

Tracy handed me a cup of coffee. "So, Mrs. McClure, what did you want to talk about?"

"I'd like to ask you about that argument in front of my bookshop with Clifford Conway."

"Oh, that." She blushed with embarrassment. "I went a little crazy. Okay, a *lot* crazy. But I had to say something after all that man's done to scam me—and so many others."

"Does this have anything to do with what happened at the reading group the other night, when you were upset?"

"Yes, Mrs. McClure, it has everything to do with that."

Tracy went on to tell me what she told Conway, but without the rage. She recounted how she'd written and illustrated a fantasy novel. She wanted it published and found Conway's slick advertisements on the web. Tracy was interested but couldn't afford the fees. To earn some cash, she naively sold Conway the rights to license one of her best pieces of fantasy art—and that's when the heartache started.

"I guess most of Conway's clients aren't savvy enough to know they're being cheated. I certainly wasn't. But apparently, one of his clients did realize her 'exclusive' book cover art was on three other novels! When she complained to Conway, he blamed *me* for reselling my work over and over to some underling at his company who couldn't tell I'd 'doctored' it with superficial changes. It was a total lie. Conway himself bought my art, added different backgrounds and color schemes, and resold it multiple times. I was the honest one. He was the cheat. He hurt my reputation terribly. I was called awful things in social media and thrown out of my favorite online fantasy groups."

She squared her shoulders. "But I'm not giving up, Mrs. McClure. I can't afford an attorney to fight for me, so I'm going to post my side of this story, the *true* story, wherever I can. At this point, people may not listen or even believe me, but I'm going to try my best to stand up for myself." She took a deep breath. "As for that scene in front of your store, well, I can't deny I felt betrayed by Mr. Conway, and I wanted to hurt him. But my big brother calmed me down after our shouting match. He explained how it's better to forgive than to hate, that carrying all that bitterness and anger inside will damage me far more than the man who wronged me. Dennis told me Conway would pay for what he's done, in God's time, not ours."

"Well, Tracy, I have some distressing news to share. If you believe in divine justice, you may have gotten it. Mr. Conway was murdered tonight."

Tracy stared at me a moment in frozen disbelief. "Murdered?" she whispered, voice barely there. "How?"

"He was beaten to death."

I waited for her reaction. It was not what I expected.

She burst into tears.

CHAPTER 38

Reach Out and Touch Someone

The telephone is a good way to talk to people without
having to offer them a drink.

—Fran Lebowitz

AFTER I SPENT an hour convincing a guilt-stricken Tracy
Mahoney that she did not "wish" Clifford Conway dead,
Seymour and I said good night.

On our way across the rickety bridge, I began to feel
woozy, and by the time we reached my car, I was so fuzzy I
actually let Seymour take the wheel. When we hit the highway, he took a detour. In the mother of all ironies, Seymour
drove me to the hospital.

After a few tests, the doctor told me my weak spell was
due to dehydration and the fact that I'd neglected to eat more
than a few bites of food for the entire day—and *not* because
of my head wound. So, after a medicinal dose of Silva's
Seafood Shack's famous oyster po'boy with steak fries, Seymour got me home.

My son was tucked into bed and my aunt asleep on the
couch during a Mystery Classics Channel marathon of *Iron-
side* reruns—a relief because there was too much information to share, and I was too exhausted to do it. The apartment

was so quiet I took a hot baking soda bath with a cold compress on my head to ease the many aches and pains.

I longed to crawl into bed and end this harrowing day. But there was a terse voice mail message from Deputy Chief Franzetti I had to return.

Eddie's mood was not good.

"Where the hell did you go, Pen? One minute you were at the Comfy-Time; then you're gone."

"I felt lightheaded. I had Seymour drive me to the emergency room."

"Nice try, but I called the hospital. You weren't there."

"I did go to the hospital, eventually. First I followed a lead."

"One you'd care to share with the Quindicott Police?"

"No, sorry, it didn't pan out . . ."

There was another reason I didn't tell Eddie whom I'd followed and what I'd discovered. I'd already told him about Tracy's public argument with Conway. I knew she was innocent of any wrongdoing, and her brother had good reason to be at the Comfy-Time, so there was really nothing to tell.

"How about you, Deputy Chief? Any suspects?"

"We're looking at the security footage from the Comfytime. The only two working cameras are aimed at the front desk inside and the parking lot outside. There are comings and goings we'll have to look into, but we've got no solid leads yet."

"And what about the phone I told you about?"

"You were right, Pen. The mobile device found on the dresser did not belong to Clifford Conway. It belonged to Walter Waverly. I spoke with Sheriff Taft, who was about to close the Waverly case up in Blackstone Falls. She says with this development, she's going to take a second look."

"What about Walt's notebooks, Eddie? Did you find them in Conway's room or his van?"

"No. And we did a thorough search."

Something wasn't right, I thought. Conway could have tossed the notebooks after he got what he needed—to avoid incrimination. But why take and keep Walt's phone? It didn't make sense.

"Have you talked to our friend Barney Finch?" I pressed.

"He hasn't called me back. In the meantime, my officers canvassed the guests at the motel and took statements. The state police crime scene unit confirmed your witness statement to me. There was a second glass. They found a dried ring of spilled champagne on the table."

"And?"

"We're going with that lead for now. Champagne suggests a romantic liaison, as does the bedroom location of the body. So I sent Officer Tibbet to the Gentleman's Oasis to see if Conway came in looking for a little relief from loneliness. I've got Bull McCoy asking the same questions at the Go-Go Lounge in Millstone."

As Eddie talked, it became disappointingly clear that he'd completely rejected my theory that the murder was connected to Harriet's portrait. He wasn't even looking in that direction.

"Eddie, I understand why you're pursuing those leads, but I doubt Conway's murder was about some random pickup and a robbery, though I'm sure the killer wanted the police to think it was. Conway was a shady businessman, and his latest scheme, whatever it was, had something to do with the artwork Seymour bought from the late Walter Waverly. Harriet McClure's portrait seems to be the key. It could be why Conway was killed, our friend was attacked, and Old Walt's life was cut short."

"So you say."

"Why don't you believe me?"

"Let me put it this way, Pen. I don't *dis*believe you, especially on the possibility that the killer wanted the scene to look like a pickup gone wrong. But face facts. If it wasn't a blind date from hell, then the motive for Conway's murder is far more likely to be this guy's shady business dealings than a dusty old painting. The brutality of that beating tells me it may have been personal."

The deputy chief's words gave me pause. There were so many leads, so many possibilities. But I couldn't let go of my gut feeling. Harriet's haunting portrait had something to do with all of this. I didn't know what, but I was too tired to continue arguing.

"I'm signing off, Eddie. I'll be sure to come by the station and look over that first-floor guest list. Good night."

I climbed into bed, my mood now as sour as Eddie Franzetti's.

Why so glum, Penny?

Because we've got no answers. We're right back where we started.

Not quite. Now we got two stiffs instead of one.

And two lumps on the head, if you're keeping count.

Hey, buck up. Considering what you had to work with, you did a good thing tonight. I mean, let's face facts. Your PI skills are still hinky. But you had the gumption to pursue a lead and eliminate a suspect. That's not small potatoes. No decent gumshoe wants to send some poor sucker up the river without a paddle.

Believe me, Jack, I feel bad enough that I implicated Tracy in my original statement to Eddie.

Lucky you collided with that blue-haired girl artist, then. Otherwise, you would have left that building thinking you found Murder Incorporated's secret headquarters—

And it turned out to be a church, of all things! Thank goodness I didn't run off and tell Eddie that Reverend Mahoney was a killer with a meth lab in the woods. He'd never trust me again.

Lesson learned. Circumstantial evidence is sometimes just that—circumstantial. Until you prove otherwise, appearances can be deceiving, and a collection of facts don't always add up to the truth. To use your lingo, you shouldn't judge a book by its cover.

I yawned. *Very funny, Jack. At least your reference is apropos.*

It's more than that.

What do you mean?

I'll be glad to show you. But you'll have to close your eyes first.

Another dream?

Another memory. But the same case. And while we're back in my time, I'll give you some PI pointers.

Like what? How not to stick my nose where it doesn't belong?

Nix to that. "Sticking your nose in" is practically the credo of my profession, which is why I'm going to show you how to make your nose look like it belongs.

Huh?

Never hesitate to investigate, doll. You weren't wrong to want to look inside that mystery building tonight—see if illegal activity was taking place. Only next time something like that comes up, you have to be prepared.

I yawned again, so hard this time my eyes watered.

Close those peepers, Penny, and I'll show you how a professional does it. But first, we need to visit a little diner with a name that's out of this world.

Out of this world? Like you, huh, Jack?

A deep, vibrating chuckle was the last thing I heard before my world faded away.

CHAPTER 39

Intelligent Life on Pluto

The coffee shop smell was strong enough to build a garage on.

—Raymond Chandler, *Farewell, My Lovely*

IN TOTAL DARKNESS, I heard Jack's voice. It seemed to come from far away.

"Ready for that cuppa joe I promised you?"

"Coffee?" I moaned. "You'll have to drag me out of bed first."

"You're sleeping back there, doll, but you're awake with me. Just open your eyes."

I did, and along with my vision, all my other senses returned—with a vengeance. We stood on the sidewalk of Manhattan's Eighth Avenue in the middle of a bright October afternoon. Boxy cars and trucks in hues from black and green to muddy brown crowded the busy street. I could smell the diesel exhaust from a Greyhound bus, hear the traffic noise, and feel Jack Shepard's strong, reassuring arm wrapped around my waist.

"The diner's right down the block." Jack pointed. "The Pluto isn't much to look at, but the java's good and hot."

Releasing me, he took a few gigantic strides that left me in the dust.

"Slow down, Detective, I can hardly walk in these shoes!"

"They're ankle-strap wedges. Veronica Lake strolls around in them all the time."

"I'm not a Hollywood star!"

"Maybe not. But you got the gams of Betty Grable."

I shot Jack a look. He appeared amused as he watched me negotiate the sidewalk in my narrow pencil skirt. Finally, I caught up.

"So, doll, you remember the case we're working on back here?"

"Of course. It's about that beautiful blue-eyed blonde, Ruby Tyler."

"Give me the facts."

"Let's see . . . Ruby came to New York from a West Virginia mining town and wound up working as a glamorous hostess at the Albatross nightclub. A talented young artist named Nathan Brock was arrested for her murder. But Nathan's fiancée, Shirley, didn't believe it. Desperate and pregnant, she hired us to find Ruby's real killer."

As I recited the facts of Ruby's case, her haunting image came back to me, the one that Nathan Brock had painted for that stunning pulp cover. I could still see his skillful brushstrokes sensuously defining Ruby's naked curves, her sassy blond bob and apple red lips. I also remembered what was lurking behind Ruby in those saffron yellow curtains. I'd never forget that big, rough-looking man with pockmarked cheeks, raising his deadly dagger.

I was shivering with the memory when Jack announced—

"We're here. This is the joint."

The Pluto was a pretty typical boxcar-shaped hash house. It had stainless steel siding, a tacky neon sign, a row of wooden booths against the windows, and a line of cushioned stools along a well-worn counter. At this hour, the lunch crowd was gone and the place was pretty quiet. I figured Jack timed it that way.

"Is this the same diner Shirley Powell told us about?"

"Right on the money, Penny. Miss Powell followed her fiancé here. This is where she saw him meet up with Ruby. Now, let's go . . ."

As Jack pulled open the glass door, a tidy middle-aged woman frying bacon on the grill noticed us and shouted over her shoulder.

"Kosmo! We have customers."

Tidy was not a word I'd use to describe the hulking man in a dingy food-stained apron who came up behind her, carrying a sack of potatoes. His dark hair was greasy, his nose hawklike, and his expression grim as a gangster's as he sucked on the cigarette dangling from his lips. When I saw that build and the pockmarks on those rough cheeks, I knew.

"Jack, that's him!" I fanatically whispered. "That's the man with the knife from Nathan Brock's painting!"

"Yeah." Jack calmly nodded. "He's the guy in the painting, and that's a fact."

"Why are you so serene? Isn't he the one we're looking for? Didn't he kill Ruby?"

"Kosmo, a killer?" The detective laughed. "That man is so gentle he doesn't even own a fly swatter."

"Gentle or not, he gave me a fright."

"The only thing to fear in this joint is the grub. Like I warned you, doll, don't judge a book. And call me 'Mr. Shepard' from now on. You're supposed to be my secretary, remember?"

"Secretary again? Can't you introduce me as your trainee? Or better yet *associate*?"

"I use words like that in here, they'll think you're my mistress."

"Fine. *Secretary* it is, Mr. Shepard." With a sarcastic salute of my white-gloved hand, I knocked my pillbox hat off. Jack caught the silly thing before it hit the floor and set it back on my head. Then he led me to the counter.

"Penny, meet Kosmo Spanos. He's the owner of this establishment."

"What'll it be, gumshoe?" Mr. Spanos asked in a voice reminiscent of Popeye the Sailor.

"Two cups of joe."

Jack gestured to a stool and we both sat down. When Kosmo served us, Jack slapped a five-dollar bill on the counter. "I'm here for more than coffee, Kosmo. My secretary and I need some information. What do you know about Nathan Brock?"

He stared at the crinkled bill. "The skinny kid artist? What do ya want to know?"

At Jack's prodding—literally an elbow to the ribs followed by a wink—I took over the conversation.

"Mr. Spanos, we were told Brock was here last week to meet a woman. Is that true?"

"Easy to meet women. Lots of dames come here. Most of them just got off the bus with stars in their eyes. And there's a whole booth full of the more seasoned variety in the back." He gave me the once-over. "You're a looker enough to join them. A little old, but you're okay."

"Gee, thanks." I followed Kosmo's gaze to the back booth.

Three bored women in their twenties lingered over coffee. One chewed gum while filing her nails. Another read the paper. A third was poring over pages of a play or script. Their shabby-chic outfits showed off their figures, and they all seemed to be waiting for something.

Jack nudged me again.

"Mr. Spanos, do you know the name of Nathan Brock's latest acquaintance?"

"Do I look like a stool pigeon, lady?"

"No, you look like a concerned citizen who's helping in the investigation of a young woman's murder."

Kosmo Spanos shifted his gaze to Jack, then back to me. Finally, he snatched the fiver and stuffed it into his apron pocket.

"You must be talking about Ruby Tyler. Sweet kid. She worked for me once upon a time. Visits now and then, too. But I didn't know she'd been clipped. Really sorry to hear it."

"It didn't make the papers," Jack explained.

"Ruby was a decent waitress and easy on the eyes. Her charms kept the cabbies and bus drivers coming back, that's for sure."

I leaned close to Mr. Spanos. He smelled of raw onions.

"Was Nathan Brock with Ruby the last time you saw him?"

"Yeah, she met Mr. Artist here. It was before the lunch crowd showed. Maybe eleven. They had coffee and sinkers and left together. I haven't laid eyes on Ruby since. Was he the guy who did her in?"

Jack spoke up. "Any chance you know where they went that day?"

"I heard mention of the Forrestal on Park Avenue." He leaned close and spoke in a conspiratorial tone. "I gotta say it wasn't the first time I heard that place mentioned, either."

"What do you think they did there?" I asked.

"How should I know? My cousin used to work at a sewing shop in the basement. A bunch of gals do costumes for Broadway. But I doubt Ruby and Brock were there for a fitting, if you know what I mean."

"What else can you tell us about Brock?" Jack asked.

Kosmo shrugged. "Not much. Just that Mr. Artist was a fixture around here for months before he met Ruby. He'd eat a sandwich, order coffee or a milk shake, and sit around, lurking."

"Did he do anything else," Jack said, "besides *lurk*?"

"Take pictures."

"With what?" I blurted.

"A camera, what else?" Kosmo looked at me like I was a dim bulb.

I glanced apologetically at Jack, who covered his eyes and shook his head. *Sorry, Jack, I forgot.* This was 1947, a little too early for iPhones, drones, and GoPros. At least my question kept Kosmo talking—

"Brock has one of them fancy cameras, like reporters use. He snaps pictures of all sorts of customers."

"What sort?" Jack asked.

Kosmo shrugged. "Rubes just off the bus, cabbies, steam-fitters from the dock, creeps and panty sniffers from who knows where—usually New Jersey." Kosmo chuckled. "Brock even took pictures of me once. But mostly he photographs dames. Young ones. And those gals who only come out at night."

Jack jumped in again to steer the conversation. "You said you heard the Forrestal mentioned before? When was that?"

"The first time was a few months ago, the day Nathan Brock came in with a woman old enough to be his mother."

"Is that right?" Jack rubbed the scar on his chin. "Can you describe her?"

"Maybe fifty. Long gray hair swept up like a school-teacher, even had a pencil behind her ear. Classy manners, but her duds weren't posh like the ladies with leather luggage. She was dressed regular, like your secretary here." He gestured to my plain cotton blouse. "The two of them sat at my counter and watched the crowd. I was busy, but I over-heard the dame make a crack about how great it would be to get some of them dolls in my diner up to the Forrestal."

"Why?"

"Search me, gumshoe. But it started happenin'. That same gray-haired dame showed up plenty o' times since. She chats up some young doll or even a gaggle of them. Then they all hop a cab and off they go."

"Go where?" I demanded.

"Ain't you listenin', honey? The Forrestal apartment building on Park Avenue."

Kosmo's testimony sent my thoughts into a tailspin. What began as a cut-and-dried case of a man two-timing his pregnant fiancée, and being falsely accused of killing his mistress, started to look like something else entirely. *What*, I didn't know. A secret bordello? From the grim look on Jack's face, he seemed to think so.

"One more thing," Jack said. "Do you have Ruby's address? There's another five-spot in it."

Kosmo nodded and went back to the kitchen. While he was gone, I leaned toward Jack and whispered—

"Why did you ask for Ruby Tyler's address? Wasn't it in that envelope Shirley Powell gave you?"

He shook his head. "When Miss Powell followed Ruby and her fiancé to the Forrestal, she mistakenly assumed Ruby lived—and died—in that building. But I knew Ruby could never have afforded an apartment on Park Avenue. Kosmo doesn't remember, but I knew Ruby from her days working here at the Pluto. She used to serve me. That's how we met. I was the one who helped get her a spot at the Albatross, after putting in a good word with Hugo."

"Then why didn't you go to Hugo for Ruby's address?"

"Because I didn't want him knowing I was on the case. Loose lips sink ships—and I didn't want Hugo tipping anybody off before I got some background legwork in."

Before Jack could say more, Kosmo returned with a piece of paper.

"That address is almost two years old. Don't come crying to me for your money back if this isn't Ruby's place no more."

Jack slid the fiver across the counter, and we hit the street. But we didn't go far. At the end of the block, I stopped him.

"Where are we going now, Detective?"

Jack folded his arms. "You're the *trainee*. You tell me."

"Well . . . we could stake out the Pluto and wait for that older woman to return."

"That would take time and too much of it. Think smarter. What do we want to know more about?"

"The Forrestal. Whatever was going on between Nathan Brock and Ruby Tyler happened in that building. It also sounds like illegal activity might be going on with all those pretty young girls. I think we should check it out . . . Is that what you did?"

Jack nodded. "That's what I did—and that's what *we're* going to do."

"But if it's a posh building on Park Avenue, there's sure to be a doorman. How do we get in?"

"I'll show you. But first close your eyes."

"What?"

"You heard me. We need a change of costume and lo-cation."

"If you say so," I told him, and down my eyelids went.

CHAPTER 40

Finding Forrestal

You know how damned life-like Pickman's paintings
were—how we all wondered where he got those faces.

—H.P. Lovecraft, "Pickman's Model"

"SHAKE A LEG if you want to get past the doorman. I've
got my ticket."

I opened my eyes—and almost fell on my face.

"Steady, girl."

I blinked against the noonday sun. From the traffic noise,
the smell of leaded car exhaust, and clouds of tobacco smoke,
I knew I was still in Jack Shepard's time.

"Where are we now?"

"The other side of Manhattan. You okay, Penny?"

"It's these shoes! Why do you keep insisting I walk on
stilts?"

"Sorry, doll, it's the fashion. And right now you've got to
look fashionable because we're on Park Avenue."

I looked down and down even more, at my far-too-daring
neckline. My face suddenly felt hot.

"Jack, this is way too risqué for me."

"That's the point. If you want to get past the doorman,
you've got to look the same as those other dames who get

brought here from the Pluto. Like I said, I already have my ticket."

I took my first real look at Jack—and burst out laughing.

The PI had costumed himself in a white button-down shirt with SPEEDY DELIVERY splashed in bold letters across his broad back. Baggy white pants and a jaunty cap cocked to one side completed the uniform. As an accessory, Jack clutched a brown paper bag that smelled of pickles.

"You're the most unconvincing sandwich boy ever."

"It'll get me through the door."

I took one last look at my tarted-up self. "At least I'm not the only one who looks silly."

"Gee, thanks."

"So, *Mr. Shepard*, what's the plan?"

As Jack briefed me, I took some experimental steps. I felt wobbly, but by the time we hoofed it to the Forrestal's front door, I'd gotten the hang of it. I also got a few leering winks and wolf whistles. Then I laid eyes on the doorman and nearly lost my nerve.

His uniform would have done Mussolini proud, all knife-edged creases with epaulets and gold-trimmed collar and cuffs. His arms were crossed in front of him, his complexion was ashen gray, and his expression was a sneer meant for all of humanity.

And *this* is the guy I was supposed to sweet-talk? Climbing Everest in these heels might be easier!

Despite my trepidations, I dived right into my role, doing my best to achieve a street-girl persona.

"Hey, mister!" I paused to chew some imaginary gum. "This is where we girls go in, right?"

The doorman's face remained rigid, but he flicked his hand like a fly buzzed his ear.

"Come on," I pleaded. "I know this is the place. Can't you be a sweet guy and let me in?"

"Amscray, before I whistle for a beat cop."

"Don't give me that. I was supposed to meet the gray-haired lady at the Pluto. But I was late."

"You mean Gwen?"

"Yeah, Gwen."

His face remained stony, and he didn't budge an inch.

I was about to double down with my pathetic act when I felt a presence behind me. It was Jack, arriving right on cue.

"I got a delivery for the costume shop," he announced, lifting his paper sack.

The doorman turned suspicious. "I never seen you around here."

"My regular sandwich boy came down with the grippe. I'm the kid's boss, but deliveries gotta be made, don't they?"

Stone Face grunted. "Take the stairs to the basement. You'll see the door on the left." Then Stoney shifted his gaze to me. "You take the elevator on the right to the penthouse. Suite 1201. And *don't* stop on any other floor or talk to any of the tenants. Got it?"

"Sure, mister, no problem."

Now I knew where all those young women went, and so did Jack.

As we both hoped, once we were through the door, the gatekeeper forgot we existed. Jack feinted left, dodged right, and followed me into the elevator. The doors closed and we were alone.

"Jack," I whispered as he pulled off his cap, "did you just say the regular sandwich guy has an STD—"

"A what?"

"Isn't the grippe a venereal disease?"

"No, it's influenza." He made a face. "Focus on the job, will ya? Think you can pull this off and get inside?"

"I'll do my best. And given what happened to Ruby, I'm glad you're going in with me."

With a ding, the elevator arrived on the top floor. The doors opened, and we stepped out. The entire floor was occupied by only three apartments. Twelve-oh-one had a sturdy oak door. I read the name above the doorbell.

ROLAND PRINCE

I stopped Jack before he touched the button.

"I know that name! There's a painting by Roland Prince among the artwork that Walt lent to our shop. It's a picture of a cowboy fighting a dinosaur. This man is a top-notch pulp artist—he's painted over five hundred covers!"

"You don't say," Jack replied with a raised eyebrow.

He pressed the bell, and the door was almost instantly yanked open by a slender bald man wearing a vest and no jacket. The sleeves of his wrinkled white shirt were rolled up, and he clutched a phone with an ink-stained hand. In the middle of a conversation, he motioned us in with a wave.

I expected a luxury apartment, perhaps with a whole suite of rooms. But what I saw more resembled an artist's assembly line.

The living and dining areas were occupied by rows of easels with artists (male and female, young and old) working hard at their craft. Some used live models, others worked from photographs, and all of their efforts were in various stages of completion, from rough sketch to final touches.

Bare bay windows let in strong sunlight, and I noticed naked bulbs strung up overhead by their own wires—presumably to keep the artists working late into the night.

Jack whistled. "What do you think?"

"Looks like Prince has turned his apartment into a pulp factory."

"Factory," Jack repeated, thinking over my term. "No smokestacks. But, yeah, I get your drift." He put his cap back on his head. "And what about those dames being brought here from the Pluto? What do you make of that, trainee?"

"It's clear enough. They're being hired to work as artists' models. And that's obviously what Ruby was doing here with Nathan Brock."

"And there's your lesson again," Jack said. "No matter the story you're told, check the facts."

While we gawked, the little bald man barked into the phone.

"What do you mean Dolly can't make it? The cover for next month's *Cowgirl Belle on the Range* is due on Tuesday. Dolly's been the face of Belle since the first issue!"

He listened a little and replied. "Okeydoke, if Dolly needs more money, we'll squash the deal and use the photos we took of her from now on."

He slammed the phone down so hard the bell inside dinged. Then he turned away from a cluttered table to give us a stare.

"What can I do you for?"

Jack was about to announce a delivery, but I had a better idea.

"I'm here to see Gwen," I said. "This is my big brother. He's on his break and came along to make sure this job is on the up and up."

"Sure, I get it," the man replied with a benign smile. "A looker like you can't be too careful. But don't worry your pretty red head. We're straight as an arrow around here."

The bald man pointed. "Gwen's at the fourth easel on the right."

He shifted his gaze to Jack. "Don't stick around long, *brother*. The boss doesn't like strangers—or boyfriends pretending to be family. Got it?"

Gwen was the woman Spanos had described: fiftyish, gray upswept hair, classy manners, and plain clothes. We found her propped on a stool, adding the finishing touches to a pen-and-ink drawing depicting a female pirate swinging her sword at a sea monster.

She smiled when she saw us and followed my gaze to her picture.

"Yes, I know. The outlines are absurdly thick, but that's the only way they'll show on cheap pulp paper." She extended her hand. "I'm Gwen Thomas, and you are?"

"I'm Penny and this is Jack."

She closed the inkwell and tucked her pen behind her ear. Then she folded her arms and studied us with an appraising eye.

"So, what does Roland want from me today? Let me guess. I'm to paint a sultry housewife seducing a delivery guy cover for *True Scandals*."

Jack stepped up. "Mrs. Thomas—"

"Miss."

"We're not here to pose. My name is Shepard. I'm a detective investigating the death of one of your models. A girl named Ruby Tyler."

Unruffled, Gwen never lost her smile. Looking Jack up and down, she made a crack about Sherlock Holmes never pretending to peddle pickles.

Jack arched an eyebrow. "Got me in here, didn't it? Now tell me what you know about Ruby."

"Let's see . . . dazzling smile, cerulean eyes, skin tone like ripe peaches and virgin cream. I knew the girl, but not well. Roland Prince might be able to help you. Ruby Tyler was very pretty, so he was probably *better acquainted* than I."

"And this is his studio?" Jack assumed.

"That's what Roland calls it. I see this place a bit differently."

"How?"

"It's a sweatshop, darling—one with very skilled workers who are getting unskilled wages and no credit." Gwen sighed wistfully. "It's not like my glory days, but it's a paycheck, and at least I can practice my craft."

"I recognize this business model," I said. "Does Mr. Prince claim credit for all this work?"

"Of course he does. And if you question that, he'll be sure to school you: 'You don't see my signature on your check until my name is on your painting.'"

"Do you know Nathan Brock?" Jack asked.

"Sure, he's Roland's golden boy."

I wasn't surprised. "Is that because Brock's paintings are so much better than all the others?"

Gwen snorted. "Are you kidding? Honestly, I don't think Roland could tell the difference between a decent piece of art and one that's stinko. All he cares about these days is cabbage, and Nathan Brock is golden because he saved Roland a bundle by telling him about the Pluto. There are always unique faces and pretty girls at the diner with stars in their eyes, reading the trades for Theater District auditions. We grab them for modeling work, they're paid in cash under the table, and Roland gets them for a song. No more professional modeling prices or agency fees."

Gwen shrugged. "See what I mean when I say sweatshop?"

"Where can I find Mr. Prince?" Jack asked.

"That's an easy one, Sherlock. End of that hall behind the big door marked PRIVATE. But right now, that door is *closed* . . ."

She let the rest of the sentence fade, but you didn't have to be a detective to understand her meaning.

"Don't worry," Jack said. "I won't disturb Mr. Prince . . . much."

CHAPTER 41

Prince of the Pulps

He sniffed invisible winds of art and commerce.

—William Gibson, *Count Zero*

AS JACK AND I approached the door to Roland Prince's office, we heard a man's husky voice and a woman's girlish giggles.

I glanced at Jack. "Now we know why Mr. Prince doesn't want to be disturbed. Should we wait?"

Jack lifted his fist and knocked, hard. "Delivery!" he bellowed. "Special delivery for Roland Prince."

A hush fell over the couple inside. A moment later the door opened, and a blushing brunette with Betty Boop eyes pushed past us. Straightening her dress, she retreated down the hall.

A jowly middle-aged man with black oily hair and a tiny mustache appeared in the doorway. He was jacketless, his tie was askew, and though his shirt was crisp and white, one of the flaps was untucked, and the cuff on his left sleeve hung loose, covering a meaty hand.

"What's the meaning of this interruption?" he growled.

"I brought lunch, Mr. Prince." Jack put the flat of his hand on the man's chest and pushed him backward. "You like ham on rye, right? I even splurged an extra two cents for a pickle."

I followed the pair into a nicely appointed sitting room with several overstuffed chairs and a couch that seemed to have gotten a lot of use. Unlike the factory on the other side of the door, the windows in here had curtains on them, and they were shut tight.

In the corner an easel was set up beside a standing full-length mirror. The portrait displayed was only half-completed and appeared to be a prop, the canvas neglected so long it collected dust.

Meanwhile, Jack kept the hand pressure on until Roland Prince dropped into a chair.

"The name's Shepard." Jack flashed his PI license. "I'm investigating the murder of Ruby Tyler, one of your models."

Prince swiped his shiny hair.

"My studio provides color and black-and-white illustrations for twenty-five magazines a month. I employ dozens of models and artists. I can't be expected to know their names."

As Jack began describing Ruby's physical characteristics, Roland Prince rose and began putting himself together. In the middle of tucking his shirt, he leered at me.

"Pardon my appearance . . . I didn't catch your name."

"Because I didn't offer it," I replied.

"Hey, you're talking to me right now, not my secretary," Jack warned. "So don't jump the rails. I asked about *Ruby Tyler.*"

"And I told you I never heard of her."

As Prince fiddled with his loose shirtsleeve, I noticed the cheap cuff link he used didn't match the much nicer one in place—it was gold, with the initials RP inlaid in black onyx.

"You're missing a cuff link, Mr. Prince," I told him.

"I fear it's at the bottom of one of the paint pots around here."

"More likely down your friend's dress," Jack cracked.

"I don't care for your insolent tone, Mr. Shepard, or your interference."

"And I don't like the way you do business."

Prince's smile was smug. "What do you know about my business? You're nothing more than an ambulance-chasing, divorce-sniffing bloodhound for hire."

"I'll tell you what I know. You find poor slobs with plenty of talent and no cabbage. You buy them on the cheap, passing their work off as your own. I know you take advantage of poor girls struggling to survive and pay them pennies on the dollar so your bankroll can get fatter."

"Funny, I never hear complaints." He studied his fingernails. "And if I do, they know where the door is." He looked up. "So do you. I suggest you go back through it before I call the authorities and report you as a trespasser."

Jack folded his arms. "You're not going to do that."

"And why not?"

"Because this little factory of yours isn't something you want the 'authorities' to know about—or the *respectable* tenants in this building."

Roland Prince approached the half-finished portrait, but only to check his reflection in the mirror beside it. When he spoke again, Mr. Prince dialed back his outrage.

"What do you want, gumshoe, a payoff?"

"I want you to stop making excuses and answer our questions."

"Fine, if it will get you out of here faster. What do you want to know?"

Jack glanced at me. The trainee was on. I cleared my throat. "What can you tell us about Nathan Brock?"

"Brock?" The man tapped his chin, appearing to puzzle over the name. "Oh yes, that skinny blond kid with the camera. Weird boy. I've seen him in the studio. I think he's one of the artists."

"And?" I asked.

"Employment here is temporary. People work for me as long as they need to and are free to leave at any time. Under that sort of arrangement, you can't expect me to know a particular artist or the name of one of Hugo's girls, now, can you?"

Jack's eyes narrowed. "No. Guess not."

I can't believe it, I thought. *Jack missed Prince's slip of the tongue.*

"Mr. Prince, how do you know about—"

"That's enough, Penny," Jack said, abruptly cutting me off. "We've wasted enough of this man's time. Let's breeze."

Before I could protest, he hooked my arm and dragged me out the door. Jack didn't let me speak again until we were outside and down the block, where a traffic jam made the cars, trucks, and buses on Park look as if they actually were parked.

"Roland is lying about everything!" I cried, voice raised over the honking traffic. "He wouldn't admit he knew Brock. Yet Gwen said he was Roland's 'golden boy.' And I can't believe you missed that sleazeball's slip of the tongue about Ruby being one of Hugo's girls!"

"You think I *missed* it? Penny, I cut you off to keep you from making the mistake of tipping him off!" The honking cars wouldn't let up. In frustration, Jack took my hand. "Let's get out of here."

Pulling me along, he turned the corner and headed down a quieter side street. Jack's expression was grim when he faced me again.

"Look, you have to understand. People have all sorts of reasons for lying to cops and investigators. Knowing Ruby isn't a crime. And neither is lying about it. The question is, *why* was Prince lying?"

"I don't know. I guess we'll have to find out. But at least we got something out of this trip. After seeing what's really going on upstairs at the Forrestal, we can deliver the good news to Shirley Powell that her fiancé wasn't stepping out on her. He was just trying to earn a little extra money for their future."

Jack doused my plan with ice water. "We can't tell Miss Powell anything because we haven't *proved* anything. And we certainly haven't cleared her fiancé of murder. No, honey. This case is far from over—"

Just then, the rumble of a subway train rose from the grate beneath us, drowning out the rest of his words.

"So what's next?" I asked.

The PI put a hand to his ear and shook his head. I asked again, louder this time, but the train's steel wheels were mangling my words into gibberish.

The gumshoe grabbed my hand again. "Come on!"

We turned another corner, but the subway noise never let up. Suddenly a shaft of steam shot up from a manhole. When he moved to dodge it, our connection broke, and his hand slipped away.

"Jack?" I called. "Jack!"

I looked for him, but he was gone. The traffic vanished and the buildings, too. Then the full-color world of Jack's memories faded, until all that was left were wisps of steam and the haunting rumble of a faraway train.

CHAPTER 42

Wake-Up Call

Never get out of bed before noon.

—Charles Bukowski

THE HAUNTING RUMBLE continued into darkness like an endless train chugging through an infinite tunnel. It rumbled and rattled until it transformed into something else—a buzzing, but not like a bee. More like a clattering buzz.

I opened my eyes to the sound of my smartphone vibrating itself to the edge of my night table.

Shoot! Rolling onto my stomach, I reached out and grabbed the thing before it went off the cliff.

"Hello?"

"Pen! Thank God you picked up."

Barely awake, I yawned as my mind scrambled to place the voice. "Fiona? Is that you?"

"I'm sorry to bother you so early, but it's about Barney . . ."

Barney? I thought, still fuzzy, until I realized she was talking about her husband, Barney Finch.

Longtime friends of our family, the Finches were beloved in the town of Quindicott and scrupulous caretakers of the late Harriet McClure's magnificent Queen Anne Victorian, which they ran as a bed-and-breakfast.

Fiona herself was a slight, fastidious woman in her fifties. From the day she'd taken the Finch name, she'd begun collecting a vast assortment of pins and brooches in the shape of feathered friends. She herself had sparrow-brown hair, which she often coiffed as high as a rooster's crown. Why she was calling me about her husband on a weekday morning (at 6:45 A.M.!) I had no idea, but it couldn't be good.

Sitting up quickly, I was painfully reminded of the bumps and bruises I'd gotten the night before.

"Is Barney okay?"

"I don't know! He's been gone all night. I called his phone, but all I got was voice mail. Have you seen him?"

I hadn't seen the man, not lately. But I had seen his *name*, scribbled in Clifford Conway's appointment book:

Barney Finch, 7:30 P.M.

Closing my eyes, I took a breath and asked the question I was dreading—

"Fiona, did Barney have a business meeting last night?"

"No! Last night was Barney's bowling night. He never misses it. He and his friends get together every week at Millstone Bowl-a-Rama. He usually gets back late, but he's never stayed out all night—not after bowling, anyway."

"Have you tried contacting any of his other bowling pals?"

"I sent messages but haven't heard back."

"How about Linda at the bakery—"

"Of course!" Fiona cried. "Barney and his friends might be there right now, stuffing themselves with doughnuts."

Twenty minutes later I joined Sadie and Spencer at the breakfast table and gently broke the news of Conway's death to them both.

After getting my son off to school, I gave my aunt the disturbing details—including my head making an unfortunate connection with a Comfy-Time doorjamb right before I found the man's battered corpse.

Sadie cringed, then worriedly fussed over my wounded noggin. As she did, I could sense her relief. Neither of us said it out loud, but we were thinking the same thing. With Conway dead, the threat of his lawsuit against us was gone, too.

I SPENT THE rest of the morning in the privacy of our shop's stockroom, preparing for our upcoming book launch with the Palantines. Paging through *By Its Cover*, I pulled out passages to create information cards for each of the cover art paintings on display. These cards would replace Walt's price tags.

Since "Nathan Brock" had no listing in their book, I selected some general comments about the days of pulp publishing to caption his brilliant rendering of Ruby Tyler as victim and Kosmo Spanos as killer.

When I got to the listing on Roland Prince, I shuddered.

With new eyes, I saw the similarities between Nathan Brock's signed work and the so-called Roland Prince painting of the cowboy shooting a T. rex. My hand passed over the small B in a circle, placed in the lower right of the painting, which Prince had nearly obliterated with his bold signature.

I now knew what that little B stood for. It stood for Brock, and so much more . . .

That little B was Nathan's own secret message to the future, not unlike Da Vinci's or Caravaggio's or the messages of countless other artists who left something behind, a spirit they hoped would haunt their canvas long after they were gone, a bridge from one time to another that said—

"I was here. I existed. I did this."

I couldn't prove that, of course. Some proofs and truths were destined to be lost in time. Like what really happened to Ruby Tyler and Nathan Brock.

As images from my dream rushed back to me, so did my feelings of anger and frustration. Jack Shepard must have been frustrated, too, all those years ago, trying to get answers out of that smug man.

Roland Prince had pretended he knew nothing about Nathan or Ruby when he obviously did.

What did you do next? I asked the ghost. *Were you able to save Nathan? And find Ruby's killer?*

I waited for an answer, but none came.

The ghost had vanished. Jack did that sometimes, especially after a powerful dream. It seemed to sap his energy. It certainly drained me of mine.

Shaking myself out of my reverie, I went back to work.

CHAPTER 43

Feathered Friends

Friendship is the hardest thing in the world to explain.

—Muhammad Ali

OVER THE NEXT few hours, I finished printing out the cards, unjammed the printer twice, and had begun fulfilling online orders when Sadie knocked on the stockroom door.

"Pen, I thought you should know. Barney and Fiona Finch are in the event space. They came to see Harriet's painting."

"So the Prodigal Innkeeper finally returned from bowling night?"

"Apparently, Barney showed up after Fiona called you. He claimed he drank too much and slept it off in his car—which shocked the heck out of me. That doesn't sound like the Barney I know."

"It's not the Barney I know, either."

"Well, they're both here now."

"Don't you find that odd, too?" I said. "You'd think Barney would be more interested in nursing his hangover than rushing over here to see a work of art."

"I think the message Seymour left Fiona got them all riled up."

"Message? What message?"

Sadie sighed. "Fiona called Seymour this morning looking for Barney. When he called back with no news, he took the opportunity to gloat about discovering the new Harriet McClure."

I threw up my hands. "That portrait really is cursed. It's going to sour relations between Seymour and Fiona worse than they already are."

"Those two have been goading each other for as long as I can remember. A silly old picture isn't going to change a thing."

Your auntie's on the money, honey.

Jack! You're back! The return of the spirit lifted my own. With all the turmoil going on, the ghost's cool presence felt reassuring. And his next observation was so blunt I had to bite my lip to keep from laughing.

That cluck Seymour and Fiona Finch are birds of a feather. Two know-it-all eggheads in one small-town nest is one too many.

Nobody's perfect, I told the ghost. *And you should be glad Barney is here. I finally have a chance to ask him about his connection to Clifford Conway.*

Jack agreed and breezed along with me as I followed Sadie to the event space. On the way, Sadie told me about another visitor.

Leo Rollins, our local electrician, had stopped by earlier to view the Harriet painting. Like Seymour, Leo was also taken with the young woman's arresting image.

"She deserves better lighting," he announced.

Since Leo was willing to pay for the changes himself, Sadie agreed, and he worked his electrician's magic, adding a whole new bank of LEDs to the event space. The results were awe inspiring. The new lighting of Harriet's portrait created an even more powerful impact, which appeared to mesmerize Fiona and Barney.

The unforgiving glare also emphasized a stain on the lapel of Fiona's autumn gold pantsuit, though she gamely attempted to mask it with a pretty pin in the shape of a nightingale. I assumed she was coming straight from lunch service at Chez Finch, the French restaurant she and Barney had built adjacent to their inn. It was Fiona's pride and joy. For the last few years, she'd focused her exacting efforts on designing, building, and running it. But the usual fussy energy she exhibited in all her ambitious endeavors was subdued as she gazed at Harriet's portrait.

"Seymour has good reason to gloat," Fiona conceded. "I've never seen a portrait of Harriet when she was young. She seems so . . ."

"Unhappy?" Aunt Sadie prompted.

"Lovely." Fiona's features curled in bafflement. "I see our inn is beautifully rendered in the background, but I don't understand all the numbers and letters, or the musical notes. And those brash colors. They're so . . . strange."

I nodded. "Like an illustration in a children's book."

Barney Finch's weathered face twisted into an angry scowl. "This is *not* Harriet's work. It's a forgery, some art student's idea of a joke!"

Tall as a beanpole and nearly as thin, with squared shoulders that would do a cadet proud, Barney had more energy than most men pushing seventy. Right now, it was being expended in an ugly direction.

"This so-called Harriet McClure is an insult!" he declared, his complexion growing redder than his flannel shirt. "You'd have to be a fool to think it's the real thing!"

A taciturn New Englander by nature, Barney was exhibiting more emotion than I'd ever seen from the man.

Jack noticed, too.

The old-timer's blowing more smoke than a '22 Stanley Steamer chugging up a steep incline.

"But, Barney," his wife countered, "you can *see* the top of Harriet's signature peeking up from the frame."

"If you can forge a picture you can forge a signature." Barney faced me. "You tell Seymour he got hornswoggled. He should have the crook who sold that piece of junk to him arrested for fraud."

That would be a challenge, the ghost observed.

Fiona laid a calming hand on her husband's shoulder. He shook it off. "I don't have time for this nonsense, Fiona. There are chores to be done, and I've already lost the morning. Remember that busted light fixture in the hallway?"

His wife nodded timidly.

"I'm heading over to Napp Hardware to get a replacement."

Stop him! Jack cried in my head. *You can't let that cranky old coot get away. Not before you ask him why he met with Conway.*

"Barney, wait!" I shouted.

But the man kept going, stomping right past Bonnie Franzetti at the register and out our front door.

Go after him! Jack urged.

No, I told him, putting my foot down. Given the man's mood, I wasn't willing to risk another public argument in front of our store. And I doubted very much I'd get straight answers out of him, anyway. *It would just be another Roland Prince stone wall, with me bashing my already-throbbing head against it.*

Begrudgingly Jack agreed.

I'll let Eddie deal with him, I told the ghost. *Maybe Barney will show a little more patience when he's talking to the deputy chief of police.*

CHAPTER 44

The Trouble with Money

I've got all the money I'll ever need, if I die by four o'clock.

—Henny Youngman

AS SOON AS Barney was gone, Fiona profusely apologized for her husband's surliness. "He's under a lot of stress. On top of that, I doubt he got much sleep, cavorting with his pals like some teenager. That's the second night this week he was out all night—"

Sadie stopped her. "The second night?"

"Barney was out Monday night, too. He was on the road when the storm hit, and he had to pull over and ride it out. He didn't get back from Upton until Tuesday morning."

That got my attention. Upton and Blackstone Falls were a stone's throw apart. "Did you say Barney was on Route 126 Monday night?"

Fiona nodded. "I couldn't reach him. I was worried sick. When he got home, he said he forgot to charge his phone."

"What was he doing in Upton?" I pressed.

"Trying to sell our sterling silver tea service."

My aunt was astonished. "Not the Revolutionary War–era set on display in your tearoom?"

"It's back now," Fiona replied. "The fellow in Upton changed his mind. I asked Barney what happened, but he said he was too tired to talk about it."

"Why would you sell such a beautiful heirloom?" Sadie said with concern. "Your great-grandmother brought it all the way from Scotland."

"Because . . . the truth is . . . we need the money." As she choked the word out, Fiona's lower lip began to tremble. Then tears flooded her eyes.

"Goodness!" Sadie put an arm around the innkeeper's quaking shoulders. "Come, sit down. Let's get you some tea, and we'll have a talk."

Fiona protested, but Sadie was adamant. While I opened folding chairs and settled Fiona in one, Sadie returned with a tray holding a box of tissues, a plate of shortbread, and three cups of Earl Grey.

"It's all my fault," Fiona began. "When we first got married, turning our home into a bed-and-breakfast was my idea. That should have been enough to satisfy me. But these last few years, I stretched our finances when we bought the Lighthouse and remodeled it into a luxury beach bungalow. Then I pushed things too far when I opened Chez Finch. Now the restaurant is in trouble, and I haven't had a guest in the Lighthouse since the end of July."

"How was the lunch crowd today?" Sadie asked.

Fiona huffed. "We stopped serving weekday lunch a month ago. No one noticed because no one was coming anymore. The Sunday brunch is still popular, thanks to the after-church crowd. But it's not enough . . ."

Fiona noted the direction of my stare and self-consciously shifted the pin.

"I had it dry-cleaned but—what can I say? I'm hardly a four-star hostess these days, so no bother. Besides, we decided to close the restaurant tonight due to a lack of reservations."

"It's that bad?" Sadie whispered.

"Dinner service is still good on the weekends, but week-nights have been dismal, and the contract with our chef pays him whether we have a full house or not. We've weathered lean times before, but these days, I lie awake at night and dream about finding buried treasure." She sighed. "Anything to get Finch Inn out of its financial situation."

"Wait a minute," I interrupted. "Two weeks ago Brainert had to host an out-of-town lecturer at his home because your inn had no vacancies."

"It was a fluke." Fiona blew into a ball of tissue. "A bunch of thrill seekers checked in last minute because that couple from Providence who saw Harriet's ghost made the regional news."

She sniffed. "Even that didn't lift our bottom line. Today's young people don't spend money! They always ask about Groupon discounts. They're not interested in fine dining or Chez Finch."

Fiona sipped her tea. "We're considering closing the restaurant, but even that's not our biggest problem."

"My goodness, Fiona, what could be worse?"

Fiona's face was stony. "The town council just imposed a new tax that is going to ruin us."

"What?!" Sadie blanched.

"Late last week, they passed the law in the dead of night. Anyone who owns *developed* land within a mile of the Atlantic coastline has to pay a special fee for beach maintenance."

Death and taxes, Jack cracked. *They're the only sure things in this world—and I should know.*

Shush, Jack.

"There are five miles of shoreline within the city limits," Fiona said, "but only a half mile has been *developed*. That half mile just happens to include our inn, lighthouse, and restaurant."

That stinks like Bowery fish on a summer afternoon, Jack groused. *It's the same sad story I've heard since the stock market crashed in '29. And guess what, doll? It always ends the same. It's a good thing there are no tall buildings in this town. Otherwise Barney and his wife would end up as a pair of sidewalk pancakes—*

"Jack!" I was so shocked by the ghost's cynicism that I'd spoken out loud.

Fiona eyed me strangely. "You said something, Pen?"

"Er . . . yes . . . I was about to ask how much they *jacked* up your taxes."

"It *doubles*, and just when our business is suffering."

It's a land grab, sweetheart. Jack's voice had an angry edge. *Dollars to doughnuts somebody with plenty of dough bought that town council. That's why the tax was passed in the dead of night. And I'll bet whoever corrupted those Alvins is angling for the Finches' nest, because the best way to get the jump on prey is to wait until your mark is on the nut—*

The nut?

Dead broke, Jack replied. *Then you hit them with more debt until the Finches have to fly away—*

And whoever wants the property grabs it at a distressed price—

And then bribes the town council again to repeal the onerous tax—

And suddenly someone, who did nothing to build it, gets to own the most enviable dwelling and business in all of Quindicott.

Nobody ever said you weren't smart, baby.

And the losers are the poor Finches.

Finches? More like plucked chickens. Or dead ducks.

I felt a rush of shame. This had to be fixed for the economic health of the town and for the sake of our friends.

Fortunately the shopkeepers along Cranberry Street had organized the Quindicott Business Owners Association in an effort to counter the often shortsighted decisions of our local politicians. We had our monthly meeting coming up within days, and I knew I could count on them to do something.

Do *what* exactly? I didn't know, but despite the fact that our association spent more time arguing than anything else—hence the nickname, "the Quibblers"—I knew we'd find a solution.

"There must be a way to fight this," I told Fiona. "A higher authority to petition for repeal. Or a way to expose any corrupt motives behind it."

"Oh, Pen, those are fine thoughts. But we don't have the first idea how to do those things—or the money for an attorney to try." Just then, Fiona's smartphone chirped. "It's Barney. I have to go. He's waiting for me in the car." Fiona rose and smoothed her pantsuit. "I must look a fright. That won't do for a dinner service . . . What am I saying? I forgot, we'll be closed tonight."

She faced us. "Thank you for letting us view the portrait. I hope Seymour isn't counting on selling it to us—"

"He's not." I leaned close. "Just between the three of us, I think that portrait is the love of Seymour's life."

Sadie laughed, but Fiona offered only a forced smile.

"And please forgive Barney for being so rude," she added. "At his age he should be enjoying retirement, not fretting over our financial future. I ruined everything—"

"Fiona, you can't blame yourself! You have more gumption and work harder than anyone I know."

"And what good did it do us? I was the one who convinced Barney to expand the inn into the Lighthouse and open Chez Finch. Now we're going to lose it all, and he's taking it so hard."

Tears again flooded Fiona's eyes. "He's lost heart. And we all know what happens to men his age when they lose heart."

Fiona suddenly straightened up and dabbed away her tears.

"You know what? I'm fine with selling the Lighthouse and closing the restaurant and even losing our beloved home. If that's our fate, then so be it. But I just can't lose my Barney, and I'm terrified this financial pressure will be the death of him."

CHAPTER 45

Bye-Bye, Alibi

A man always has two reasons for what he does—a
good one, and the real one.

—J.P. Morgan

FIONA WAS HARDLY out the door before we got another
visitor.

"Heyyyy-ooooo," Vinny Nardini, our Dependable Delivery man cried as he rolled in an empty dolly. "So, you've got
a pickup for me, young lady?" he asked Sadie, grinning
through a beard the color of tree bark.

"Right here, Vinny." Sadie gestured to a stack of
boxed-up returns beside the door.

While Vinny stacked the boxes on his dolly, Sadie talked
(okay, *gossiped*) with him about Barney Finch. "I understand he's in an awful bind, but no matter the situation, Barney shouldn't have gone on a bender at the Bowl-a-Rama.
Fiona was worried sick."

Vinny shook his head. "Poor guy. I feel bad for him. Hey,
when times were tough for me, I used to drink myself silly
there, too. Still, I was sorry to see the place go under."

"What place?" I asked in confusion. "What went under?"

"The Bowl-a-Rama in Millstone," Vinny said and

scratched his beard over our baffled expressions. "You guys didn't know? That place went out of business a month ago. They're closed for good."

I pressed him. "Are you *sure*, Vinny?"

"Oh yeah, Pen. Our league is itching to start bowling again. Good thing a Lazy Lanes is opening nearby soon. There isn't a bowling alley within an hour's drive of Quindicott, and we were nearly ready to throw in our hand towels."

My aunt and I exchanged glances. I held my tongue until Sadie signed the manifest and Vinny wheeled the boxes away. Then I let loose—

"Barney lied!"

Sadie pulled the glasses off her face and let them dangle on their chain. "He's in a bad situation, Pen—"

"There's more to it than that!"

I finally told Sadie what I knew about seeing Barney's name scribbled in Clifford Conway's appointment book. "And now Barney's outright lying to his own wife. We both know he wasn't bowling last night!"

"This isn't the Barney Finch I know." Sadie shook her head. "But what can we do? And what do we really know? Should we tell the police?"

"I already told Eddie Franzetti about seeing his name in the appointment book . . ."

As Sadie digested that disturbing news, I thought over what Jack told me in last night's dream, about people having all sorts of reasons for lying to cops and investigators. The question was: What would Barney say in his statement to the police?

"Pen, this is bad." Sadie wrung her hands. "If Barney lies to Eddie with the same alibi he gave his wife—"

"I know. It's only a matter of time before he's found out."

"Do you really think Barney murdered Clifford Conway? And slammed your head into a doorjamb on the way out?"

"If you asked me yesterday, I'd say absolutely not. But I've never seen our calm, easygoing friend acting as agitated as he did today, looking at Harriet's portrait."

"So you *do* think Barney is a murderer?"

"I don't know what to think. Maybe Barney didn't kill Conway. But what if he knows who did? What if he was involved in some way?"

"How in the world are we going to find out?"

"I'm not sure. But our friend is obviously in trouble. We have to help him. We need to find a way."

My aunt and I fell silent, trying to come up with a solution. At last, Sadie announced—

"I've got it! According to the Quindicott Business Owners Association charter, any three members can call an emergency meeting."

"So?"

"So why don't you, Bud Napp, and I call the meeting? We'll use the Finches' tax problem as an excuse, but our real goal will be to get to the bottom of whatever's going on with Barney."

I blinked. "Like an intervention?"

"Whatever you want to call it, we have to do something."

"Works for me."

"I'll call Bud at the hardware store right now." Sadie glanced at her watch. "It's still early. Maybe he can schedule the meeting for tonight."

As Sadie went off to call her beau, I struggled to keep an open mind. I tried to continue believing that my old friend and a pillar of Quindicott's business community could not be involved, that Barney Finch was incapable of murder, that he had no motive to kill anyone.

But there was one more thing I'd learned today that I hadn't told my aunt—

According to Fiona Finch, her husband was near Blackstone Falls on Monday evening, which meant Barney could very well have been the mysterious Harriet McClure buyer who'd pounded on Walt Waverly's door.

I didn't want to face it, but if I was honest with myself, then rationally, logically, and circumstantially, Fiona's harried husband might just be a prime suspect in not one but *two* homicides.

CHAPTER 46

Intervention

Those who in quarrels interpose, must often wipe a bloody nose.

—John Gay

"I CALL THIS emergency meeting of the Quindicott Business Owners Association to order!"

Bud took off his Napp Hardware cap and slammed his ball peen hammer. The folding table groaned and nearly collapsed from the blow.

The man's New England accent was particularly thick tonight, a sure indication of the seriousness of the matter before us.

As secretary, Fiona Finch called roll. It didn't take long because only a third of our members were able to attend the last-minute Thursday night meeting—along with one invisible participant.

So you think this sorry bunch of gum-flapping, penny-pinching shopkeepers are going to put the finger on old Barney?

They're here to help, Jack. So lighten up. Anyway, it's really up to me.

You're going to shine a light on this mess? You're better off using a dim bulb than this bunch of bumpkins.

I have a plan.

So did Wrong Way Corrigan.

I try to think of tonight's meeting as an episode of Perry Mason—

Mason? What good is a bricklayer going to do you, doll?

Perry Mason is a fictional lawyer, Jack, and it was Spencer who gave me the idea.

Taking advice from a grade school attorney? That should pay off.

I detect your *sarcasm, but I'm on a mission to get to the bottom of Barney's secrets, and I plan to carry out this intervention like a criminal trial. I'll be playing Perry Mason, with Bud Napp as the judge, Barney Finch as the defendant, and everyone else as the jury.*

A kangaroo court if you ask me.

Pipe down, Jack, the proceedings are starting.

"We're going to dispense with formalities, as this is an emergency meeting," Bud began. "But I do want to thank Cooper Family Bakery and Buy the Book for supplying tonight's refreshments and meeting room."

Bud was being polite as they weren't much.

Though I managed to supply coffee and Linda Cooper-Logan brought what was left over in her pastry case, I didn't have time to hang the association banner behind the presiding table. Instead, the portrait of Harriet McClure hovered above Bud's head like a spectral magistrate.

"I'm sorry to disrupt your businesses," Bud continued, "but this is a time-sensitive situation—"

"Hell, you're not disrupting anything," Leo Rollins of Rollins Electronics returned. "I had two contracts canceled this week, so it's here or Donovan's for beer."

Colleen the hairdresser winked at the young veteran. "If you've got time on your hands, soldier boy, you can drop by my salon for a trim of that lumberjack beard."

There was laughter and whistles all around.

"Order, please," Bud insisted, bringing the Napp Hardware hammer down again. "We'll skip the minutes and continuing resolutions, too, so we can get right down to business."

Fiona, who'd taken a seat in the front row, cradled her husband's hand as Bud enlightened everyone about the onerous new shore tax. Gasps and groans filled the room. No one had a clue the legislation had been proposed, let alone passed. Then Bud leaned across the table and spoke directly to Fiona and Barney.

"I've consulted with a tax attorney friend, and the news is positive. There are a number of ways we can fight this. *Together!*"

Fiona sighed visibly. Barney, however, remained as taciturn as ever.

"But right now, we have other business," Bud declared, moving on. "It's on a personal level, but it also involves Barney and Fiona Finch."

As I rose and faced the couple, Barney's icy exterior cracked.

"What's going on here?"

"Barney, you were on the road to Blackstone Falls the other night, and you didn't return until morning. Would you mind confirming this? Trust me, it's important."

After shifting uncomfortably, Barney admitted he'd gone north on Monday. "I had business in Upton. I was selling something, but the man I met with decided not to buy. Then the storm hit, and I got stranded on the side of the road."

"Honey," Fiona said, squeezing his hand. "That man from Upton called the inn this afternoon. He asked why you never showed up to meet him. He said he's still interested in buying the tea set—"

"He . . . he must have changed his mind again—"

"But he told me you were *never* there!"

"You heard *wrong*, Fiona, that's all."

I jumped in. "The same thing happened last night, Barney. Your wife told us you were out all night. She was worried sick—"

"I was bowling in Millstone!"

Vinny Nardini timidly cleared his throat. "Sorry, Barn. Millstone Bowl-a-Rama closed last month. To make double sure, I drove past the place this afternoon. The building is boarded up, and there's a demolition order on the door. What's more, there are no bowling alleys operating within an hour's drive of Quindicott. Our league would have used one if there had been."

Barney yanked his hand free of his wife's grip and jumped to his feet. "Why do you people care? How does this concern any of you?"

He's cracking, doll, don't let up. Keep hammering!

"Tell us the truth!" I demanded. "Did you or did you not have a business meeting last night at the Comfy-Time Motel with a man named Conway?"

"Conway?" Barney stared in confusion a moment. "Clifford Conway?"

"That's right!"

Barney scratched his head. "There was no meeting. All we did was speak on the phone. Ask Fiona. I think it was seven, maybe seven thirty—"

Fiona nodded. "That's when Mr. Conway called. I answered the phone myself and handed it over to Barney."

"That's right," he said. "Mr. Conway was looking for a corporate-looking-type conference room to tape an infomercial. I told him the Finch Inn didn't have a space like that. I suggested he consider renting out our restaurant, but he said that wouldn't do and hung up. That was the end of it."

I was not convinced. While Fiona backed up his explanation, his answer didn't explain his lie about Monday night or the Bowl-o-Rama alibi, and I said so.

"I don't understand any of this," Barney continued. "What are you accusing me of, Pen?"

This time Seymour Tarnish spoke up. "Look, Barney, we're all here to help. Just tell the truth. Hey, it's not the end of the world if you've got some hot Betty White–type babe on the side. I'm sure Fiona would forgive you if you come clean now."

"Shut your yap, mailman!" Barney sputtered angrily as Fiona burst into tears.

Looking to the ceiling, Sadie wrapped her arm around the sobbing woman.

Leave it to the postman to wring twice more waterworks than necessary out of this train wreck of a trial.

Barney faced his wife. "Fiona, stop crying! You know that's crazy talk. Sure, I get a kick out of those *Golden Girl* reruns, but that's it!"

Fiona's sobs became a wail. Barney reached out to comfort her, but she pulled away. Barney's shoulders sagged, and his expression softened.

"All right," Barney rasped, barely above a whisper. "I'm done with pretending. I'll tell you what's really going on."

Here it comes, I told the ghost. *The confession. Just like on* Perry Mason.

He faced his wife. "I spent last night at the Gentleman's Oasis."

"The girlie bar!?" Fiona's wail turned into howls.

"It's not what you think! I was there *after* closing time—"

Fiona howled even louder.

"It was just Fred Mitchell and me. None of the girls! Fred was losing customers because his saloon is an all-cash business. He needed a scanner, the software, and the accounts to accept credit cards. I set it all up at our inn, so I already knew how to do it on the cheap—"

"Son of a—" Leo Rollins cried. "I was hired to do that job, but Fred canceled on me. Said he changed his mind—"

"I needed the money, Leo, so I agreed to set up accounts at both of Fred's girlie bars for one price—"

"You undercut me at Brews and Babes, too?"

Shamefaced, Barney nodded. "That's where I was the other night. I was supposed to start the job after I met with the man in Upton who wanted to buy Fiona's tea set. But I just couldn't do it. I couldn't bring myself to sell that heirloom set. It's the most precious thing Fiona owns. So I went straight to Brews and Babes. The job took longer than I expected. I didn't finish until morning."

Rollins (and his beard) bristled. "What about the Go-Go Lounge in Millstone? I lost that contract, too."

"I'm doing that job next week," Barney confessed.

Rollins jumped out of his seat so fast his folding chair collapsed.

"What the hell kind of business association lets one member steal the livelihood of another? I have a big house and I live all alone. Do you see me setting up an Airbnb to compete with you? Huh, Barney?"

"You can if you want to," Barney shot back, suddenly belligerent.

Leo was hopping mad himself. "If you weren't seventy, I'd punch you in the mouth."

Barney balled his fists. "You could *try*, sad sack! I may have a few more gray hairs than you, but I spent ten years in the Rhode Island National Guard!"

As the two men moved to face off, Seymour leaped up and planted his big body between them.

"Guys, guys, take it easy! If you really want to fight, we ought to sell tickets. Think of the poster: Leo 'Weird Beard' Rollins versus Barney 'The Birdman' Finch. Why, the receipts alone might pay Barney's tax bill!"

Despite Seymour's earnest attempt to lighten the tension, Leo charged the exit.

"I'm out of here, and you can all go *Quibble* yourselves!"

Boldly leaping up from his folding chair, Professor J. Brainert Parker appeared to believe he could succeed where Seymour failed. "Please, Mr. Rollins. Don't leave like this. I'm sure we can—"

The burly vet swept the spindly professor aside like he was a branch on a baby sapling. Brainert crashed into a folding chair and bounced off the hardwood floor. Rollins kept right on going.

Seymour rushed to Brainert's side faster than I did.

"Are you okay, Brainpan?" Seymour fretted, helping him up. "You spun like a plugged cowboy in a Clint Eastwood Western!"

"I'm fine, I'm fine," Brainert huffed as he dusted himself off.

That went well, Jack quipped.

I was about to answer when I realized something. Fiona had stopped crying, and Barney had stopped fighting. The innkeepers were far too busy hugging each other.

"You weren't cheating on me at all," Fiona cooed, wrapping her birdlike arms around her husband's skinny neck. "You were trying to save my restaurant and tea set!"

While she rained kisses on Barney's flushed face, I brought the gavel down on my ghost—

You know what, Jack? It did go well.

CHAPTER 47

The Prosecution Rests

I didn't grow up with light. I grew up in tenements.

—Martin Scorsese

THREE HOURS LATER, I was pulling blankets up to my chin and hiding my head in the pillow. "I feel like Hamilton Burger," I moaned.

And I'd love a Coney Island hot dog. But what does chow time have to do with anything?

"It's *Hamilton* Burger, Jack. He's the DA who always loses when he goes up against Perry—ah, never mind."

I was in no mood to spar with the ghost. Frankly, I wasn't fit to be around human or ghostly company. After tonight's Quibblers' meeting broke up, I was elated that I'd cleared Barney of suspicion and revealed the altruistic reasons behind the lies to his wife. But as I folded the chairs and cleared the refreshment table, that exhilaration faded because it dawned on me that I was right back where I'd started.

"Killer, two. Me, zero. I don't like the score, Jack."

Maybe we should play a different game.

"What do you have in mind?"

Another dame. Another time. Another case.

"Ruby Tyler and the Brock painting?" I sighed. "Normally I'd jump at the chance, but not tonight. I need to focus on the here and now. I have a lot riding on a very big launch party this weekend."

So think of it as a vacation, but without the baggage.

"No, I need to lie awake here and think things through—"

If you stare at a picture too long, you can't see what you're looking at.

"Maybe," I said on a yawn. "But I need to try."

And trying too hard leads to headaches. Why not take a couple of steps back with me? Look at the case from a different angle.

"Your old case is fascinating, Jack, but it has no bearing on mine."

It does, doll. Tricks of the trade are always useful. Believe me.

I didn't. But despite my best intentions to stay awake and focus on my present reality, my eyelids grew heavier, my thoughts drifting toward dreams of the past.

"I don't want to fall asleep, Jack. I object."

The ghost chuckled. *Objection overruled.*

IN THE BLINK of an eye (literally), I was back in Jack's time, sitting in the back seat of a Checker Cab. Opening my eyes, I realized my head was leaning on the detective's big shoulder.

He grinned. "Just in time, Penny. We're here."

Here was the home of Ruby Tyler, a weather-beaten brown brick tenement on the southern tip of Hell's Kitchen. Three rickety wooden steps led up to the paint-blistered front door.

Gaslighting the doorman wouldn't be a problem, as there wasn't one. Gaining entry was a snap, too. The locks on both the outer and inner lobby doors were broken.

Once inside, Jack scanned the bank of brass mailboxes.

"I found it. Apartment 414. And there's another name on the box, too."

"Audrey French," I read aloud. "A stage name?"

"Yeah. French by way of Canarsie, Brooklyn."

The halls were narrow and poorly lit, with empty milk bottles and old newspapers beside every door. From somewhere inside the building, we heard an infant crying. In another apartment, a man and woman yelled at each other in a foreign tongue.

We'd climbed the stairs to the fourth floor before we spied our first resident, an emaciated man who wore shabby clothes and shoes two sizes too large. Head twitchy, skinny shoulders slumped, he stared at the floor and muttered to himself. When he spotted us, he slunk off in the opposite direction.

Jack knocked on the flimsy wooden door of Apartment 414. Inside, the radio went mute. He knocked again, and I noticed a spear of light at the far end of the hall where an eye peered through a chained door. When the observer realized they were being observed, the door abruptly closed.

Meanwhile, a woman's muffled voice emanated from within.

"If you're the Fuller Brush Man, I ain't buying!"

"I'm a detective, Miss French."

The lock clicked, and a slim woman opened the door. Her ebony pageboy had not a hair out of place. As for her attire, she wore a long silk robe and obviously nothing else.

She gave Jack the eye.

"You're better-looking than the other flatfoots."

Then she spied me and frowned. "I hope you have better manners," she added, tying her robe tighter.

"You're Audrey French? Ruby Tyler's roommate?"

"Who are you?"

He flashed his license.

"A PI, huh? Who are you working for? It sure isn't Ruby's family, because she hasn't got any."

Jack brushed her question aside. "What do you know about Ruby's murder?"

She scanned the empty hallway, with an extra glance at the peeper's door.

"Come inside, I don't want the whole building to know my business."

The apartment was far less shabby than the building's exterior—but sad compared to the glamour that was the Albatross. "Miss French" led us to a living room with Japanese screens, lacquered blackwood chairs, and tables with brass fittings.

Our hostess stopped in the middle of the room and met Jack's stare. Then she pointed to the stained Persian rug under her bare feet.

"I found Ruby lying here when I got home that night. The coppers said she'd been knocked around and hit her head against that table there."

She pointed to a solid-looking end table with sharp corners.

"Ruby was still breathing when the ambulance took her away. But I got a call the next morning that Ruby wasn't expected to live more than a few hours."

"Who called?" Jack asked.

"Ruby's boss—"

"Hugo Box?"

"Yeah, that creep."

"Do you have any idea who might have done this?"

"Sure I do. And I fingered him to the cops, too. It was that skinny kid artist Ruby was modeling for. Nathan Brock."

"How do you know? Did you see them together?"

"He always walked her home after a modeling session. She posed for him that very afternoon. I figured he walked her home that day, too—"

"You may have figured wrong," I said.

She shot me a cold stare. "Look, toots, I'm never wrong. I even told the cops I was willing to testify that Brock killed her."

"Ruby didn't know other men?" Jack pressed. "She didn't have a boyfriend or a sugar daddy?"

"Lots of guys were after her at the Albatross, but she kept her life private from that bunch. Never told them where she lived. It would have ruined the fantasy, anyway. Nobody wants to think 'glamour girls' live in run-down tenements."

Jack asked a few more questions, but it was clear he'd hit a wall. So he slipped Miss French his card, and we left.

In the hallway it was Jack who spied the peeper this time. Again, when the peeper saw us looking, the door closed. Jack didn't let that stop him. He walked right up and knocked.

The door barely opened a crack, this time not even enough to strain the chain. From what little I could see, the peeper was an older woman, gray hair undone, a scowl on her weathered face.

"Who are you?" she demanded, voice like a scratched LP.

"A detective," Jack replied.

Her eye narrowed suspiciously. "You might have fooled that young girl, but not me. You're not a real copper."

"You're right," Jack said brightly. "Because no real copper would hand you a five-spot."

Jack sparkled with charm as he waved the bill.

I wasn't surprised. As Jack had once told me, *The laws of physics are upside down in the PI game. A piece of flimsy green paper opens doors faster than the biggest crowbar in your toolbox.*

Sure enough, the peeper's eye widened at the sight of Jack's offer. Then it narrowed again. "What do I gotta do for it?"

"Just tell us what you saw and heard the night the ambulance took Ruby Tyler away, because I'm willing to bet you heard and saw plenty."

Jack shook the bill again. "If I like your story, there's more cabbage where this came from."

The door opened wider. I caught a whiff of cigarettes and whiskey. A clawlike hand reached out and snatched the wrinkled bill.

For a moment I thought the woman was going to slam the

door, but the enticement of another payoff was too much to resist.

"I *did* see and hear plenty," she said, "but I ain't gettin' involved. You understand? If you tell the cops I told you this stuff, I'll tell 'em you're a liar."

CHAPTER 48

See Evil, Speak Evil, Hear Evil

There are no innocent bystanders . . . what are they
doing there in the first place?

—William S. Burroughs, *Exterminator!*

"I DIDN'T SEE Ruby and the guy arrive, so I don't know
when they got to Ruby's place. But around eight o'clock, I
heard them arguing, real loud."

Jack leaned toward the cracked door. "Who's the guy?"

"Some older man in a fancy suit who doesn't look like he
belongs in this neighborhood."

"What did you hear?"

"I couldn't make out the words, but pretty soon, that Ruby
girl was screaming 'no, no' over and over again."

"And what was the man saying?"

"He just laughed, like he was playing a game. Then,
pretty soon he wasn't laughing no more. But Ruby kept on
saying 'no, no.'"

"What did you do?"

"What could I do? I couldn't call the coppers. The phone
is four floors down, and I got rheumatism. Besides, there's
always some chump using it."

"Okay, you're pure as the driven snow," Jack said, a disgusted scowl on his face. "Then what happened?"

The woman's eyes widened. "After a minute or two, I hear this crash, and after that, things got real quiet. That's when I opened my door."

"What did you see?"

"Nothing at first. Maybe a whole minute goes by before a man comes out. That's the older man in the fancy suit. He closed the door real quietly, and that's when he dropped a quarter."

"A quarter?"

"I heard it clang on the floor. The guy looked around for a minute, desperate like he needed it for cab fare. But then Benny came shuffling down the hall, and the fancy dresser took off in a hurry—"

"Who's Benny?"

"The nut who lives in the basement. Messed up his head with Sterno or something. Benny never sleeps; he just wanders the halls night and day."

"What else do you remember about the older man who came out of Ruby's apartment?"

"I told you. He had a real nice suit—like Cary Grant or something, only this guy was stout, and his face was round."

"What color was his hair?"

"Black, slicked back, and varnished, and he had a little black mustache."

I touched Jack's arm. The picture this woman painted didn't match the skinny-blond-kid description for Nathan Brock. But it sure did match someone we'd met at the Forrestal.

"Did Benny see this guy?"

"He must have. I know he found the quarter. I saw him pick it up and tuck it in his pocket."

Jack fell silent.

"So?" the woman said belligerently. "Was my story worth another five bucks?"

Jack shoved the bill at her. She snatched it and shook her finger.

"Just remember, gumshoe, if you send the coppers to talk to me, I'll tell 'em you're lying!"

As she slammed the door, I turned to Jack.

"That woman just described Roland Prince."

"Yeah, and you heard her threat. She'll button up for the cops if we send them. But maybe this Benny will talk. A juicer makes for a lousy witness, but it's better than nothing."

We went down to the basement. The less said about that experience, the better, so I'll use three little words: bad smells and spiderwebs. But no Benny. We could find no evidence he ever was there—not at first.

"Look at this," Jack called. "It's a hatch to the coal room."

"So?"

"So this building has a gas furnace and steam heat."

Jack jerked the handle, and the steel hatch popped open.

We heard the echo of a whimper float to us from the other side of the metal door. I peeked through the narrow opening. The room beyond was large, dark, and empty and smelled of coal dust.

Once again, we heard a whimper.

"Come on out, Benny," I called gently. "Don't be afraid. We won't hurt you."

We heard a shuffling sound, and suddenly Benny scrambled through the opening and dropped to the floor in front of us. When he looked up, I saw bald spots and ravaged scars on the left side of the man's head.

"He's no juicer," Jack whispered. "That's a war wound."

Jack knelt down beside the man. Benny's head twitched, and he refused to meet Jack's stare.

"Were you army? The marines?"

"Navy," he stammered. "*Y-Y-Yorktown.*"

"You were in it, then."

The man nodded.

Jack clapped his hand on the man's shoulder like Benny was an old friend. "How would you like to earn a little dough, sailor?"

Benny smiled and shrugged.

"The lady upstairs tells me you saw another man in the hall the night the police came. Is that right?"

He nodded.

"Did you mention it to the cops?"

Benny shook his head. "I hid. If they found me, I'd get thrown out. Bad on the street . . ."

"Don't worry about that. We won't rat on you," Jack promised.

I jumped in. "The lady told us you found something the man dropped. A quarter, she said."

Benny shook his head. "Not a quarter." He offered us a crooked smile. "I could have used a quarter."

We watched as he reached into the pocket of his dirty flannel shirt.

After fumbling for a moment, he pulled out three metal jacks, a thimble, and a Buffalo nickel. Then he reached into his scuffed workpants for something else. He held the shiny object up so we could both see it.

Between coal-dusted fingers, Benny clutched a gold cuff link with inlaid initials set in black onyx.

RP.

Roland Prince.

CHAPTER 49

The Ties That Bind

My feeling about in-laws was that they were outlaws.

—Malcolm X, *The Autobiography of Malcolm X*

WHEN MY ALARM went off Saturday morning, I jumped out of bed and hurried to shower and dress. Gulping down a cup of tea, I read the to-do list Sadie had left on the kitchen counter. There was still so much to be done before the Palantines' launch party this afternoon!

All day yesterday, store work had kept me busy. Still, I tried discussing my dream with Jack. I asked about his next step in the Ruby Tyler case—but there was no answer and, last night, no new dream. Now the weekend was here, and I was too busy to think about anything but our store event.

Downstairs, morning light poured through our shop windows, and it was luminous. My aunt's sunny disposition mirrored the weather.

"We got more sign-ups on our website last night." She was almost giddy. "We're nearly at capacity, never mind last-minute walk-ins. This has become one of Buy the Book's biggest events. Let's hope the fire marshal isn't one of the ticket holders."

"I better start setting up chairs," I said. "We're going to need all we have and then some."

"Spencer carried up the extras from the basement. He's in the event space now, getting a head start."

As I turned to go, Sadie stopped me. "One more thing, dear. The Saturday *Quindicott Bulletin* was delivered a few minutes ago. Prepare yourself for the front page."

"Tell me it's not about Conway's murder."

"We should be so lucky." Sadie displayed the screaming headlines.

GHOST HAUNTS FINCH INN!

GUESTS SPOT SPECTER IN WOODS, SECOND SIGHTING THIS MONTH

HAS HARRIET MCCLURE RETURNED FROM THE GRAVE?

My aunt clucked. "I'm afraid this news will only feed Seymour's obsession."

"You noticed how strange he's been acting?"

"Who hasn't?" Sadie sighed. "He delivers the mail. People talk."

The rest of the morning passed in a blur.

Linda delivered boxes of cookies and pretty little tarts from her bakery. Then Spencer's friend Amy Ridgeway arrived for her weekend visit. After settling in upstairs, she excitedly returned to the shop to help me and Spencer set up the refreshment table.

At half past one, the partygoers began to trickle in, Seymour among the first. Brainert arrived with his visiting professor friend, Violet Brooks.

The tall, mop-haired art historian was once again dressed flamboyantly, this time in a tan dress decorated with big cubistic patches of red, yellow, and green. Her glasses were gone today, and I presumed she'd switched to contact lenses under those thick dark bangs.

As Brainert waved hello to me, Violet barely noticed. With singular focus, she made her way over to the Harriet McClure portrait, where she remained.

By two fifteen, with forty-five minutes to go before Liam and Sally Palantine kicked off the party, the store was at capacity, and we had to close the doors to all but ticket holders. Those who managed to tear their eyes away from the art exhibit were already grabbing seats.

The Palantines had promised press coverage, and they delivered. Along with reporters from New York, Boston, and Rhode Island, Reuters and *Publishers Weekly* sent stringer photographers. A famous newscaster and her video crew added to the excitement—and the crowding.

As the party was about to begin, I felt confident that things were under control. That's when Sadie sidled up to me and whispered two words that dashed cold water on my afternoon.

"Ashley's here."

Ashley McClure-Sutherland, my late husband's older sister, called Manhattan home and the family's Newport mansion her "summer place." She rarely deigned to show her face within the Quindicott city limits and had never before attended one of our bookstore events. Yet there she was, resplendent in pastel separates, mingling with the journalists.

Like a silent shadow, husband Bertram Sutherland hovered in the background, his stony gray features frozen in a perpetual bland grimace.

Someone else was with Ashley. Violet Brooks appeared to be locked in an intense conversation with my sister-in-law.

"Oh God, Sadie. I pray Ashley doesn't notice—"

"Penelope!" Ashley warbled, her right arm bobbing in a limp-wristed wave. "Do you have a minute?"

What sharp eyes your sister-in-law has, Jack cracked, finally making an appearance. *Be on you guard, Penny. You already know the dame has sharp teeth, too.*

As I crossed the floor, I felt as deflated as a dancing balloon man with a broken air pump. I hadn't seen Ashley in a

year or more, and I found her blonder, thinner, and more
tanned than ever. Her expression seemed welcoming—but
Jack's warning was on the money. Ashley's placid features
masked a condescending attitude and calculating mind.

As I approached Ashley, I noticed Violet Brooks quickly
melting into the crowd. I was sorry to see her go. I was hoping the art historian would blunt this encounter.

But to my dumbfounded surprise, my sister-in-law did
not start in with her typical veiled insults. Instead, she showered me with air kisses, then proceeded to compliment the
store, the event, and the turnout. I smiled with all the gra-
ciousness I could muster, while I waited for the other shoe
to drop.

It was my jaw that dropped instead.

"Bertram and I were so impressed to see this store on last
week's CBS *Sunday Morning*, weren't we, Bertie?"

Bertram Sutherland issued a faux-British-aristocrat
murmur—sort of a baby's *yum-yum* sound.

"Sally and Liam speak quite highly of you. Don't they,
Bertram?"

Mr. Sutherland yum-yummed again, but this time, his
granite features cracked into a weak half-smile.

Well, well, Jack quipped. *Looks like you've got the Mc-
Clure stamp of approval. If I were you, I'd start worrying.*

Sure enough, a moment later, Ashley leaned close.

"Penelope, it's obvious you've brought an air of urban
sophistication to this tiny town of small minds. I don't know
how you managed it, but it was your vision that began the
renaissance of Quindicott. Bertram and I won't forget, and
we promise that you won't be left behind when this town
changes direction."

"Changes? How?"

Ashley prattled on as if she hadn't heard me.

"Since Bertram's left the firm, we've been searching for
new horizons, new challenges, some way to improve our
community and leave our mark on the world. Fortunately we
found it right here, in this quaint little town where the Mc-
Clure family's legacy began."

Her grin revealed pearly whites. "That's why I want you to be the first to know. Penelope, we're going to be neighbors! Bertram and I are moving to Quindicott."

Yikes! Jack cried.

Yikes, indeed.

CHAPTER 50

There Goes My Neighborhood

Neighbors are frightening enough when they're alive.

—George A. Romero, filmmaker

THOUGH I WAS completely gobsmacked by my sister-in-law's announcement, I managed to form a coherent monosyllabic sentence in response—

"Why?"

"Honestly? We were stuck in a rut." Ashley shook her blond mane and spoke in a conspiratorial half whisper. "You were so right to get out of the city when you did. Manhattan's become such a mess, so we've put our town house up for sale.

"Of course, our son will still attend Manhattan Prep. The campus is isolated from the common people, and it's by far the finest boarding school in the Northeast."

Brace yourself, doll.

"There's always a berth for Spencer, you know. Bertram is on the board; I'm sure he can arrange a full scholarship due to your financial . . . *situation*."

You want me to blow cold smoke up her skirt? Jack asked.

I had to admit, it was a tempting offer—Jack's. Not Ashley's.

"You *must* think of your son's future," my sister-in-law argued. "Boarding school would be far superior to a public education. He'd socialize with a better class of people, and that's a definite plus. No more troublesome locals like Spencer's little blue-haired babysitter."

"Tracy? What do you know about Tracy?"

"Oh, look!" Ashley cried, gesturing to a cluster of people across the room. "My friend Marjorie's arrived!"

Another ding-a-ling makes an appearance.

Marjorie Binder-Smith, mayor of Quindicott, was surrounded by several members of our town council, well-known to be her political puppets. The woman's typical disapproving countenance—which Sadie once described as "Mrs. Grundy 2.0"—had brightened considerably, and I quickly saw why. She was chatting up that famous television newscaster.

Meanwhile, Ashley continued to gush all over me.

"I'm so excited about our impending move!"

Well, I'm not, the ghost groused. *So you better warn that pretentious petunia, if she moves anywhere near this place, I'll scare her into next week.*

Biting my cheek to keep from laughing, I asked, "Where exactly are you moving, Ashley? Larchmont Avenue, I presume?"

"*Actually*, Bertram and I have our eyes on a magnificent Queen Anne, right on the pond . . ."

As Ashley went on describing Fiona and Barney Finch's property, right down to the beachfront Lighthouse, her husband visibly winced.

"Nothing is settled yet," Bertram interjected pointedly, cutting off Ashley's careless words. But it was too late.

See that, doll? Jack declared in triumph. *The truth will out!*

Jack was right. Just like shaky Benny in that tenement basement, Ashley had given me the verbal equivalent of a monogrammed cuff link—without having any idea what she was handing over.

Now I knew who was behind the outrageous local tax on

the Finch Inn. I did my best to hide my reaction, but inside I was absolutely fuming!

Buying off their political friends, my sister-in-law and her husband had set out to ruin my friends and defy the last will and testament of Harriet McClure by claiming the estate she'd left to the Finch family—property that was now an absolute treasure, thanks to the painstaking work Fiona and Barney had done to improve and beautify it.

This underhanded ploy is classic Ashley! I told the ghost.

Yeah, getting others to do your dirty work keeps your fingerprints off the knife. But cheer up. This is what I call the bright side of the gumshoe's tunnel.

Bright side?

Learning the real truth not only gets you out of the dark; it gives you an advantage in the ring.

How?

Same way those two vultures are taking out the poor Finches. If your opponent can't see you, knocking them out is a whole lot easier.

I don't know if that's true, Jack. But I sure wish I could KO Ashley.

I was so angry I might have done it, too. Good thing Sadie stepped into the middle of the shop and announced that our authors had arrived.

"Take your seats, everyone. Our launch party is about to begin!"

AFTER EIGHT OF the busiest hours of my life, capped by the overwhelming success of our book launch for the Palantines, it was time to celebrate with a lavish dinner at Chez Finch.

Not that I was feeling the least bit festive.

I was still seething about Ashley's scheme to grab the Finch Inn. I myself wanted to grab my sister-in-law by her skinny neck, but I knew it wouldn't accomplish anything. Instead, I was desperate to grab Fiona and Barney and tell them everything.

But right now I had to fulfill my professional role, put on a happy face for my guests, and keep my lips zipped as Fiona Finch played the perfect fine-dining hostess and seated us.

After everyone settled in, we ordered drinks, and I excused myself to "visit the ladies' room." On the way, I waved frantically to Fiona, who was sorting menus at a service stand. She followed me around the corner, into the empty hallway.

"Pen? What's the matter?"

I told her everything.

Fiona scowled. "I knew something was going on behind the scenes. But I never suspected Ashley McClure-Sutherland!"

"Believe it, Fiona. Ashley talked about moving into your property as if it were a done deal."

I could see Fiona was upset about the news. Legal battles didn't come cheap. Sure the Quibblers were willing to band together and back the Finches. But we didn't have bottomless bank accounts. Not like the McClures. They were one of the richest families in the region, and when they wanted something, they usually got it.

I began throwing out suggestions, looking for some kind of leverage.

"There's something else that I don't understand. Ashley weirdly bragged about Quindicott *changing direction* after they take over your property. Do you know anyone who might give us some answers? If we're going to fight them, we need all the information we can get."

"Sam Tibbet is here," Fiona said excitedly. "I don't think you've ever met Sam. He's a cousin of Welsh Tibbet, who your friend Eddie works with on the police force, and he runs Tibbet Real Estate. He's also on the town council. I can work on him."

"How?"

"Sam comes here to wine and dine his clients. If he closes a deal, after the client leaves, he has a bottle of Chianti to celebrate. If he doesn't make a deal, he drowns his sorrow with Chianti. Either way, he'll appreciate a complimentary bottle of the stuff—and maybe I'll ask a few *innocent* questions after the wine loosens his tongue."

"In vino veritas, Fiona, that's the spirit."

Jack was impressed, too. *She's one clever bird.*

And you were right, Jack. Fiona was glad to know who to fight, even if it feels like a match Rocky couldn't win.

Yeah, Marciano was one of the greats.

No, not that Rocky, Jack, the one from—oh, forget it.

Buoyed by Fiona's spirit, I left the alcove to rejoin my guests and nearly collided with Violet Brooks.

"Oh, sorry, Mrs. McClure!" Stepping back awkwardly, she shook her heavy mop of bangs. "I was looking for the ladies' room?"

"Right around the corner," I said, frowning as I watched her go. When I'd turned the corner, she hadn't been "looking" for anything, just standing out of sight, close to the wall.

Did you see that, Jack? First, she's chatting up my sister-in-law. Now she's eavesdropping on my conversation with Fiona.

That's one St. Bernard to keep an eye on.

CHAPTER 51

Once Upon a Palantine

The paperback field is less vivid than movie posters,
but it does have a certain charm.

—Stanley Meltzoff, illustrator

RETURNING TO MY guests, I did my best to avoid staring across the dining room at Fiona's efforts to pump Sam Tibbet for info. Refocusing instead on my professional duties, I tried to enjoy our celebratory meal. It wasn't difficult: The food was amazing, and our guests of honor held the table spellbound with their amusing stories about their decades in the publishing business.

A large, effusive man of eighty-plus years, Liam Palantine was an impeccable dresser; a staid look counteracted his gray Einsteinesque tangle of uncombed hair. His wife, Sally, was a plump, jovial presence who laughed often, something she'd clearly done for years, judging from the lines on her gently furrowed face.

"I was just starting out when my father shifted from pulps to paperbacks," Liam told us after my aunt asked how the pair had met. "I learned that a book is judged by its cover. That's why I hired Sally as Palantine Publishing's first art director."

Sally nodded. "I'd made a study of book cover designs, even back then. It's hard to believe these days, but in the first twenty years of modern mass-market paperbacks, there were really only five stylistic trends."

She happily went through them all, starting with surrealism. "The original cover of *The Maltese Falcon* was a good example."

"I remember it well!" Aunt Sadie said. "The cover showed a silhouette of the falcon statue with disembodied hands grasping for it."

"That's right," Liam said. "That image told the story and sold the story. Unfortunately the Rex Stout and Erle Stanley Gardner covers sometimes looked like Salvador Dalí painted them, and readers didn't always get it."

"When World War II ended, styles did a one-eighty," Sally said. "Covers became colorful and humorous with jolly typefaces typical of animated cartoons. Then the Cold War began, and covers changed with the country's mood, returning to the violence and sensationalism of so many Depression-era pulps."

"By 'sensationalism' you mean sex, right?" Seymour asked bluntly.

"Don't be rude, Seymour," Brainert scolded.

"No, your friend is right," Liam said. "Even the most innocent novel had to have a scandalous cover."

On that note, Sally told us about the fourth trend. "They were known as the keyhole covers. Penguin originally created it for an Erskine Caldwell novel in 1946—an innocent illustration of a hole in a picket fence, and through it you could see a family home. By 1950 the keyhole idea had been 'borrowed' by every other publisher, but this time they used an actual keyhole to create a feeling of voyeurism."

"I remember those, too!" Aunt Sadie noted. "And the ones I recall weren't so innocent."

"No, they weren't," Sally said. "Those keyhole covers typically showed a scandalous scene: a woman in a state of undress or a couple in a compromising position."

Just then, our beautiful Chez Finch desserts arrived, and

we all dug in. Then more wine was poured, and Bud Napp cleared his throat.

"I've been keeping count on those trends of yours, Mrs. Palantine. You covered four so far. You still have a fifth to tell us about."

"Yes, please go on," everyone insisted.

Sally smiled, pleased to know we were all so interested.

"Let's see, the fifth trend . . . that came along around the mid-1950s, when publishers decided to target the serious reader. By then, they all hired art directors who crafted a distinctive look for each company's publications. And by the time the 1960s rolled around, the styles became genre-specific. A surreal image could sell science fiction, but Gothic romance readers demanded a realistic depiction of their heroine—"

"Yeah," Seymour said, laughing and nodding. "In the dead of night, wearing a negligee, and fleeing a sinister old house on a hill."

"Or better still, a *castle*," Sally said. "There are hundreds of variations of that cover. An editor at Ace Books determined that a single lighted window on that castle could jump sales by five percent."

"I think Harriet McClure would have made a fine romance illustrator," Seymour declared.

"She was certainly accomplished," Sally conceded. "But from what you told me back at the shop, Harriet had issues. You can't rely on someone who works only when the mood strikes them. And in any profession, mental instability is a liability. Let's face it, no art director wants their hire to pull a Van Gogh and hand you their ear."

"Actually, that's not accurate," Violet Brooks said. There was a dead pause around the table. This was the first time Violet had spoken during the entire dinner.

"What's not accurate?" Liam Palantine asked with genuine curiosity. "Sally's remark about Van Gogh?"

"No. About Harriet McClure. I've been doing a little research into her life and background."

"Really?" Seymour got excited. "Tell us what you've discovered, Ms. Brooks."

"From what evidence I've found, everything people repeated about Harriet McClure's psychological state appears to be a slander—a lie."

"But we've heard the same stories for years," Brainert countered, "about Harriet's continual painting of self-portraits, her reclusiveness and midnight strolls in the woods. You're saying the woman didn't have psychological problems? What's your evidence?"

Violet rested the flat of her hands on the tablecloth.

"Harriet McClure was a complex woman. Intelligent, talented, introspective, rebellious even—but she wasn't mad. I would guess that Harriet was as psychologically sound as anyone at this table."

"Seymour excluded," Brainert quipped.

The mailman rolled his eyes. "Let the lady speak, Brainpan."

Violet cleared her throat. "The Newport Historical Society granted me access to Robert Morehouse McClure's papers. Harriet's brother was twelve years her senior and raised her after their parents died in the 1889 flu pandemic."

"Robert Morehouse McClure, now, there's a name from the past," Aunt Sadie blurted, a little tipsy after sharing a second bottle of wine with Bud. "The old-timers used to say he was a bit of a rogue."

"Not the word I would use," Violet said coolly.

"Oh? What word would you use?"

"Monster."

CHAPTER 52

Ghosts

Insanity is relative. It depends on who has who locked
in what cage.

—Ray Bradbury

"I SPENT TWO days perusing that awful man's papers,"
Violet revealed. "His many crimes aside, I found no evidence a physician ever declared Harriet unfit. It was her own
brother who was responsible for Harriet's reputation. A slander that persists to this day."

Seymour looked stunned. "Why would her own brother
do that?"

"The McClure siblings initially got along. Robert even
encouraged her interest in art. The trouble began when Harriet refused to marry the man her brother chose for her."

Seymour's brow furrowed. "But it was the twentieth century, not the Middle Ages."

"Robert considered it as the merging of two powerful
Newport families. Harriet didn't see it that way. The groom-
to-be was twenty years her senior, a known womanizer, and
diagnosed with the early stages of *bad blood*."

"What the heck is bad blood?" Bud Napp asked.

"A polite euphemism for syphilis," Brainert replied.

My aunt gasped. "Oh, that poor child!"

"For her refusal to do his bidding, Harriet was banished from the McClure's Newport home, and her legal share of the family inheritance was co-opted by Robert. He made it known in their social circles that his sister was 'unbalanced' and that everyone should keep their distance."

Seymour bristled. "What a stinking son of a—"

"It doesn't end there, I'm afraid. Robert intended the Quindicott home to be Harriet's prison and hired a local family to keep his sister in line. Harriet was lucky in that regard. Malachi Finch and his wife were generous, decent people."

"Harriet left the house to the Finch family," my aunt pointed out. "She was obviously grateful for their kindness."

"She had a lot to be grateful for," Violet agreed. "Harriet was given ownership of the house and property, but she arrived with nothing more than the clothes on her back, her jewel box, and a parsimonious annual stipend from her brother. It was Malachi who kept the property up and shielded her from Robert."

"She needed protection from her own brother?" Sadie cried.

"Robert was a gangster, a bootlegger, and a social climber. He was a cruel and sometimes violent man. Malachi Finch, on the other hand, was an honest, hardworking soul who made no secret of the fact that he despised the McClure family. He never let Robert near his sister after she came to Quindicott. Not even once. Not even after Robert cut off Malachi's meager salary. After Harriet died, her brother resented the fact that the Finch family inherited her grand house and property. He tried every legal means to grab it."

"And my in-laws carry on the tradition," I muttered into my glass.

"Robert coveted Harriet's jewels, too—"

"Harriet had jewels?" I interrupted, surprised. "Are you sure? None of her paintings show her wearing any jewelry."

But Violet was certain. "They're mentioned in Robert's lawsuit. He claimed they originally belonged to Harriet's mother and were family heirlooms."

"Did you discover what happened to them?" I asked.

"The Finch family claimed they were lost, but it's more likely they were sold over time to keep Harriet's household going." Violet frowned. "In any case, after Robert lost his lawsuit, there was no further mention of the jewels." She paused. "That's about all I've uncovered thus far, other than what happened to so many of Harriet's paintings after her death. Really, the only blight on Malachi Finch's kindness to her was his destruction of so much of her art. I understand it was done out of desperation—a harsh winter, a lack of fire-wood, but still . . ."

Violet's voice trailed off and the table got very quiet. Suddenly Seymour startled everyone by pounding his fist on the table.

"No!" he cried. "That can't be the whole story. There's more to Harriet's life that we don't know, a secret that she's trying to tell the world, to tell *me*. Harriet wants the truth to be known!"

After that disconcerting slip into *The Twilight Zone*, the party broke up. Liam and Sally bid us good night, and accompanied by Violet Brooks, they strolled along the lovely lighted path that led back to the Finch Inn.

After they were gone, my aunt chided Seymour.

"What were you thinking? Telling our guests that a dead woman is trying to talk to you?"

"Sadie's right," Bud Napp chimed in. "You sounded . . . well, crazy.

"As a loon," Brainert added.

When Seymour scowled, Sadie squeezed his hand. "I'm not trying to be cruel. I'm worried about you, that's all. You're letting your imagination run wild. This obsession with Harriet's portrait is consuming your life."

"Listen to the lady," Bud advised. "You used to be a level-headed guy. A little weird, but that's what makes you a mail-man." Rising, he slapped Seymour on the back. "We just want to see our old pal again. The guy we know and love. Think it over, son."

Sadie took Bud's hand. "We're going to stroll down to the Lighthouse."

But Sadie and Bud weren't gone more than five minutes when I heard my aunt's scream through the open windows of the nearly deserted restaurant. I rose to my feet as she burst through the door and rushed to our table.

"We saw it . . . Her!" Sadie stammered. "Out there, in the woods!"

Bud Napp was so shaken he had to take a seat and a few deep breaths before he could speak.

"We were walking toward the Lighthouse," he gasped. "That's when the ghost appeared, plain as day—"

"It was Harriet!" Sadie squealed. "She was in the woods. We could only see the top half of her body as she glided by. She was floating—"

"The ghost was maybe twenty feet away," Bud said. "Dressed all in white, with that long scarf-type shawl thing flowing behind her—"

"When I screamed, I swear Harriet's stark white face stared right at me!" Sadie cried.

Seymour suddenly looked smug. Crossing his arms, he loudly cleared his throat. "So which is it? Are both of you mental? Did you let your imaginations run wild? Is the ghost of Harriet consuming your life? Or maybe you just sucked down enough vino to drown a fish?"

CHAPTER 53

Midnight Confession

Three may keep a secret, if two of them are dead.

—Benjamin Franklin

I AGREED WITH Seymour on one thing. My aunt and Bud had had way too much to drink. As for the ghost sighting, I was far from an impartial juror. Whether they saw Harriet's spirit or not, I wanted them to get home safely and was glad Brainert offered to drive them.

I didn't go with them. Instead, I stayed behind, hoping to hear what (if anything) Fiona had learned from the town's Chianti-loving Realtor.

When I joined her and Barney at the bar of the deserted restaurant, they were discussing Aunt Sadie's outburst.

"I hope she isn't going to blab all over town about how she saw Harriet's ghost," Barney complained. "We don't need another article in the *Bulletin*."

Fiona saw me and quickly changed the subject. "Pen, sit down and join us! I'm so glad you told me about your sister-in-law."

"I'm glad, too. Did you get any news from Sam Tibbet?"

"Yes!" Pouring me a ginger ale, she declared, "Some-

thing is definitely going on in this town. Sam told me he
made three sales this month, all to out-of-town buyers. Nobody even came to look at the property. They just paid the
asking price."

"Anything else?"

"Charting is being done along Quindicott's shoreline.
Sam talked with a pair of surveyors at Linda's bakery. They
said they were hired by a law firm in New York, so he
checked it out. It's Bertram Sutherland's firm."

Barney cursed.

"Sam began to dig, and from what he gathered, Ashley
and her husband are planning to turn Quindicott into a
Newport-like resort town. Once they force us out of our own
property, they're going to expand the inn and develop the
shoreline. They also plan to use their financial influence on
the mayor and town council to pressure the existing shop
owners to sell, so 'high-end' retailers can lift the town out
of its 'middle-brow' doldrums."

I felt sick. "It's worse than I thought. We'll have to fight
them, starting with your inn."

"I'm ready for that fight!" Fiona said.

I couldn't contain my outrage. "What nerve they have. I
can't get over how Ashley spoke about your property as if
she'd be moving in next month without any hitch. How
could she be so confident?"

"She's confident because she's got something she can use
against us," Barney said.

"The tax?" Fiona assumed.

"I think it's something more. Something I never told you.
Never told anybody." Suddenly Barney faced me. "Is Seymour in on this scheme? I know Tarnish and Fiona poke
each other every chance they get, but I never thought the
mailman would stoop so low—"

"What are you talking about, Barney?"

"That portrait of young Harriet McClure. It appeared out
of nowhere. Who gave it to Seymour? Why is he showing it
off now?"

"No one gave it to him. He bought it. I was there when

Seymour first laid eyes on it. And are we talking about the same painting you claimed was a *forgery*?"

Barney's cadet-straight shoulders sagged. "I've been doing a lot of lying lately, and it's brought me nothing but grief."

He took his wife's hand, but Barney's eyes never left mine.

"It's not a forgery," he confessed. "That portrait is the real thing. So real it can ruin us."

"My God, Barney," his wife cried. "How can that be? It's only a painting!"

"It's more than that . . ."

Barney confessed that when he was just twelve years old, he was puttering around in the attic of what is now the Finch Inn when he found a crawl space. Inside he discovered several paintings by Harriet McClure, including the one that hangs in their lobby today.

"My father demanded I show him. When he saw they were all portraits of Harriet in her last years, he relaxed. But then he saw one that had numbers and letters on it. It looked like the one Seymour bought. Had strange colors and images drawn in the rocks and on the clouds. I didn't even think it was a picture of Harriet because the girl was so young and striking."

Barney paused. "My father told me if I ever saw a picture of this young woman with strange writing and symbols, I should do what he was about to do. Then he took the painting to the incinerator and burned it."

I was appalled. "Did he say why?"

"He told me there were secret things on that painting. He said that if anyone in the powerful McClure family ever found out that secret, they would bring a curse down on us."

"Didn't your father give you any hint as to what that secret was?"

"He only said that my grandfather Malachi had burned a bunch of paintings just like the one he burned. And when he did, Malachi gave my father the same warning he was passing on to me." With a heavy sigh, Barney went on. "I can only think Ashley or that bastard of a husband got hold of one of those paintings. Figured out the secret and is about to blackmail me, or worse—"

"Wait a minute," I said. "If that's really their plan, then Ashley and Bertram don't need another painting. Not if they have the digital images of the one Seymour owns."

As I explained my theory to Barney and Fiona, I realized my in-laws were sounding more like outlaws. But were they capable of double murder—or paying someone to do it for them?

"One more thing," I said. "Violet Brooks mentioned Harriet's jewels. She said they were part of her brother's lawsuit to reclaim the house after Harriet died. Violet thought the jewels might have been sold to keep the household going. But a few jewels would have brought a great deal of money. Isn't it possible that not all of those jewels were sold? What if the remainder were hidden somewhere on the property?"

Barney shook his head. "Nice theory, Pen. I wish that were true. But we stripped most of this house down to its bare walls and rebuilt the foundation. If there was a box full of jewels hidden in this old building, we would have found it."

CHAPTER 54

A Criminal Investigation

There is nothing more deceptive than an obvious fact.

—Arthur Conan Doyle, "The Boscombe Valley Mystery"

DESPITE MY LATE night, I volunteered to open the bookstore on Sunday morning. Sadie was "feeling a little tired and would be down soon."

Translation: My aunt had had too good a time drinking wine and needed to recover. I was only too happy to give her a break. Unfortunately, my first customer of the morning didn't give me one.

"Deputy Chief Franzetti. What brings you here so early?"

Eddie's face was haggard, his five-o'clock shadow pronounced, and I assumed I knew the reason why he looked so unhappy.

"I'm sorry, Eddie. I've been busy with the launch event. I know you wanted me to look at the Comfy-Time guest list—"

"That's not why I'm here. That guest list is no longer relevant, anyway. Is your son around, Pen?"

I felt a jolt of maternal panic. "Why do you want to see Spencer? Has he done something wrong?"

"No, but I need to speak with him about a criminal investigation."

That didn't comfort me one bit. "He's upstairs having breakfast with his friend Amy. I'll call him down."

I phoned upstairs, and a few minutes later, my son bounded into the shop. When he spied the deputy chief, he stopped dead.

"Do you have your phone with you, Spencer?"

Spencer's brows knitted in suspicion. "Why?"

"Because I was told you recorded something on Cranberry Street the other day, and the police need to see it. What you recorded might be evidence relating to a crime."

Spencer looked at Eddie, then at me. I could tell by his stricken expression that my son and I were thinking the same thing—the authorities wanted to see Tracy Mahoney's public spat with Clifford Conway. Which meant Spencer's favorite babysitter was a suspect—maybe the *only* suspect.

I spoke up. "If you're planning on confiscating Spencer's phone, you're going to need a warrant."

"I have a warrant, Pen. I was hoping to avoid using it."

"Even if Spencer did record what you call 'evidence of a crime,' I don't see how you can use it in court. You need consent from the person being recorded, right?"

"Under Rhode Island statute, consent is not required when a communication is spoken without a reasonable expectation of privacy. I don't think anyone expects privacy in the middle of Cranberry Street on a busy afternoon."

"You think Tracy did something wrong, don't you?" Spencer cried. Eddie met my son's accusing glare.

"Look, son, for justice to be served, we have to get to the truth, no matter where that truth might lead. I know you understand, and I hope you'll cooperate."

After a long, awful pause, Spencer reached into his pocket, expression grim, and handed over the phone.

"We'll try to get this back to you as soon as possible, okay?"

My son just stared at the floor.

"Spencer, go upstairs and finish your breakfast. I'll be up to talk to you in a little while."

When he was gone, I faced Eddie. "You said the Comfy-

Time's first-floor guest list was no longer relevant. What did you mean by that?"

"We've already made an arrest." Eddie's frown made him look ten years older. "Tracy Mahoney."

"You can't be serious!"

"You're lucky it's not you."

"What?!"

"You were in the room. That bump on the head could have happened in a struggle with the victim—"

"You don't believe that."

"No, but the state police did, until they found other evidence."

"What evidence?"

"There are only two security cameras at the Comfy-Time. One covers their front desk. The other is pointed at their parking lot, and the exterior camera clearly shows Ms. Mahoney entering and leaving around the time Conway was murdered."

"Her brother had a business meeting at the motel—"

"But Reverend Mahoney has no idea why Tracy was there."

"She was excited about the concert promoter from Nashville meeting with her brother. She wanted to be the first to know how it went."

"Or so she told you."

"No other vehicles entered or left the parking lot?"

Eddie shook his head. "Just yours and Seymour's."

"You know it's possible someone came and left using that service staircase right next to Conway's room. It leads to the back of the motel, and there's a walkway back there that will get you to the McDonald's. Have you checked the McDonald's parking lot camera?"

"The only exterior camera at that McDonald's is aimed at the drive-through pickup window—and before you start arguing another angle, you should know we found an eyewitness."

"Who?"

"A guest on the first floor went to the vending machines. On his way there, he spotted a redhead going into Conway's room—that was you. He even described what you were wearing. Apparently, you struck his fancy because when he got change, he asked the office clerk about you. On his way back to his own room, he was watching Conway's door, hoping to see you come out again, but you didn't. Instead, he saw another woman exit Conway's room."

"He identified Tracy?"

"He couldn't make a positive ID, but he was sure it was a woman. He said she kept her head down and wore a Kelly green plastic rain parka, which is exactly what Tracy Mahoney was wearing when she rode in—"

"Like the ones Mr. Koh sells at his grocery store for three dollars a pop, you mean? I have one. Aunt Sadie has one. You probably have one!"

"We *also* recovered the murder weapon."

"What?" I felt a chill go through me—and for once it had nothing to do with Jack.

"It's an umbrella heavy enough to be a club. It looks old, like something she picked up at a secondhand store. It was strapped to the saddlebag of her Yamaha, parked in back of the church, and it has Conway's blood on it."

"You found it out there in the woods? It could have been planted to frame her. What did Tracy say when you arrested her?"

Eddie frowned. "What they all say. 'The weapon isn't mine; I didn't do it.' Then she became hysterical. So hysterical, we took her to the hospital for a psych evaluation."

My anger flared again. "You're driving that poor girl insane. I'll bet you haven't found the stuff stolen from Conway's room. And what's the name of this male witness who identified Tracy?"

"I can't talk about an ongoing investigation."

"You just did!"

"That was a courtesy because you were personally involved. But no more. From now on, this is police business."

"But I'm a witness to that business."

"And? What are you getting at, Pen?"

"Just do me one favor. Send over a copy of that Comfy-Time list of guests from the first floor. I'd like to see it."

"Fine." With a tired nod, he glanced at his watch. "Now I've got to go. I have a lousy day ahead of me."

Think how lousy the day's going to be for Tracy Mahoney, Jack whispered in my head. *That poor kid, locked up in some crazy ward.*

It's going to be a lousy day all over, Jack, because now I have to go upstairs and talk to another poor kid.

Breaking the news to my son about Tracy's arrest was one of the toughest things I'd ever done. But town gossip was inevitable, and Spencer would find out one way or another. I wanted him to hear it from me so I could help him process it. The worst part was that my son took Tracy's arrest even harder than I did.

"I recorded that argument to *help* Tracy," he said, his lower lip trembling. "I thought that Conway man was going to hurt her. But I was the one who hurt her. It's my fault this happened!"

"No, honey." I pulled him close. "You didn't do anything wrong."

"I did, Mom, I did," Spencer cried. "Now we have to fix this. We have to help Tracy!"

"We will. I promise."

Even as I made the vow, I knew there was only one way to truly help our young friend. I had to find the real killer. And with that understanding, Deputy Chief Franzetti's words came back to haunt me.

For justice to be served, we have to get to the truth of what really happened, no matter where that truth might lead.

CHAPTER 55

Artful Clues

Art is not what you see, but what you make others see.

—Edgar Degas

AFTER MY PRIVATE talk with Spencer, I suggested he and Amy get some fresh air and gave them money to rent bikes for the day at Quindicott Pond.

By late afternoon, Sadie felt well enough to relieve me in the bookshop. I picked up Spencer and Amy, took them out for pizza, and finally settled them upstairs with their favorite video game.

Eddie had yet to send over that motel guest list, which troubled me even more after I received an e-mail from Sheriff Augusta Taft, informing me that Walter Waverly's son, Neil, was back in town to deal with his father's estate.

I gave him your contact info, she wrote as a courtesy, *and I expect he'll be in touch about the paintings you borrowed.*

My mind was now swirling with even more theories as I brewed a pot of tea and stewed alone in the kitchen, trying to puzzle out what I could possibly do next to help Tracy— and the Finches.

When the ghost had had his fill of my ping-ponging prospects, he made a blustery appearance.

Enough already! Give it a rest.

With a shiver, I told him he could rest in peace if he liked, but I was determined to help my friends.

Then stop sipping tea and do some legwork.

That's the trouble. I don't know where to start.

Look, doll, there was a reason for these murders, wasn't there? And for your postman pal's bump on the head.

Yes, I said. *The killer was after Harriet's painting.*

Yet the painting is still hanging downstairs.

Okay, you're right. The killer took the digital photos from Cliff Conway's motel room, which means it wasn't the painting but the secrets buried in the painting's images that the killer wanted.

And what are those secrets?

I have no idea.

Well, don't you think you should try to find out? The killer knows what they're after, but you still don't have a clue.

Actually, Jack, you're wrong about that. I have dozens of clues. I just don't know what they mean! But I'm going to find out . . .

After a few phone calls, I went downstairs to the empty event space and waited for my two best friends to arrive— the very companions who'd begun this bizarre journey with me a full week ago.

Though there wasn't a rocket scientist among us, I hoped our combined knowledge would solve the riddle of the cursed portrait.

It's good that you're the brains of this outfit, Jack cracked. *I doubt Laurel and Hardy could find the powder room if you gave them a map.*

Competent or not, they were certainly eager.

Professor J. Brainert Parker came armed with his computer tablet. Seymour arrived looking as exhausted as Deputy Chief Franzetti. He confessed that he hadn't slept a full night since he laid eyes on Harriet's self-portrait.

I began by swearing them to secrecy and then revealing what Barney Finch had disclosed.

"So those really are decipherable clues embedded in the painting!" Brainert exclaimed.

Seymour scowled. "I've been telling you there's a secret message for days, Brainpan. Why are you suddenly so convinced now?"

"I'm sorry, Seymour, but you failed to convince me because you're, well . . . *you*. But Barney Finch had ancestors who actually knew Harriet McClure, and he's a stable and dispassionate party—"

"Are you kidding me?" Seymour returned. "The other day Barney 'the birdman' was ready to go three rounds with a man half his age and twice his weight!"

Brainert breathed a patient sigh. "By 'stable and dispassionate,' I meant someone who *isn't* obsessed with a dead woman."

"Okay, you two!" I said, channeling Jack's firm attitude. "Knock it off and help me get this painting out of its frame . . ."

Within minutes we were all studying the painting, including and especially the writing and symbols on the edges that had been covered by the frame.

Seymour frowned. "It doesn't help that I can't read music."

"It's Brahms' 'Lullaby,'" I said, remembering Georgia Gilder's comment. "I think it must be tied to that two-headed baby."

"There's no two-headed baby," Seymour countered. "That's *two* babies lying close together."

Brainert ran his fingers along two pencil-thin lines on the canvas.

"These were invisible behind the glass, but now we can see where they lead. From this baby's head to the Mars symbol, and the other line goes to the symbol for Venus."

"So we're talking a boy and a girl." Seymour shook his wool-capped head. "Let's move on to the tiny writing on the cloud. We'll need a magnifying glass. I can hardly read it."

"No," argued Brainert. "The fish is much more important. It says—"

"Stars like dots in the sky," I interrupted. "Whatever *that* means."

"Google it, Pen," Seymour suggested.

"I did. I got 'blue field entoptic phenomenon.' That's the scientific term for seeing spots."

"Okay, what about this word?" Seymour pointed to the interstellar design around the frame. "It must be important. It's repeated over and over between these stars and planets. But what the hell is a *laedo*?"

Brainert's grin was smug. "Here is where a *classical* education proves invaluable. Any schoolboy who read Virgil's *Aeneid* in Latin would recognize that word." The professor arched an eyebrow in my direction. "Perhaps you should have Googled *that*, Pen."

Seymour frowned. "And the translation is . . . ?"

"*Laedo* is a verb meaning to hurt, wound, strike, smash, or bash. Quite common when describing ancient warfare—"

Seymour sniffed. "The *Iliad*, the *Odyssey*, and the *Aeneid* are Hellenic murder porn, if you ask me. I can't believe Harriet got a thrill from splatter punk."

"Yet an educated woman of her class would certainly have learned Latin and been familiar with Virgil," Brainert countered.

"What could she mean?" Seymour cried. "Hurt, bash, smash."

"How about *dash*?" I offered.

"As in 'dash to the ground'?" Brainert nodded. "It could mean that—"

Seymour suddenly waved his arm excitedly. He could hardly get the words out. "Stars like dots . . . with the Latin word *dash* in between. As in dots and dashes, as in—"

"You're right!" I cried. "It's code!"

Brainert frowned. "As in *The Da Vinci Code*?"

"No, Brainpan, Morse code, which I can read!"

"Since when do they teach postal employees Morse code?"

"They don't. But the Boy Scouts do." Seymour grinned in triumph. "I earned a merit badge in it."

"Of course you did," Brainert muttered.

"I'm also fluent in American Sign Language, braille, trail signs, and sports-officiating hand signals."

"Thank you, Mr. *Jeopardy!* Champion." Brainert rolled his eyes. "Now can we get back to business?"

"Seymour, how do you send Morse code on a painting?" I asked.

"Morse code can be communicated lots of ways, Pen. You can turn a light on and off, honk your horn, or just simulate the dots and dashes on a piece of paper—which is what I'm going to do right now."

Seymour grabbed a pen and paper. "I'm a little rusty, so this might take time."

CHAPTER 56

Mapping Out Solutions

Without geography, you're nowhere!

—Jimmy Buffett

BRAINERT AND I left Seymour to work. At the front of the store, we found Sadie fretting about Tracy's arrest.

"The girl with blue hair?" Brainert nodded. "Some of my students are in her reading group. Quiet type. But you never know what they're thinking. Still waters run deep."

"Oh, poo on that!" Sadie spat. "I made that mistake myself, misjudging the girl. But she's a creative soul. She's overly emotional because she's sensitive. She's different because she's an artist."

Sounds like another artist dame we know, the ghost observed, *the one who cast a spell on your mailman.*

A few minutes later, our enchanted postman charged down the aisle and proudly slapped the paper on the counter. "*Voilà!* Morse Code translated from Harriet-ese."

We all stared at Seymour's dots and dashes.

-- .- .-. ... .

.... --- ..- ... .

... - --- -. .

- ..- .-. -. .-. .. -.- .

"What does all this mean?" I asked.

"Yes, in the King's English, please," Brainert insisted.

Seymour pointed out each set of dots and dashes.

"This means 'marsh.' And these marks here spell 'house,' and here's 'stone,' and finally 'turnpike.'"

Brainert blinked. "Marsh House Stone Turnpike. That's all? Only four words."

"They are repeated over and over, just like that Latin word *laedo*."

"Riddles within riddles," Brainert muttered. "What does it mean? Is it a location?"

"Yes!" Seymour said.

"Well, I've never heard of it," Brainert said.

It perplexed me as well. But not my mailman.

"We postal workers know a thing or two about roads, streets, and addresses," he said tucking his thumbs into his belt.

Brainert smirked. "Well, please do enlighten us with your good-enough-for-government wisdom."

"When the state took over the turnpike system, they assigned the roads the numbers we use today. But a few dozen byways were no longer traveled, so the government left them out of the official Rhode Island road system, essentially abandoning those lanes to time and the elements. One of those forgotten roads is Stone Turnpike."

"And where is this turnpike?" Brainert was already consulting Google. He held up his computer tablet. "Stone Turnpike isn't listed."

"That's because it's an abandoned road. Modern maps aren't going to list it. What we need is a really, really old map. And there's a hundred-and-eighty-year-old road map of this area just a ten-minute drive from here. We can check it right now."

"Really?" Brainert scoffed. "And where is this ancient

map, Indiana Jones? The library isn't open on Sunday night and neither is the local historical society."

"It's not at the library or the historical society. It's on display at the Finch Inn."

Sadie was closing up the bookstore when I told her where I was heading. "Would you like to come with us?" I asked. "I can bring Spencer and Amy along."

But after her supernatural encounter the night before, Sadie automatically shivered. "You go on over with your friends. I'll be happy to keep an eye on Spencer and Amy until you get back."

FOR THE SECOND time in a week, Brainert and I piled into Seymour's VW. The drive was easy until we reached the gates of the Finch Inn, where we joined a parade of cars moving slowly along the weeping willow–lined drive.

"Barney and Fiona are raking in the dough tonight," Seymour declared. "Is there a Sunday special at Chez Finch I should know about?"

"I think this crowd is here because of Harriet's ghost," I said. "Fiona had a spike in business the last time there was a sighting."

Seymour chuckled. "Ha! Harriet's a tourist attraction."

Brainert eyed his frenemy. "You're surprisingly sanguine about these apparitions."

"It's a mistake. Or a drunken hallucination."

He sounds almost normal, Jack.

Wait for it.

"Harriet is talking to me and nobody else," Seymour emphatically insisted. "If these ghost stories were true, I'd be the one she'd visit."

Sound familiar, doll?

Settle down, Jack.

After Seymour parked the VW, we approached the Finch Inn.

From the freshly painted Victorian clapboards to the wraparound porch, stained-glass windows, gabled roof, and dramatic turret, the Queen Anne had been restored to authentic perfection by Fiona and Barney.

Through the antique glass doors, we were greeted by a polished staircase worthy of a royal ball. One turn led to the library and common room; another took the visitor to the carved mahogany front desk.

The Queen Anne was incredibly quiet. It appeared all the activity tonight was going on at the inn's restaurant. We even found the common room deserted, its Tiffany lamps set on dim. Seymour led us to a faded brown map mounted behind a glass frame. After a minute studying the antique document, he jabbed a finger at a tiny faded line.

"Look, the Stone Turnpike ran past Finch Inn. It veered inland and ended in Millstone." Seymour whooped. "And look at that, Marsh House! It's right there on the map."

Brainert nodded. "It looks like the only homestead along the whole turnpike. The family cemetery is there, too. It's indicated by the tiny cross."

"That's where Harriet wants me to go," Seymour declared, taking a photo of the map with his mobile phone.

"Don't get your hopes up." Brainert shook his head. "Marsh House is probably long gone."

But Seymour remained undaunted. "We can get close to the place on back roads, but we might have to hoof it a mile or so."

"Not in the dead of night," I said.

Seymour agreed. "Let's start early tomorrow. What do you say?"

Brainert was practically jumping up and down. "I'm going to dig out my L.L.Bean waders. I plan on getting some rubbings off those old gravestones, too!"

This was becoming a grand adventure.

As we headed back to Seymour's van, the men continued making plans. They were certainly in high spirits. Unfortunately, in his excitement, Professor Parker tripped on a paving stone. I caught him before he broke his neck.

Some grand adventure. Jack laughed. *Egghead can't*

negotiate a sidewalk, and the mailman's half-delusional. Tomorrow you're off to the woods with no help for miles.

Don't worry, Jack, I'll watch their backs.

Replace "watch their backs" with "babysit" for honesty's sake.

"So, what time are you picking me up?" I asked Seymour.

"We start our journey at seven sharp!" he said, his whoop echoing through the night air.

"It will be like old times," Brainert said. "Perhaps we'll find a hobbit."

"I just hope we find our way back home . . ."

CHAPTER 57

The Road Less Traveled

Not all those who wander are lost.

—J.R.R. Tolkien, *The Fellowship of the Ring*

THE NEXT DAY, Seymour picked me up at seven sharp—and promptly drove to Cooper's Family Bakery, where Brainert was already ordering us fresh doughnuts and hot coffee for the road.

Sufficiently fortified with carbs and caffeine, we hit the highway.

Seymour had worked out the route in advance. Watching his speedometer closely, he made a turn onto an unmarked side road. We drove a few more miles, and he turned again, this time onto a two-lane blacktop that I hadn't even known existed.

"What do we know about Marsh House?" I asked. "I tried a search online but came up with nothing."

"I texted Violet Brooks last night, but she said there was no mention of the house in her Newport research on Harriet. I have an idea. Let me check a source . . ."

Brainert tried using his computer tablet, but a weak Wi-Fi signal foiled the attempt.

Soon Seymour pulled off the road at a clearing ringed by

trees. When he cut the engine, the only sounds we heard were wind and the chatter of birds.

"I can't believe this is Rhode Island. It looks like a national forest."

"You shouldn't be surprised," Seymour replied in his *Jeopardy!* contestant voice. "The Rhode Island Homestead Bureau says two-thirds of the state is completely forested."

Brainert nodded. "The homestead bureau is exactly the source I was going to check for Marsh House. They list dozens of abandoned farms and their histories. Let me try again . . ." But once again, he failed to get a signal. Meanwhile Seymour checked his Boy Scout compass.

"We head due north for half a mile."

Hiking was easy. We found a narrow path and discovered we weren't its only travelers.

"Gad, what a stench," Brainert groused. "Is it skunk?"

"Deer," Seymour replied.

"And how do you know, Chingachgook?"

"Because you're standing in a pile of droppings."

I'll bet that isn't the first time the egghead stepped in it, either.

I'm relieved you're here, Jack.

The great outdoors is hardly the pavement I pounded. But considering these two, I'm all you got.

The path ended at a grassy clearing. As we crossed the space, I stumbled—and of course both men were too preoccupied to catch me.

I spit dirt as Seymour helped me up. "What did I trip over?"

Seymour pointed to a gray chunk of granite nestled in the brown grass. "It's a gravestone, Pen."

"I see more graves." Brainert pulled a pad and charcoal out of his knapsack. "I'm going to grab some rubbings. I'll catch up with you."

Seymour and I pushed forward through another thicket of trees. When the branches parted, we found another clearing.

"Look!" Seymour cried. "It's Marsh House!"

Ruins was a more fitting description, though the stone chimney still stood tall above the trees. The outlines of the structure were visible, but the floors inside those four crumbled walls were covered by ivy that climbed over the remaining stonework to engulf the old house.

"The only thing standing is the hearth," Seymour noted. "Let's check it out."

We circled the ruined walls until we reached the chimney, where tendrils of ivy crawled across the weathered stone.

"The fireplace is intact," I marveled. "There's even a rusty hook to hang a cooking pot."

Seymour spied something under the ivy. "There's a carving, Pen."

He hacked at the vines with his Swiss Army knife until a single flat stone was exposed. The letter M and a bird symbol had been carved into its surface. Seymour retrieved his phone and showed me a detail from Harriet's portrait—a bird hovering above her house.

The outline of the bird in stone and on canvas were identical.

"I thought the bird was a seagull," Seymour said. "Brainert insisted it was an albatross and the M meant *Rime of the Ancient Mariner.* We were both wrong. The M stands for *Marsh.*"

Seymour frantically dug at the seams around the stone until he could pry it loose. Behind it was a dark hole. "There's something in there!"

Seymour reached into the depression and dragged the object into the light of day—an iron box the size of a brick, its hinges welded shut. A scarlet glass heart about the size of a quarter was embedded in a blob of hardened metal on top of the box.

He frowned. "Geez, how are we going to open it?"

Brainert showed up a moment later. His pride over his "fantastic rubbings" evaporated when Seymour showed him the box. Even the prickly professor was impressed.

CHAPTER 58

Dreaming Up Solutions

I shut my eyes in order to see.

—Paul Gauguin

ON THE HIKE back to the bus, we debated our next move. Without the tools to open the box, we didn't know what we'd found. But we were well aware of the fact that Walt and Conway might have been murdered to get what was inside, which jacked up our paranoia pretty good.

And speaking of Jack . . .

You're smart to be wary, he said. *You ain't out of the woods yet.*

In more ways than one, I thought.

As soon as we reached the VW, Brainert searched for a phone signal. He cursed. "Nothing. If we need help, we're doomed."

Meanwhile Seymour stuffed the iron box into an old gym bag and passed it to me.

"Keep it at your bookstore, Pen. You have the best security system out of all three of us, and I don't want the box stolen before we get a chance to see what's inside."

When we hit the road again, I was relieved to be going home.

"I've finally got Wi-Fi!" Brainert announced.

With Seymour busy driving and Brainert searching the web, I stared into the glass heart as if it were a crystal ball.

What do we do next, Jack?

Something will come to you, Penny. In the meantime, take five. You're going to need your strength.

The sunlight dancing inside the crimson heart along with the gentle rocking of the VW made me drowsy, and I drifted off to dreamland . . . or in this case Jack's land . . .

OPENING MY EYES, I found I'd gone back in time again—to Jack Shepard's time. Behind me was Ruby Tyler's rundown tenement building, standing next to a decrepit row of others just like it.

I remembered how we'd questioned Ruby's "glamour girl" roommate and her "peeping" neighbor, who'd described the brutal attack on Ruby and the man who'd accompanied her home that night—*not* a skinny kid artist by the name of Nathan Brock, but a stout middle-aged man in a suit. A man with slick dark hair and a little mustache. A man whose description precisely matched Roland Prince with an RP, the exact initials on the monogrammed cuff link that was picked up by Benny, the poor guy who'd been living in the building's basement.

With that cuff link now in Jack's possession, I assumed we'd be heading to the police station.

"Shake a leg, Penny. We're going uptown." Jack threw me a wink as he gallantly held open a taxi door.

"Police station?" I assumed, sliding across the big taxi seat.

"No, we're going to talk to Hugo."

"Hugo Box? Ruby's employer at the Albatross? Why?"

"Because now that I know he's not involved, I can trust him. And I need his help."

When we arrived at the Albatross, Jack took me around the back to Hugo's office, but Hugo wasn't there. Jack spoke quietly to his secretary, explaining how he was investigating the case of the attack on Ruby Tyler.

The secretary told us to wait in the club's lobby while she got in touch with Hugo. Fifteen minutes later, a giant bouncer appeared wearing a pinstriped suit and a menacing expression.

"Where's Hugo?" Jack asked.

"Mr. Box says you gotta take a ride with me."

"I'm not going anywhere with you."

"Sure you are, gumshoe." A second man came up behind the giant. He was smaller and thinner—and pointing a gun. "Go out the front door and get in the limo parked there. That goes for your pretty pal, too."

"Jack, what's going on?" I whispered.

"I don't know, Penny, but we're going along with it— for now."

We climbed into the back of the limo, and Hugo's gunsels drove us crosstown to a posh doorman building. Inside the elevator, Jack began to lose his temper.

"What the hell are we doing here?"

"You'll see," the gunsel grunted. "Have a little patience, will ya?"

We exited the elevator, crossed the carpeted hall, and knocked on the polished oak door. When it opened, Hugo Box appeared.

"Come in, Jack. Sorry for the secrecy, but when my secretary told me about the case you're investigating, I had to bring you here. There's someone you need to talk to . . ."

I could see Jack was completely confounded by Hugo's behavior as he led us down the hallway. Then we stepped into the front room, and I gasped when I saw her.

Ruby Tyler sat in a lounge chair beside an open window. Crimson curtains fluttered around her in the cool autumn breeze. Though she was obviously alive, she was far from well. The faded remnant of a black eye was clear to see, and her blond head was swathed in bandages thick enough to rival Seymour's wool cap. Three fingers on her left hand were in splints, and her arms were bruised from IV needles. But despite it all, the lively blue-eyed vitality captured in Nathan Brock's brushstrokes still burned behind her pain.

Ruby even managed a smile when she saw Jack. "I know you, don't I? Yeah, you're a private dick."

"Her memory's sketchy," Hugo said. "You'll see."

We soon learned what the club owner meant by "sketchy." Ruby couldn't remember most of the events of that night. She recalled modeling for Brock and someone taking her home, but this time it wasn't Brock.

"We rode in a cab," Ruby said. "I remember that."

Ruby didn't recall this man's name, what he looked like, or anything that happened after the ride was over.

"Sometimes, when I'm falling asleep, I can almost see his face—"

"Think you'd recognize the guy if you saw him again?" Jack asked.

Ruby shrugged, then turned to face the red-curtained window.

Jack led Hugo to the corner. "Now I know why Ruby's murder wasn't in the papers."

"No one thought she'd pull through, Jack. Not the cops, not the docs. But she did. I brought Ruby to my place as soon as she woke up. Got a whole staff of nurses to take care of her and a brain doctor who makes house calls, too."

"Sure, you did swell, Hugo. But why the concern?"

"You know I protect my girls. I do it because there was one I couldn't protect. That was a long time ago, and I was just a kid . . ."

Hugo's voice trailed off but came back stronger a moment later.

"So, gumshoe, are you going to tell me what you know?"

Without hesitation, Jack dropped a dime on the Prince of the Pulps. He told Hugo about the cuff link and how he got it, too.

"I was hired to clear Nathan Brock. I got what I need to do that—"

"It's not enough and you know it," Hugo shot back. "If you let Roland Prince walk away from this, he'll do it again to some other dame."

"What do you want from me?" Jack asked.

"It's like you said. If Ruby confronts this lug, face-to-face, she might recognize the son of a b—"

"I think I can help you," Jack said. "How about you help me, too?"

"Money?"

"Naw. There's a guy I know. He's a vet, living in a coal cellar. He needs a job and a place to sack out."

"Sure, I can help with that. I got custodial work at the club, and there's a room in the attic he can use. Okay?"

"That'll do."

"So what are you going to do for me?"

"I have an idea."

Jack made a phone call while I stood beside a silent Ruby and stared through the rippling red curtains. Soon those curtains surrounded me, engulfed me until my world turned a deep, dark red.

I squeezed my eyes shut to clear them.

When I opened them again, I found myself standing in front of that familiar Forrestal apartment door on Park Avenue marked ROLAND PRINCE.

Without Jack ringing the bell, the door opened.

"Ten o'clock, right on cue," Jack whispered. "You're a doll, Gwen."

"Prince is alone in his office," Gwen Thomas replied, her purse under her arm. "I think you know the way, Sherlock."

Though she'd finished her work, Gwen still had a pen stuck under her long gray hair. I tugged it free and handed it to her.

"Jack told you what this might mean, right?"

"Don't worry about it." She shrugged. "The pulps are on their last legs anyway. I've already decided to look for work at one of those new paperback houses."

As the elevator doors closed on Gwen, the other players emerged from the shadows. Ruby, in a simple white dress, followed Jack and me through the factory door. Hugo Box brought up the rear.

The suite was deserted, the overhead lights dark. All the windows were open to clear the studio of the day's heat. The windows were open in Prince's office, too. Lifted by the dry autumn breeze, the lacy white curtains reached out like spectral hands.

Roland Prince lounged on his couch, scribbling in a ledger book. He jumped to his feet when Jack and I barged in.

"What's the meaning of this?" Prince sputtered.

"You owe me for a sandwich," Jack replied. "I brought along this nice waitress to collect."

On cue, Ruby entered with Hugo.

Roland Prince paled and took a step backward when he recognized her. As we'd hoped, she recognized Prince, too, but her reaction took everyone by surprise.

"You're the one!" she yelled. "You attacked me! You almost killed me and left me for dead!"

Before Hugo could stop her, Ruby charged forward, the fingers that weren't broken curled into claws.

No one was more stunned than Prince. As Ruby rushed him, his expensive oxfords got tangled with the end table. The Prince of the Pulps pitched backward, bounced off the side of the open window, and then plunged through it. His scream ended abruptly, on the sidewalk far below.

Jack barely managed to pull Ruby back before she followed Roland into oblivion. The girl struggled until Hugo wrapped her in his arms.

Ruby's sobs mixed with the wailing sirens on the street below.

As Hugo gazed at the open window, his grimace morphed into a smile. Then he spoke his first words since we'd entered the factory.

"That's that."

CHAPTER 59

Farm Report

Very few of us are what we seem to be.

—Agatha Christie, "The Man in the Mist"

"THAT'S IT! THAT'S what I was looking for!"

"What, Brainiac?"

The voices seemed to come from far away. As the crimson haze abruptly lifted, I knew I was back in Seymour's Volkswagen.

"Are we home?" I asked, rubbing the sleep from my eyes.

"Almost." Brainert waved his computer tablet. "I found some important information on the Rhode Island Homestead Bureau website."

Seymour braked for a rabbit. "What? *The Farm Report*?"

"In a manner of speaking, yes. I found a history of Marsh House and the man who owned it in Harriet's time."

"Then make like an audiobook and read," Seymour commanded.

"I'll just jump to the end," Brainert said. "The last owner of Marsh House was Jacob Ezra Marsh. He left his family's farm to attend Annapolis and served as first officer aboard the USS *Rhode Island* until the warship was decommissioned. Retiring from the navy when he was forty, Marsh purchased a tramp steamer christened *Mariner* and became an importer of luxury goods catering to Newport families. For three years he divided his time between the farm and the sea."

"He and Harriet must have known each other," Seymour said. "I'll bet he was the one who taught her Morse code, and she obviously hid her deepest secret inside his house."

"I'm betting they were more than friends," I said. "What happened to Jacob Marsh?"

"*Mariner* sunk in a typhoon off Japan. Lost with all hands. Marsh House was not even a working farm by then, and the house was abandoned along with Stone Turnpike." Brainert sighed. "That's the end of the entry."

I lifted the heavy box and shook it. There was something inside, but it didn't rattle. "I'm pretty sure there are no jewels in here."

Seymour shrugged. "The killer wants it anyway. If they hear about it, they'll come for it."

"Then why don't we set a trap and use this box as bait?"

Brainert brightened. "You have a plan, Pen?"

"Yes. In fact, you might say I dreamed up quite an idea . . ."

I RETURNED TO Buy the Book dirty, sweaty, and hungry for more than the Tootsie Pops Seymour brought in his fanny pack. I tucked the mailman's gym bag under the counter and covered it with my jacket.

"So," Sadie said as she untangled ivy from my hair. "What did you find in the woods?"

I told my aunt about the box.

"Where is it?"

"Here." I pointed to the gym bag under the counter. "Seymour left it with us."

"Well, I won't tell a soul. My lips are sealed."

"No. I want you to *spread the word*. That's what Seymour and Brainert are doing. Call everyone you know. Tell them we found Harriet's lost jewel box, it's here in our shop, and we're going to open it in front of the whole town tomorrow morning."

"All right," she said with a shrug. "I'll spread the word. Oh, before I do, is this something you need?" She handed me an envelope. "Eddie Franzetti dropped it off while you were out."

Inside the envelope were the names of all the registered guests for the first floor of the Comfy-Time Motel on the night of Conway's murder. This was the list I'd been waiting for. As I scanned the names, one stood out from all the others.

Jack, do you see what I see?

Yeah, I see it. Plain as day. But like I keep trying to tell you, things aren't always what they seem. You're going to need more proof than this.

Well, I'm setting the trap. Let's hope our killer walks into it.

CHAPTER 60

Boxed In

Any mortal at any time, may be utterly mistaken as to
the situation he is really in.

—C.S. Lewis, *A Grief Observed*

IT WAS NEARLY nine P.M., our closing time, and our store
lights inside were low. I waited alone by the register with no
customers in sight. For the tenth time I made sure Seymour's
gym bag was under the counter.

As I hoped, our killer walked through the door a few
minutes later.

"Violet Brooks, you're back," I said pleasantly. "How
have you been?"

"Busy," she replied. As she scanned the store, both of her
hands remained suspiciously in the pockets of her purple
jacket. "It's quiet tonight; are you alone?"

I shrugged. "Look around."

"I stopped by because I heard the news. Professor Parker
texted me about Harriet's box, and I'd like to know—"

As I grabbed Seymour's bag and dropped it on the counter, Violet's right hand came out of her pocket, clutching
something black and shiny.

Seymour instantly popped up from behind our John

Grisham display. "I wouldn't use that gun unless you're planning on shooting us all!"

"Violet Brooks, I'm shocked!" Professor Parker suddenly rushed out of the True Crime aisle. "What are you after? And why did you resort to murder to get it?"

"Murder?!"

Violet's eyes were so wide I could see their whites through her heavy dark bangs and purple-framed glasses. She threw up her hands, displaying a tiny handheld recording device.

Relieved she wasn't armed, I pressed on. "Yes, Violet, murder. Walt Waverly died suspiciously on Monday, and Clifford Conway was beaten to death at the Comfy-Time Motel the day you first laid eyes on Harriet's self-portrait."

"I don't know who Walt Waverly is. And I had no idea Mr. Conway was murdered!"

"How could you *not* know?" I challenged. "The police were all over that motel. And I see your name right here, plain as day—" I waved the Comfy-Time guest list at her. "Violet Brooks."

"Yes, I was checked in at that motel, but I didn't spend the night there. Right after my lecture, I drove to Newport and barged in on a fellow academic. I wanted access to Robert Morehouse McClure's papers, and I knew he could help me. My friend put me up for the night and in the morning introduced me to the right people. When I got back to Quindicott, I checked *out* of the Comfy-Time and took a room at the Finch Inn. After reviewing Robert's papers, I was eager to sleep under the same roof as his sister once did."

"Why, what are you looking for?"

"A *story*. Harriet McClure's life, her legacy, and that remarkable self-portrait are worthy of a piece in the *Atlantic* or the *New Yorker*. Maybe even a book." She displayed the recorder again. "I was about to interview *you* about finding Harriet's lost jewel box."

Seymour was still skeptical. "Okay, Ms. Brooks, let's say you have an alibi for Conway's killing. But where were you on *Monday* night when Old Walt Waverly got the ax?"

"On Monday evening, I was in Boston, lecturing at the Institute of Contemporary Art. They posted my talk on their website. Take a look! After the lecture, I went out with a group to a local pub. We closed the place around three A.M., and I crashed at my host's town house."

In the ensuing silence, Jack offered his opinion. *This Violet isn't wilting. Maybe she's got nothing to hide.*

I used the store computer to verify her alibi. Violet was telling the truth. The institute had even posted a video of her lecture.

It's over, Penny, Jack asserted. *You threw the dice and came up with snake eyes. It happens to the best of us.*

She looked so guilty—

So did Nathan Brock, another artsy dupe who fit the frame.

While I stifled a frustrated groan, Violet pointed at the gym bag.

"May I see it? Have you opened it? Because I doubt you're going to find any jewels."

"Really?"

Violet nodded. "I spent the last two days at the local library, researching public legal filings, historical documents, and old newspaper reports. I discovered Harriet's brother cut off her stipend; it happened around the time that one of his late mother's necklaces had been sold."

"So?"

"So I followed the thread. After Harriet lost her stipend, she began selling off the McClure family jewels in her possession to a local pawnshop. She did this over a period of years to keep her house running. This pawnshop donated its old ledger books to the library as part of its historical collection for the town. That's how I was able to trace the sales. And it appears whenever she sold a piece of the family jewelry to this shop, the shopkeeper turned around and sold it right back to Robert."

"Are you saying there are no jewels left?" Seymour asked with disappointment.

"Highly doubtful," Violet said, "although when Robert

tried and failed to sue the Finches after his sister's death, he seemed to think so, which is why I'm anxious to see: What *is* inside the box?"

"We don't know yet," I told her. "It's welded shut. Come back tomorrow and you'll find out, along with everyone else."

As soon as Violet was gone, I called a halt to the evening's proceedings.

"False alarm. Somebody please tell Sadie."

My aunt emerged from the stockroom a moment later, still clutching Spencer's baseball bat. "So, what did I miss?"

"An epic fail," Seymour groused.

"What do we do now?" Brainert asked.

"We open the box tomorrow in front of the whole town. Maybe something inside will help us get to the bottom of all this."

CHAPTER 61

All That Glitters

Adventures are not all pony-rides in May-sunshine.

—J.R.R. Tolkien, *The Hobbit, or There and Back Again*

AFTER EVERYONE LEFT, Sadie locked the back door and headed upstairs. "Don't forget to set the store alarms," she called down. "If you need me, I'll be in bed with a good book."

With our cat Bookmark slung over my shoulder, I turned the OPEN sign to CLOSED and was about to lock the front door and activate the security system when the marmalade scamp leaped out of my arms and darted into the darkened event space.

"Come on, cat. I'm too tired for this. I can't leave you down here, or you'll set off the motion detectors!"

Her reply was a taunting mew.

"Okay. I'm coming in there!"

As I walked into the large, empty room, shadows played across the images on canvas, all those faces from long ago, and the longest was young Harriet McClure.

I still didn't know all her secrets or what was in her jewelry box. But thanks to Violet's research, I now knew why there were no earrings or necklaces adorning her poses in all those self-portraits—or rattling around in the box we'd found. She'd sold the gems to keep her household going.

That's when Violet's words came back to me about Robert McClure secretly buying back Harriet's jewelry from the local pawnshop here in Quindicott.

"The local pawnshop," I repeated, pausing to consider that phrase. "Jack, I know the history of the stores in this town, and there's only one that began as a pawnshop."

You don't say.

"Gilder's Antiques."

The very same shop that's now run by your old friend?

"Georgia Gilder was never a friend, only a classmate."

My mind worked overtime, thinking back on Georgia's entrance into this very room, how she'd immediately recognized the musical notes in the painting, how she'd been on the street to witness Conway's argument with Tracy and my son's filming of that confrontation.

Chills went through me that had nothing to do with Jack's presence, and I felt a sudden urgency in setting that security alarm. After a few minutes of cat and mouse (though who was the cat and who was the mouse is anyone's guess), I grabbed Bookmark again.

When I returned to the store, my nostrils flared. Jack whiffed it, too. And in that instant, I remembered—

La Chienne Number 5!

The preferred flower juice of the Georgia peach.

I could have kicked myself for two reasons: not getting that front door locked sooner and misjudging the faint floral aroma in Conway's motel room.

Sacre bleu, Jack cracked. *French fries masked the French perfume!*

I remained outwardly calm, even as I fought to tame my panic.

Georgia must have slipped through the unlocked front door and hid herself while I was chasing Bookmark. What do I do now?

There are two ways to look at this. Either you're trapped in here with her, or she's trapped in here with you.

Jack's meaning came through loud and clear.

I locked the door and activated the security system, including the motion detectors in the event space. Then I set Bookmark free. The cat gleefully scampered back to the art exhibit, tail held high in feline triumph.

With creepy silence, Georgia Gilder stepped out of the shadows clad in baggy pants and an oversize jacket with the hood pulled up. One gloved hand pointed a rose pink pistol at my heart.

That's a snub-nosed .38, Jack cautioned. *It's a pretty little ladies' pistol, but it has enough punch to put you in the morgue.*

"Where is it?" Georgia demanded. "I know you have the lost jewel box. Your friends were bragging about it all over town."

"You really think you'll get away with this?"

"You'd be surprised what I've already gotten away with. Now, where is it?"

Keep her talking, Penny. That cat of yours is going to trip the alarm any minute.

"I'll tell you where it is if you answer one question. Why is it so important to you?"

"I'm going to buy my future with it, *that's* why. I know all about Ashley McClure's upscale plans for this town. These little family businesses are finished, and good riddance! I'm done, too. I never wanted to come back here."

"Then why did you?"

"Let's just say I got a raw deal, but that Harriet legacy is my winning ticket out of here and back to the life I deserve."

"The life you deserve?" I laughed in her face. "Good luck. You're not going to get much capital from an iron box."

"You stupid idiot." Georgia sneered. "You figured out *part* of Harriet's message, so you think you know everything. Clearly you don't."

"I know *much* more than you. I always did, you pretentious dimwit."

Showing Georgia my own proud sneer was like waving a red cape at an agitated bull. It did the trick and kept her talking.

"Here's what I *do* know," she spat. "It was *my* grandfather who bought jewelry from Harriet McClure, right on her estate. That's how he learned about her crazy coded paintings. He even sold some of them for her. When she died, old Malachi Finch called my grandfather up to the house. For years, that insane spinster kept her jewel box hidden. Before she croaked, she confessed the box still contained her 'most precious treasure,' and the map to finding it was written into her early paintings. But Malachi and his simple wife couldn't figure it out, so he asked my grandfather to help. They came close to cracking it, too, until my grandfather stupidly mentioned his clever business dealings with Harriet's brother, who Malachi hated. After hearing that, Malachi stopped trusting him and burned the paintings, right before his eyes."

"So your grandfather was the one who spread the false gossip about why the Finches burned Harriet's paintings."

"Of course! He wasn't going to tip anyone else off to the truth. On his own deathbed, he gave my parents all his notes and told them to keep looking for those weird early paintings. My parents never had any luck, but they never stopped trying to find Harriet's treasure."

"Not all treasures are gold or jewels. Whatever is inside that box—"

"I don't give a damn what's inside that box. I want the jewel!"

"You mean the red glass heart embedded in the top?"

"You jackass, that's a ruby!" She smirked. "Without Conway's digital files, you nerds couldn't blow up the script on the cloud big enough to read it. If you had, you'd have seen the chemical compound for the crystalline form of aluminum oxide, aka a sapphire or *ruby*."

She huffed. "Do you know what a pure ruby is worth? The Queen of Burma sold for three million at auction. The Graff Ruby for eight million. The Sunrise for thirty!"

"And did you tell Clifford Conway about the ruby, or did you just bring the champagne and seduce your way into his suite?"

"Men are easy. He died thinking he was the luckiest guy in town. And he was the perfect dupe to frame for the old man's murder. You have to admit, planting Walt Waverly's mobile phone in his motel room was genius."

Acting confused, I shook my head. "How did you even get Mr. Waverly's phone?"

"You really are stupid, aren't you? All I had to do was set up my search engine's alert for Harriet's name. When I saw the watermarked thumbnail image on the old guy's website, I contacted him, but the fool sold it out from under me! Then he refused to tell me who he'd sold it to. I had to act, so I pretended to purchase a painting in the entryway and up the ladder he went. You know, I tried to get rid of that walking encyclopedia friend of yours, too, but Seymour's head was too hard." She laughed. "How's that lump I gave you? Still throbbing, I hope."

My fists clenched. "I forgot what a vain workout queen you were. Do you still spend hours in the gym, trying to hold back the inevitable?"

"I'll tell you what's inevitable." She waved that pink gun again. "Tell me where that box is, and I won't make you suffer in horrible pain before you die. It'll be over quick."

"No, it won't." I folded my arms. "And you're going to spend the better part of your life working out in a prison yard."

Furious that I still refused to act as cowed as I had in high school, she tried to menace me by stepping closer. I moved backward, until my spine touched the counter.

"It will look like a robbery." Georgia bared white teeth. "Everyone in town knows about that jewel box, including the junkies at the Wentworth Arms. I'll leave the gun there and see to it one of them gets blamed."

"Like you planted that umbrella on Tracy's bike? Eddie said it was old, from a secondhand store. But it was really an antique, wasn't it?"

"The box, Penelope! You have ten seconds left. Then I'm going to pull the trigger and look *upstairs*. Your old auntie and that cute little boy of yours still live up there, don't they?"

That's it, the ghost insisted. *Time to act!*

I've been *ready, Jack, but that blasted cat isn't doing her part!*

I'll fix that . . .

A sudden draft of supernaturally cold air swept into the event space. A second later, Bookmark let out an outraged howl and tripped the motion detectors.

The shrill alarm and blinking lights startled Georgia.

Go for it, Penny!

I snatched the gym bag off the counter and swung it as hard as I could at Georgia's head. The pink pistol flew in one direction; the smug woman went another. As the gun rattled across the room, Georgia crashed into our Butcher Block Mysteries display and dropped to the floor, out cold.

I released the gym bag, and the decoy brick spilled out. (Harriet's jewelry box had been safely hidden under my mattress.)

The alarm brought Sadie down to the shop, followed by Spencer, rubbing sleep from his eyes. Outside, a police car rolled up, and Deputy Chief Franzetti rushed in.

"Are you okay, Pen?"

"Better than okay," I said, "because I finally know who killed Walter Waverly, who murdered Clifford Conway, who framed Tracy Mahoney, and who gave Seymour and me our blasted bumps on the head."

Pointing at the figure sprawled on the floor, I knew one more thing: how incredibly relieved Hugo must have felt when he looked out that pulp factory window and said—

"That's that."

CHAPTER 62

All in the Family

Painting is just another way of keeping a diary.

—Pablo Picasso

GIVEN THE CHAOTIC hours and days following Georgia Gilder's arrest for double murder, attempted murder, and the burglary of Seymour Tarnish's home, we postponed the public opening of Harriet's lost jewel box.

There were too many other things that took priority, starting with freeing poor Tracy Mahoney from the local hospital's psych unit. Thanks to Eddie Franzetti and a cooperative judge, Tracy was soon released with all charges dropped and back home in her brother's loving care.

The recovery of Walt Waverly's color-coded notebooks was high on the priority list, too. They were found, along with more damning evidence against Georgia, including a notation in her parents' ledger for the purchase of the Victorian-era antique umbrella that doubled as a cudgel. The perfect defensive accessory for gentlemen in crime-ridden London had served Georgia's purpose. It rained the night of Conway's murder, and he wouldn't have blinked twice when she showed up clutching a parasol.

Of course, Georgia's arraignment didn't solve everyone's problem.

Though the town was now alerted to the machinations of Ashley McClure and her husband, there was little anyone could do to stop them. For Fiona and Barney Finch, the situation was particularly dire, since they remained in the Mc-Clure crosshairs.

"That awful shore tax is still hanging over our heads," Fiona told me after the murders were solved. "Business has improved at the restaurant, but not enough to get us through the winter." With a sad voice, she admitted it felt like a losing battle against superior forces. "I just don't know how long Barney and I can hold on."

Based on her current experience with the McClure family and their powerful friends, Fiona also had a strong opinion about the fate of Harriet's lost box and that ruby.

"If there is anything of value inside, the McClure family will use their influence to grab it, just like they're maneuvering to attain the ruby. I heard their lawyer was at the courthouse yesterday. I'll bet papers are already filed to snatch whatever is revealed."

That reveal was the talk of the town. We fielded so many phone calls about Harriet's treasure box that Sadie took out an ad in the *Quindicott Bulletin,* informing the public that the box would be opened on Saturday afternoon at three P.M.

That morning, while Bonnie and Spencer were setting up chairs for the big event, a heavyset young man with a shaved head and full beard walked through our bookshop's door. Even before he introduced himself, I recognized the mirror image of the twinkle in Walt's eyes.

"Mrs. McClure, I'm Neil Waverly, and I'm here to thank you."

Neil was grateful for my help not only in solving his father's murder but also in the recovery of Walt's precious notebooks.

I expressed my condolences as I led him into the event space to see the works from his father's collection. He barely glanced at the Harriet McClure and instead focused on the Nathan Brock painting.

"I'm glad Dad didn't get around to selling this one. He was in such a rush to unload everything, I didn't get a chance to tell him to hold on to it—"

"If you don't mind my prying," I interrupted, "why exactly did you move to Los Angeles? My aunt Sadie was under the impression your father was training you to take over his business."

Neil confessed that though he worked with his dad, his dream was not to sell art but to make it. He'd spent years honing his skills as an illustrator and had a few small successes in the comic business, which helped him make connections in Hollywood.

"I sent my portfolio around and got hired by an animation studio."

Neil told me his father was upset about his move. But Neil had been upset with his father as well, and that's why he'd left so suddenly.

"The ugly truth is I objected to the way Dad couldn't stop hustling on the convention circuit while my mother was sick and dying. He got stuck in denial, I guess; kept acting as if nothing was wrong. He wasn't even home when my mother took her last breath."

"I'm so sorry."

Neil shook his head. "I wanted to put that behind me, Mrs. McClure. A couple of weeks ago I called Dad to reconcile. He told me, right then and there, that he was going to retire, sell his collection, and use the money to move to California to be near me. He had a change of heart. He said he was sorry we'd fought—and from now on his family was going to come first."

As for Walt's art collection, Neil vowed to sell it with care. "I'll make sure every one of Dad's beloved pieces finds a good home." Then he asked me to ship what I had to his address in LA, where he knew he'd locate appreciative buyers.

One work, however, he wanted sent elsewhere.

"The Nathan Brock painting shouldn't go to me. I'll give you an address in New York. That's where it really belongs."

"I'm curious. Does the New York addressee have a connection to the artist?"

"Not the artist, Mrs. McClure, the model. That beautiful blond woman in the painting was my mother's aunt."

"Ruby Tyler was your great-aunt?"

"Ruby who?" He blinked, baffled. "You must be thinking of another painting. The woman in this painting is Mabel Boggs. Our family's very proud of her history. As a young woman, she moved all alone to New York from West Virginia and got a job at the Albatross—one of the most popular nightclubs of its day. But her real work began with the start of her Open Arms House in the Bowery. That's where I'm sending the painting. Her daughter is the director there now."

"Open Arms?"

"It was a precursor to New York's battered women's shelters. My great-aunt started it with a friend named Shirley Powell, and the nightclub owner she used to work for helped with the financing. The depiction of Mabel in this painting was even used on their early posters. 'You are not alone'; that was their motto. 'We are here to help you with Open Arms.'"

"You know, Neil, your dad told me there was a crime story behind this painting, but he was vague about it. He couldn't recall the details."

"Dad's memory was going, Mrs. McClure. He bought the painting decades ago from Mabel herself, during one of the Open Arms fundraising drives. If there was a special story attached to it, she probably told him back then, though I never heard it. When I get Dad's notebooks back from the police, I'll look up what he wrote. He really relied on those journals. They recorded more than sales. He used them like a diary, so I'm incredibly grateful to get them back."

Suddenly I saw that familiar Walt twinkle in Neil's eye.

"Now, Mrs. McClure, let's talk business. I enjoy selling art, but I know next to nothing about rare books. Would you be willing to handle my father's book collection on consignment?" He handed me an inventory list. "Name any percentage you want, and it's yours."

I briefly consulted with Sadie, who proposed a fair deal. Neil Waverly accepted and promised to ship the books to our store within the week.

After Neil was gone, I had a talk with the ghost.

Well, Jack, now I know what you meant when you told me Ruby was "extinguished." But I thought you meant she died.

Ruby Tyler did die the night she moved out of Hugo's apartment and into her own. That's when Mabel Boggs and Shirley Powell put their heads together and hatched their Open Arms project. Hugo got a gaggle of celebrities involved to fundraise for it, and they were off to the races.

Mabel Boggs from West Virginia. I shook my head, remembering what her tenement roommate said about "glamour girl" fantasies.

Yeah, Jack cracked, *no wonder she took a stage name.*

And no wonder she let the false name die for something real, a lifetime of opening protective arms to women in need, a legacy less glamorous but far more beautiful.

CHAPTER 63

Lost and Found

Everyone must leave something behind when he dies.

—Ray Bradbury, *Fahrenheit 451*

BY THREE O'CLOCK on Saturday afternoon, our event space was filled to capacity. Even the shops along Cranberry Street closed so the owners and their employees could be present for this local historic event.

The *Bulletin* sent a reporter (editor Elmer Crabtree's fifteen-year-old nephew, Scotty), and every member of the city council attended.

The big reveal started slowly, with Leo Rollins using an arc welder to soften the metal and carefully pry the ruby loose. Then Bud Napp used a handheld circular saw to cut through the box's ancient hinges.

My sister-in-law, Ashley, fidgeted impatiently beside her husband, Bertram, ready to pounce on any discovery of value.

That's why we asked Seymour's attorney, Emory Philip Stoddard, to preside over the opening. Aware of the legal maneuvering swirling around this event, I was glad Mr. Stoddard agreed to officiate.

When the power saw stopped, we all waited in rapt silence as the iron lid was pulled off. At last, the contents were unveiled—

A few yellowed sheets of paper and an envelope.

Brainert leaned close and whispered. "I fear it's another Al Capone's vault."

Jack agreed. *Unless those papers are the deed to Fort Knox, this Easter egg hunt has been a bust.*

Amid groans of disappointment, Emory Stoddard called the room to order and within minutes proceeded to prove Brainert, Jack, and the groaners wrong.

"These papers provide a signed, written testimony from Mrs. Verna Tripp, a midwife from Quindicott. She states that on January 22, 1923, Harriet Alice McClure gave birth to twins at Marsh House on Stone Turnpike. Mrs. Tripp delivered a girl and a boy."

"That explains the two baby heads on Harriet's portrait," Seymour whispered. "And Brahms' 'Lullaby.'"

"The twins were born out of wedlock," Stoddard continued. "The father was Jacob Ezra Marsh, captain of the trading ship *Mariner*. Marsh died on Christmas Day 1922, when his ship sank with all hands. The tragic news took time to reach Harriet. When it did, the grief induced an early labor."

"What happened to the children?" Colleen called, starting a chorus of women demanding an answer to the same question.

"The girl died within hours and is buried in Marsh Cemetery—"

Moans of sorrow filled the room.

"And the boy?" This time a single, booming voice wanted an answer. Ashley's husband, Bertram Sutherland.

"According to Mrs. Tripp's testimony," Stoddard continued, "Harriet believed it would not be fair to raise a son with the stigma of being born out of wedlock and without a father, so she turned the boy over to a childless couple to raise as their own. This couple was close enough for Harriet to watch the boy grow up, though she vowed never to tell him that she was his real mother."

Stoddard paused before unleashing the firestorm. "The

boy was christened Ezra, and he was raised by Malachi Finch and his wife."

Barney Finch's eyes went wide in shock.

"He's talking about your grandparents, Barney!" Fiona cried. "That means your father, Ezra, was really Harriet's son, which makes *you* Harriet's grandson. You're a McClure!"

Our friend almost fell out of his chair. Seymour caught the man and slapped his back.

"Congratulations Finch-no-more. You're richer than King Croesus now—"

"I object!" Bertram Sutherland bellowed loud enough to be heard in Providence. "Those documents are forgeries! A pack of lies!"

"Now, where have I heard that before?" Seymour cracked, throwing a glance Barney's way.

Stoddard displayed the envelope.

"Harriet McClure provided proof, though she could not have known it at the time. Here is a lock of Ezra's hair—and her own. If Mr. Barney Finch will oblige us with a DNA sample, I believe a simple lab test can clear this family matter up."

EPILOGUE

I was never really insane except upon occasions when my heart was touched.

—Edgar Allan Poe

A MONTH LATER I sat in the storeroom with Jack, contemplating a gift sent to the bookstore by Neil Waverly—a framed vintage poster from a 1950 fundraising event for Open Arms House, held at the Albatross nightclub in New York City.

The roster of entertainers told me Hugo Box had summoned all of his celebrity friends to help. Appearing that night were Sid Caesar, fresh off his hit Broadway revue *Make Mine Manhattan*, "Mr. C" himself, RCA recording artist Perry Como, the Stan Kenton Orchestra with cool jazz songstress June Christy, and the young comedy team of Dean Martin and Jerry Lewis.

The poster itself would have done Clifford Conway proud. Though the image of Ruby, arms flung wide, was lifted directly from Nathan Brock's painting, the background replaced the menacing killer with a rendering of the sunlit Open Arms building festooned with cheerful flower boxes.

Unlike Tracy Mahoney, I doubted Nathan Brock would have objected to the transformation of his image. Considering his wife, Shirley, was a cofounder of the charity, he was likely proud of its use. But he could never have guessed the true value of his work while he was painting it—or the thousands of women he would help to realize, as the poster said, they were not alone.

"Just like Harriet, Jack. She couldn't have known the future value of those locks of hair she hid away in that iron box."

In fact, on the day her lost jewel box was opened, attorney Emory Stoddard gained a new client: Barney Finch. And when Barney's DNA test came back positive for McClure genes, the lawyer delivered the news to his horrified biological family.

All of them knew the brutal truth about their ancestor Robert Morehouse McClure. He'd made no secret that he'd cheated Harriet out of her fair share of the McClure family fortune. The McClures never cared. In their eyes, the crazy spinster was long dead. She never had offspring to fight the injustice—until now.

With Emory Stoddard on his side, Barney was able to threaten a lawsuit for a whopping *half* of the McClure trust, *unless* they agreed to his terms.

After days of legal haggling, Stoddard secured an immediate settlement, which Barney took in lieu of years of court battles. The small fortune in stocks and bonds was nice, the deed for all five miles of pristine, undeveloped Rhode Island coastline even better.

This was the strip of highly valuable shoreline, designated as a "bird sanctuary," that abutted the Finch Lighthouse, the very land the McClure family owned and *had* planned to develop once the Finches were out of the way. Now the Finches owned it.

And that newly passed beach tax? It magically disappeared, which was ironic because Barney now had the wherewithal to pay it (if he'd had a mind to).

The curse, if there was one, was lifted. Not only did Barney's settlement work out, but repeated sightings of Harriet's ghost kept the inn booked and the tables at Chez Finch filled. They were so flush that Barney hired Leo Rollins to overhaul his hinky Wi-Fi with free high-speed Internet for any visitors within range. (And since there were plenty more Finch Inn improvement jobs for Leo, the two men shook hands over their previous disagreement.)

Meanwhile, Fiona solved her restaurant problems with a "supernaturally" inspired menu on Monday through Thursday nights. Reserving fine dining for weekend guests, she embraced economical but tasty weeknight dishes like Harriet's Hamburgers, Spooky Spuds, and Spectral Spaghetti. Local families and college students were now packing the place—her Groupon specials didn't hurt, either.

Yeah, I hear customers are eating them up.

"Jack! That joke hurt worse than the lump Georgia put on my head."

Which didn't hurt nearly as much as the one you laid on her perfumed noggin.

"She only had a doorjamb, Jack. I had a brick. And it wasn't the first time Georgia found herself in an ugly situation."

After her arrest, I finally learned the reason why my former schoolmate had returned to her hated hometown. As director of human resources at the Boston law firm where her much older husband was a partner, Georgia made the reckless decision to have a fling with a barely legal college intern. When their affair was exposed, a doomsday clause was activated in her husband's prenuptial agreement. Georgia walked away with a divorce, but no money, no job, not even a reference.

"She was desperate. No wonder she wanted the ruby—"

There were two Rubies in this story, Jack pointed out. *Which was more precious?*

"A life is more precious than any jewel, and you know that, Jack."

I know, doll. I was just trying to get a rise out of you.

In truth Harriet's ruby was of mediocre quality, which is probably why it was never sold with the other gems, though

Violet Brooks found evidence that it was a betrothal gift from Harriet's doomed lover, Captain Marsh, which gave it sentimental value.

As a historical artifact, however, it was certainly priceless. That's why Seymour believed the jewel and the haunted portrait should be donated to the Finch Inn, where they are now on display in the Common Room.

"Harriet McClure wasn't resting in peace," Seymour confided, "but I'm sure she is now."

I wasn't so sure, given the periodic sightings around her old property. But I was glad to see Seymour released from his strange lovesickness.

"Solving the riddle cured my old friend of his obsession," I told Jack.

That's what happens in the mystery game. You close one case and move on to the next.

In the silence that followed, I swear I heard a ghostly girlish laughter. "Harriet?"

I listened again, but there was only silence, followed by a burst of much more human girlish laughter coming from the event space where Tracy and her reading group were meeting.

"I felt so helpless when Tracy was arrested," I told Jack, "and I imagine that's how Seymour felt about Harriet—powerless to ease the pain captured on that canvas, the suffering of a woman long dead."

In the end, the mailman did help Harriet, by protecting her offspring. And you were able to help your blue-haired babysitter.

"In more ways than one, I'm happy to report."

Do tell.

"I talked to the Palantines about Tracy's plight. Sally Palantine took a look at her manuscript and portfolio and made a few phone calls. Just yesterday, the young adult publisher Collegian hired her to create a fantasy cover for an upcoming novel. And one of their editors sent her a revision letter on her manuscript. If she works hard, she may soon be a published fantasy author, as well as an illustrator."

Another rising young artist like Nathan Brock.

"You know, I asked the Palantines whether they'd ever heard of Nathan. Since he wasn't included in their book, I thought I'd be telling them something they didn't know, but it turns out I was the one who made a mistake. Nathan wasn't indexed under the name Brock, which is a moniker he used for only a short time. 'Nathaniel Van Brock,' however, was listed as 'a gifted pulp illustrator who moved into fine art in the 1950s and '60s and enjoyed a highly successful career.'"

Hell, I thought Brock was a pretty fine artist when he painted Ruby.

"So did I, Jack. As for Nathan and Shirley Powell, they got married and stayed that way for the rest of their lives. Gwen Thomas is in the Palantines' book, too. After she quit Roland Prince's sweatshop, she became the first art director for Seahorse, a new paperback publisher that lasted until 1996, when it was bought by Salient House."

Just then, Spencer appeared in the doorway. "Mom? I need to talk to you, but you've got to promise you won't get mad."

"Why?" I asked, fearing I would.

"I know you told me not to record people's conversations after what happened to Tracy. But I kind of did, anyway, even though it wasn't exactly a conversation."

I should have convinced Eddie to keep that phone, I told Jack.

"Amy and I went ghost hunting last night," Spencer explained. "I figured if Aunt Sadie saw the ghost, it must be real. We snuck around the property and . . . well, take a look—"

The video on Spencer's phone began at sunset. A woman came to the back door of the Finch Inn on a black bicycle; even the spokes on the wheels were painted black. Fiona appeared a moment later. She passed the woman money, a wig, and a bundle of what looked like rags.

"What's going on, Spencer?"

"Keep watching, Mom."

Fiona went back inside, but the woman lingered long

enough to put on the wig and rags—really a flowing gown and a long, lacy shawl. Finally, she smeared white cream on her face.

When she slowly rode off on the bike, she headed beyond the bushes and into the trees, looking much like the specter of Harriet, floating through the woods.

"Looks like the mystery of the Finch Inn ghost is solved."

"What do we do, Mom?"

"We don't want any trouble like the last time, do we, Spencer? How about we keep this mystery to ourselves?"

Spencer nodded in agreement, pressed *Delete*, and dashed off to do his homework.

IN BED THAT night, I sorted through some final thoughts about the life of the "crazy spinster" Harriet McClure.

"You know what, Jack? I don't think Harriet's life was all that bad."

How do you figure that?

"Well, she lived in that beautiful house in a small, peaceful town with something like a family. She was able to paint to her heart's content, enjoy her woods and seafront, and be close to her son while he was growing up. For all we know, she was kindly 'Aunt Harriet' to little Ezra, able to play with him and hug him and love him every day."

Sounds like a sweet picture, all right. What's your point, doll?

"I'm saying she had good reason to sell those jewels. Love of family. True family, not a bunch of mean-spirited, status-conscious malcontents like the McClures. Sure, it wasn't Newport high society, and it was far from an exciting life, but I'll bet it was a happy one."

I pulled the covers up and snuggled into my pillow.

"I'll bet even a hard-boiled guy like you is learning to appreciate this quiet, little town."

I wouldn't make book on it, honey. But I'll make you an offer. You keep things interesting for me. I'll do the same for you.

"It's a deal, gumshoe."

Jack's laughter seemed far away, but he promised one last thing: *I'll see you in your dreams.* Then a cool breeze caressed my face as the ghost's voice faded with him, back into the fieldstone walls that had become his tomb.

ABOUT THE AUTHOR

Cleo Coyle is a pseudonym for Alice Alfonsi, writing in collaboration with her husband, Marc Cerasini. Both are *New York Times* bestselling authors of the long-running Coffeehouse Mysteries—now celebrating eighteen years in print. They are also authors of the national bestselling Haunted Bookshop Mysteries, previously written under the pseudonym Alice Kimberly. Alice has worked as a journalist in Washington, D.C., and New York, and has written popular fiction for adults and children. A former magazine editor, Marc has authored espionage thrillers and nonfiction for adults and children. Alice and Marc are also both bestselling media tie-in writers who have penned properties for Lucasfilm, NBC, Fox, Disney, Imagine, and MGM. They live and work in New York City, where they write independently and together.

CONNECT ONLINE

CoffeehouseMystery.com
🅕 CleoCoyleAuthor
🐦 CleoCoyle

Ready to find
your next great read?

Let us help.

Visit prh.com/nextread